LITERARY MASTERPIECES

ISSN 1526-1522

LITERARY MASTERPIECES

Volume 2

The Sun Also Rises

Albert J. DeFazio III

A MANLY, INC. BOOK

GALE GROUP™

Detroit
San Francisco
London
Boston
Woodbridge, CT

THE SUN ALSO RISES

Matthew J. Bruccoli and Richard Layman, *Editorial Directors*

The Gale Group

27500 Drake Road

Farmington Hills, MI 48331

ISBN 0-7876-3962-1

ISSN 1526-1522

Printed in the United States of America

10 9 8 7 6 5 4 3 2 1

TABLE OF CONTENTS

A NOTE TO THE READER

by George Garrett, Henry Hoyns Professor of Creative Writing, the University of Virginia

Think of it this way: you are about to embark on a journey. This book is, among other things, designed to be at once a reservation and a round-trip ticket. The purpose of the journey, the goal and destination, is for you to experience, as fully and as deeply as you can, a masterpiece of literature. Reading a great work is not a passive experience. It will be demanding and, as you will see, well rewarded.

What is a masterpiece? The answer is easy if you are dealing with the great works of antiquity—for example the *Iliad* and *Odyssey* of Homer, the tragedies of Aeschylus, Sophocles, and Euripides—works that have endured for millenia and even outlasted their original language. Closer in time there are the accepted monuments of our languages and culture, such as the plays of Shakespeare, the *Divine Comedy* of Dante, and the comedies of Molière. But here and now we are dealing with work that is nearer to us in time, that speaks to and about persons, places, and things that we either know at first hand or at least know about. These works are accepted by critical consensus (and tested in the marketplace and in the classroom) as among the most original and influential works of their times. It remains for you to experience their power and originality.

There is much to be gained from close and careful study of a great book. You will always find much more than you expected to, than you are looking for. Whether we know it and admit it or not, we are one and all constantly being changed and shaped by what we read. One definition of a literary masterpiece is that it is a great work that can touch us most deeply. It can be, is, if you are wide awake and fully engaged, a profound experience. Lighthearted or deadly serious, it is about things that matter to us. The Gale Study Guides are intended to help you to enjoy and to enlarge your understanding of literature. By an intense focus, these Guides enhance the values you discover in reading enduring works. Discovery is always an important part of the process. With guidance you will see how personal discoveries can be made and, equally important, can be shared with others studying the same book. Our literary culture is, ideally, a community. This book is meant to serve as your introduction to that community.

From the earliest days of our history (until the here and now), readers have looked for pleasure and meaning in whatever they read. The two are inextricable in literature. Without pleasure, enjoyment, there can be no permanent meaning. Without value and significance, there is no real pleasure. Ideally, the close study of literary masterpieces—comedy or tragedy, past and present—will increase our pleasure and our sense of understanding not only of the individual work in and of itself but also of ourselves and the world we inhabit.

There is hard work involved. What you have labored to master you will value more highly. And reading is never exclusively a passive experience. You have to bring the whole of yourself to the experience. It becomes not a monologue, but a dialogue between you and the author. What you gain from the experience depends, in large part, on what you bring and can give back. But, as great voices have told us since the dawn of literature, it is well worth all the effort, indeed worth any effort.

We learn how powerful words can be. The language of great voices speaking to us across time and space, yet close as a whisper, matters enormously. Sooner or later, our buildings will crumble; our most intricate and elegant machines will cough and die and become rusty junk; and our grand monuments and memorials will lose all their magic and meaning. But we know that our words, our language, will last longer than we do, speaking of and for us, over centuries and millenia. Listening to great voices, reading their words and stories in the enduring works of literature, we are given a reward of inestimable value. We earn a share in their immortality.

You will meet some memorable characters, good and bad, and you are going to participate in unforgettable events. You will go to many places, among them the Africa of Chinua Achebe, the England of Virginia Woolf, the China of Maxine Hong Kingston. You can visit 1920s Paris with Ernest Hemingway, the magical Latin America of Gabriel García Márquez, the Mississippi of William Faulkner, the dark side of San Francisco with Dashiell Hammett. Gale Study Guides are good maps to the literary territory. Envision the journey as a kind of quest or pilgrimage, not without difficulty, that can change your understanding of life.

ACKNOWLEDGMENTS

This book was produced by Bruccoli Clark Layman, Inc. R. Bland Lawson is the series editor; he and Penelope M. Hope were the in-house editors.

Production manager is Philip B. Dematteis.

Copyediting supervisor is Phyllis A. Avant. Senior copyeditor is Thom Harman. The copyediting staff includes Brenda Carol Blanton, James Denton, Worthy B. Evans, Melissa D. Hinton, William Tobias Mathes, and Jennifer Reid.

Indexing was done by Alex Snead and Cory McNair.

Layout and graphics supervisor is Janet E. Hill. Graphics staff includes Karla Corley Brown and Zoe R. Cook.

Photography editors are Charles Mims, Scott Nemzek, Alison Smith, and Paul Talbot. Digital photographic copy work was performed by Joseph M. Bruccoli.

Systems manager is Marie L. Parker.

Typesetting supervisor is Kathleen M. Flanagan. The typesetting staff includes Mark J. McEwan, Kimberly Kelly, and Patricia Flanagan Salisbury.

COPYRIGHTED MATERIAL IN *Literary Masterpieces, Volume 2: The Sun Also Rises* IS REPRODUCED FROM THE FOLLOWING BOOKS:

Baker, Carlos. From *Hemingway: The Writer as Artist.* Princeton University Press, 1972. Copyright © 1972 by Princeton University Press. Reproduced by permission.—Beach, Joseph Warren. From *American Fiction: 1920–1940.* Macmillan, 1941. Reproduced with the permission of Macmillan Library Reference USA.—Cowley, Malcolm. From an introduction to *The Portable Hemingway.* Edited by Malcolm Cowley. Viking Press, 1944. Copyright 1944 Malcolm Cowley. Reproduced by permission of Viking Press, a division of Penguin Putnam Inc.—Fiedler, Leslie. From *Love and Death in the American Novel.* Dalkey Archive Press, 1998. Reproduced by permission.—Fitzgerald, F. Scott. From a letter to Ernest Hemingway in *F. Scott Fitzgerald: A Life in Letters.* Edited by Matthew J. Bruccoli. Simon & Schuster, 1995. Copyright © 1994 by the Trustees under Agreement Dated July 3, 1975. Created by Frances Scott Fitzgerald Smith. Reproduced by permission of Harold Ober Associates Incorporated in North America by Simon & Schuster Macmillan.—Plimpton, George. From *Writers at Work: The Paris Interviews.* Second Series. Edited by George Plimpton. Viking, 1963. Reproduced by permission of Viking, a division of Penguin Putnam Inc.—Reynolds, Michael S. From *The Sun Also Rises: A Novel of the Twenties.* Twayne, 1988. Reproduced with the permission of Macmillan Library Reference USA.—Warren, Robert Penn. From an introduction to *A Farewell to Arms.* By Ernest Hemingway. Scribner, 1949. Reproduced with the permission of Macmillan Library Reference USA.—Wilson, Edmund. From an introduction to *In Our Time* by Ernest Hemingway. Scribner, 1930. Reproduced with the permission of Macmillan Library Reference USA.—Wylder, Delbert E. From *Hemingway's Heroes.* University of New Mexico Press, 1969. Reproduced by permission.—Young, Philip. From *Hemingway: A Reconsideration.* Pennsylvania State University Press, 1966. Copyright 1966 by The Pennsylvania State University. Reproduced by permission of the publisher.

PHOTOGRAPHS AND ILLUSTRATIONS APPEARING IN *Literary Masterpieces, Volume 2: The Sun Also Rises* WERE RECEIVED FROM THE FOLLOWING SOURCES:

From the cover of *The Sun Also Rises.* By Ernest Hemingway. Scribner, 1926. Copyright 1926 by Charles Scribner's Sons. Renewed 1954 by Ernest Hemingway. Reproduced with permission of Scribner, a Division of Simon & Schuster, Inc.

Fitzgerald's report on *The Sun Also Rises*. John F. Kennedy Library.

Ernest Hemingway, drawing, 1925. Copyright © John Rosenthal. John F. Kennedy Library.

Ernest Hemingway, head and shoulders, John F. Kennedy Library.

Ernest Hemingway, in a Red Cross ambulance in World War I, 1918. John F. Kennedy Library.

Ernest Hemingway, in a courtyard in Paris, 1924. John F. Kennedy Library.

Harold Loeb, from the collection of Harold Loeb.

Harold Loeb, in the Pamplona bullring.

Max Perkins. Princeton University Library. Reproduced by permission.

Poster, reads "Pamplona Ferias y Fiestas San Fermin," 1923.

William "Bill" Smith, from the collection of William B. Smith.

Donald Ogden Stewart, courtesy of Kevin Brownlow.

The Sun Also Rises, handwritten manuscript. The Ernest Hemingway Foundation.

ABOUT *THE SUN ALSO RISES*

The Sun Also Rises was published in New York by Charles Scribner's Sons on 22 October 1926, in the midst of Hemingway's most celebrated decade as a writer. It sold for $2. It was preceded by *Three Stories and Ten Poems* (1923); *in our time* (1924), a collection of eighteen short, untitled sketches; *In Our Time* (1925), which republished those sketches and added new stories, some of which had appeared in small magazines; and a satire titled *The Torrents of Spring* (1926). Following *The Sun Also Rises* was a story collection, *Men Without Women* (1927), and another novel, *A Farewell to Arms* (1929), by the end of the decade.[1]

PLOT SUMMARY

OVERVIEW: The narrator, Jake Barnes, was wounded in World War I, about eight years before the narrative commences, and left sexually incapacitated.[2] During his convalescence, he fell in love with his nurse, Brett Ashley, who returned his love but who also required sexual satisfaction. After the war, Jake eventually settled on the Left Bank of the Seine in Paris, where he falls in with a group of expatriates, including Brett and her fiancé, Mike Campbell. Working as a journalist, fishing, and following the bullfights, Jake tries to keep his emotions in check and adjust to life after being wounded, but his love for Brett resurfaces each time he is in her presence. Her passion for men and her iconoclastic disposition draw her away from Jake, and her brief tryst with his friend Robert Cohn causes ill feeling among the expatriates. When Jake's friends from Paris follow him to Pamplona, Spain, for the annual running of the bulls, Brett forces Jake to sacrifice his status among the aficionados of bullfighting so that she may satisfy her desire for the young matador, Pedro Romero. As the novel closes, Jake acknowledges the high price he has paid for sustaining his relationship with Brett. Early in the novel, he wishes that he and Brett could go off to the country to live together, but at the conclusion, when Brett laments "we could have had such a damned good time together," Jake replies "Isn't it pretty to think so?"[3]

Hemingway as an ambulance driver in Italy, 1918

BOOK I

CHAPTER I: Jacob (Jake) Barnes devotes the first two chapters to Robert Cohn, about whom he has ambivalent feelings. Robert is a Princeton graduate and the son of wealthy Jewish parents. In college he was a boxing champion; afterward, he squandered most of his inheritance and married "the first girl who was nice to him," only to have her leave him for a "miniature-painter" (12). He then began backing a literary review before being "taken in hand" by Frances Clyne, who hoped her fortunes would rise with the magazine, and they began living together in Paris (13). There, Cohn has written his first novel, and Frances, fiercely jealous, continues her wait for him to marry her.

CHAPTER II: Robert travels to America the following winter, where his novel is well received and the attention accorded him by women seems to have awakened his desire for romance. He has been rereading W. H. Hudson's *The Purple Land* (1916), which "recounts splendid imaginary amorous adventures of a perfect English gentleman in an intensely romantic land" (17) and prompts his desire to travel to South America. He begs Jake to accompany him, all expenses paid, but Jake declines, offering instead that they go "to British East Africa to shoot," but Robert is not interested (18). Over a drink Robert confides that he feels as though his life is slipping by and he is not really living it. Jake scolds him for thinking geography is responsible for his malaise and tells him to start living his life in Paris. Jake is sorry about Cohn's unhappiness, but believes Cohn's own stubbornness and his propensity to get his ideas from books were bound to make him unhappy. Returning to his office, Jake works and Robert, who has accompanied him there, is lulled to sleep by the typewriter. As Jake awakens him, he mutters "I can't do it," presumably a reference to Frances's plea that they marry (20). The two men go to the Café Napolitain to have an aperitif and watch the crowd.

CHAPTER III: After Cohn leaves the Napolitain, Jake catches the eye of an attractive *poule* (prostitute) named Georgette and invites her to dine with him. She reveals her disdain for Paris as well as her bad teeth. In a horse-cab en route to a restaurant, she makes a sexual advance which Jake parries by saying "Never mind" and claiming that he is "sick," later attributing his sickness to a war injury (23). His friend Braddocks calls to him from another table at the restaurant, inviting him to join his party later for dancing. The crowd, including Frances and Robert, shifts to a dancing club, an airless, working-class *bal musette* (dance hall). After dancing with Georgette, Jake observes a group of homosexuals emerging from two taxis and entering the *bal*. "With them," Jake comments twice, "was Brett," the nurse with whom he fell in love while recuperating from his wound (28). The gay men anger him. Brett approaches Jake and they exchange friendly jibes about one another's company, when Cohn interrupts to ask Brett to dance; she declines, but his interest in her is apparent to both Jake and Brett. They leave together, and the moment that they are alone in the taxi she confesses "Oh, darling, I've been so miserable" (32).

CHAPTER IV: In the taxi, Jake kisses Brett, but she pulls away. Their conversation reveals that the two are in love but that Jake's wound prohibits their having the kind of relationship that Brett requires. They drive to the Café Select, where once again they encounter the crowd from the *bal* as well as Zizi, a painter, and his Greek friend and patron, Count Mippipopolous, a fat man who is buying champagne. Jake has a headache, so he excuses himself after arranging to meet Brett at the Hotel Crillon the following day at five o'clock. In bed he reads the bullfight papers, but soon the "old grievance," his wound, troubles his thoughts, and he is reduced to tears (38). A row caused by a drunken Brett arguing with the concierge awakens him. She has been drinking with Count Mippipopolous but has rejected his offer of $10,000 to accompany him to a resort. Jake declines her invitation to a champagne breakfast; and after she leaves, he thinks to himself, "This was Brett, that I had felt like crying about" (42).

CHAPTER V: The following day Jake attends an uneventful news conference and shares a cab with two other reporters, Woolsey and Krum. Jake returns to his office to discover Cohn, and they head to Wetzel's for hors d'oeuvres. Once again their conversation belies Jake's ambivalent feelings toward Cohn, who claims to be in love with Brett. Jake bluntly tells Cohn that "She's a drunk" and adds that she has twice married men whom she did not love (46). When Cohn again expresses his disbelief, Jake tells him to "go to hell" and Cohn rises from the table, insisting that Jake "take that back" (47). Jake apologizes and they drop the subject.

CHAPTER VI: Brett fails to meet Jake at the Hotel Crillon, so he takes a taxi to the Café Select, where he talks with Harvey Stone, who appears defeated, drunken, cynical, and unkind. When Cohn approaches, the drunken Stone calls him a "moron" and a case of "arrested development." Robert's reply is to suggest that "Some day somebody will push your face in," but Harvey walks away undeterred (50–51). Cohn confides to Jake that he is having trouble with his second novel. Soon Frances arrives, takes Jake aside, and informs him that Robert has decided not to marry her. Angry, she begins scolding Cohn when she and Jake return to the café. Her tirade is so vitriolic that Jake excuses himself and leaves Robert to endure Frances's verbal barrage.

CHAPTER VII: When Jake returns to his apartment, his concierge, Madame Duzinell, gives him his mail and a telegram and reports that Brett has visited. The telegram is from Jake's visiting American friend, the writer Bill Gorton. When Brett and the count return, Jake reminds her about their date, but she was apparently so "blind" when they made the arrangement that she has forgotten it. Jake feels "tired and pretty rotten," and when Brett comes into his room, he again professes his love for her (61). She sends the count for champagne and she and Jake discuss their prospects. While he would like to live with her in the country, she knows that she could not remain faithful to him; besides, she says, "I'm going away from you, and then [her fiancé] Michael's coming back" (62). When the count returns, the trio discusses the secret of enjoying life. Later, at dinner, the count asks why Jake and Brett have not married, and they supply ironic replies: he claims to want autonomy; she, a career. After dancing with Jake, Brett suddenly feels miserable and asks Jake to take her home.

BOOK II

CHAPTER VIII: With Brett and Robert gone, Jake gets ahead at work so that he is prepared to vacation with Bill Gorton. Bill visits Jake en route to Vienna, where he spends much of his time drinking; he is still inebriated when he reappears at Jake's flat. Bill and Jake set out for dinner, where they encounter Brett. She invites them to meet Michael Campbell at the Café Select, joins them for a drink, and returns home to bathe. Mike is friendly, funny, drunk, and especially glad to be reunited with Brett. Jake and Bill head off to the prizefights.

CHAPTER IX: The following day a letter arrives from Cohn in Hendaye (in southern France, near San Sebastián, Spain), inquiring about their upcoming fishing trip, which they had first discussed the previous winter; Jake replies, arranging to meet Cohn. That evening at the Select,

Mike asks if he and Brett might come along, too. When Mike goes off for a haircut, Brett reveals to Jake that she has been in San Sebastián with Robert, and she and Jake decide that she should write Cohn to give him an opportunity to avoid the trip. Robert is keen on going, however, so Jake arranges to meet with Mike and Brett at the Hotel Montoya in Pamplona. Bill and Jake head south on a train that is packed with pilgrims headed for Lourdes. Cohn meets them at the station in Bayonne, France, and the three take a taxi to the hotel that Cohn has selected.

CHAPTER X: Jake and Bill enjoy the scenery during the drive; Cohn sleeps. They are met by Montoya in front of his hotel in Pamplona. Jake picks up the bullfight tickets and then visits the cathedral, praying for everyone but not feeling particularly religious. Because Brett and Mike fail to arrive on their scheduled train, Jake accompanies Cohn to the station to meet them. Montoya delivers a telegram from them saying that they have stopped over in San Sebastián. Jake shares the message and then confesses in an interior monologue that he hates Cohn because of his affair with Brett. The next morning Jake buys three tickets for Burguete, only to discover that Robert has decided to go to San Sebastián to retrieve Brett and Mike. Jake and Bill are annoyed with Robert, but they admit that he can be nice, too. Both men are anxious to leave Cohn's complications behind and go fishing in Spain.

CHAPTER XI: The bus to Burguete is crowded with Basques, who immediately befriend Jake and Bill. When Cohn waves goodbye, all of the Basques return the gesture. En route, a Basque seated nearby points out the fine view, which Jake and Bill also notice and appreciate. Once in Burguete, Bill and Jake locate their inn, agree upon a price for their accommodations once they discover that the wine is included, and then read and smoke in bed to warm themselves against the chill of the high altitude.

CHAPTER XII: In the morning, Jake and Bill exchange their usual comic banter, and Bill mocks America's disdain for the expatriates, telling Jake that he has "lost touch with the soil" and embraced "[f]ake European standards" (120). Bill's comic riff strikes a flat note when he says, "One group claims women support you. Another group claims you're impotent" (120). Next, they go fishing. Jake quickly catches six trout and turns to reading. When Bill returns for lunch, the pair resume their allusive dialogue about prohibition and fundamentalism. Questioned by Bill,

Jake admits to being in love with Brett "[o]ff and on for a hell of a long time" but says that he does not "give a damn any more." He also says that "technically" he is a Catholic, but is at a loss to explain what that means (128–129). Jake summarizes their stay favorably, mentioning swimming, fishing, and three-handed bridge with a companionable man named Harris (who later explains his name is actually *Wilson*-Harris). Jake remarks, "There was no word from Robert Cohn nor from Brett and Mike" (130).

CHAPTER XIII: The idyllic interlude concludes when Mike's letter arrives, attributing their delay in San Sebastián to Brett's having had too much to drink. Jake and Bill decide to return to Pamplona in the afternoon, and a cable from Cohn informs them of his planned arrival there on the next day. Bill and Jake spend their last few hours with Harris, who is genuinely saddened by their departure and gives them each fishing flies that he tied himself as a token of friendship. Back in Pamplona, they learn from Montoya that their friends have already arrived. Bill and Jake find Brett, Mike, and Cohn at a café table, and the whole crowd goes off to see the bulls unloaded. They witness a bull goring a defenseless steer, and back at the café, Cohn observes, "It's no life being a steer" (145). This comment draws a hostile response from Mike, who resents Cohn's affair with Brett. The scene ends when Bill ushers Cohn out, and Jake has to retrieve him from his room for dinner. After much wine, Jake observes, "It seemed they were all such nice people" (150).

CHAPTER XIV: Too drunk to sleep, Jake reads and reflects on his personal philosophy, which involves payments and rewards—"You paid some way for everything that was any good"—but he then decides that his goal is to learn "how to live" (152). Over the next few days, Cohn studies Spanish; Bill joins Jake in café sitting, or stays in his room to write; and Brett and Mike sleep until noon. Jake attends mass a few times and is joined once when Brett expresses an interest in hearing him give confession; he explains to her that it will be in a language she does not understand. She opts to have her fortune told by the gypsies encamped nearby.

CHAPTER XV: The fiesta "exploded" at noon on Sunday 6 July (158). Jake reminds readers that San Fermin is also a religious festival and that the mass that morning was crowded. Just before noon, Jake joins Robert and Bill at a café. They watch the rocket go up in the square announcing the beginning of the fiesta, hear the music of the *riau-riau* (sung during the traditional procession of the festival) with its fifes and drums, and see the

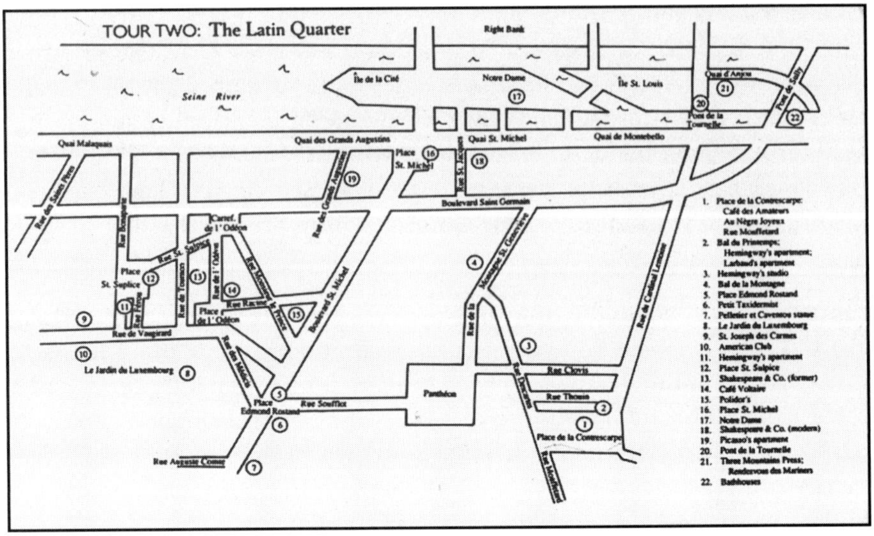

Map of the Paris Latin Quarter, where Ernest and Hadley Hemingway settled in January of 1922

dancers winding through the streets. Brett is suddenly appropriated by a group of dancers who take her to a wineshop and use her as an image to dance around. When Jake returns from purchasing some leather wine bags, he joins everyone—except Cohn, who has passed out—in eating from a common bowl. The following morning, Jake watches from the stone balcony of Cohn's hotel room (where he has slept because he could not find his room key) as the bulls run through the streets. Before the bullfight, Bill tries to explain to Cohn that he should look away if the bulls gore the horses; Cohn arrogantly rejects the advice. Back at the hotel, Montoya introduces Bill and Jake to Pedro Romero, a friendly nineteen-year-old whose extreme good looks are matched by his extraordinary skill as a bullfighter. His performance in the ring impresses everyone, and Brett is enamored of his green trousers. The next day Romero fights well and Brett grows more infatuated with him. The day following, the bullfights are bad, and none are scheduled for the day after that.

CHAPTER XVI: Rain drives the fiesta under cover, but the party continues unabated. Montoya visits Jake to explain that the American ambassador and his female friends have invited Romero to their hotel. "Don't give Romero the message," is Jake's reply, which pleases Montoya because he is afraid associating with such women will ruin

Romero as a bullfighter (176). When Jake returns to his friends, their drunkenness makes him a little uncomfortable. Seated nearby, Romero invites Jake to his table, and Brett soon joins them. Montoya, noticing Romero and Brett seated together, "did not even nod" at Jake (181). The gang drinks a toast to Romero, who then exits, leaving Mike and Cohn to argue as the fireworks display fails miserably outside. Mike joins Bill and Edna, a female friend from Biarritz. Cohn attempts to sit with Brett and Jake, only to be sent away by Brett so that she and Jake can walk together through town. She tells him that she is mad about Romero, and asks Jake to arrange a meeting between them, so he takes her to Romero at the café and sits with them a while before excusing himself. When Jake returns twenty minutes later, they are gone.

CHAPTER XVII: Outside the Bar Milano, Jake finds Bill, Mike, and Edna, who have been thrown out. The four have just sat down at another café when Cohn approaches, demanding to know where Brett has gone. Mike taunts Cohn, who then calls Jake a pimp, and a brief fistfight ensues in which Cohn easily bests both Jake and Mike. When Jake recovers his senses, he heads back to the hotel, where he grudgingly accepts Robert's apology and learns that Cohn will leave the following day. After watching a man killed during the running of the bulls the next morning, Jake learns from Mike that Cohn found Brett and Romero and "massacred the poor, bloody bull-fighter" (205). Jake is shocked. Cohn has beaten Romero severely, but Mike says the matador's refusal to quit has "ruined Cohn" (206). Mike then provides details about Brett's unhappy past: her husband slept with a loaded service revolver and threatened to kill her.

CHAPTER XVIII: At noon on the last day of the fiesta, Bill, Mike, and Jake are drinking beer and eating shrimp at a café when Brett approaches. Mike is surly, inquiring after her "boy friend" and tipping over the table as Jake and Brett depart. She explains that she feels "altogether changed" by her relationship with Romero (210–211). At the bullfight, Jake sees through the glasses that Romero's face "looked badly marked" (216). Jake says little about the bullfighter Marcial Lalanda but links another, Belmonte, in stature and prowess to Romero, commenting that neither of them "seemed to have anything in common with the others" (216). The final day of the fiesta belongs to Romero: he overcomes his personal pain, fights spectacularly, and is carried from the ring on the shoulders of the admiring crowd. At a café, Bill encourages Jake to drink absinthe after absinthe until he becomes as drunk as he has ever been. Returning to the hotel, he learns from Mike that Brett and Romero left on the seven o'clock train. Jake tries to get some sleep and thinks about the ongoing fiesta that "did not mean anything" any longer (228). Unable to sleep, he joins Bill and Mike downstairs in the dining room where "it seemed as though about six people were missing" (228).

BOOK III

CHAPTER XIX: The next morning Jake, Bill, and Mike decide to get a car to carry them as far as Bayonne. Montoya avoids Jake and his friends as they pay their hotel bill. After reaching Bayonne they continue to nearby Biarritz, where they roll dice at a bar to see who pays for drinks. Mike continues to roll and lose until he is forced to confess that he has no money, which shocks Bill. They deposit Mike at his hotel in Saint Jean, and Jake sees Bill's train off in Bayonne. At his hotel Jake dines alone and enjoys "drinking slowly and . . . tasting the wine" (236). In the morning he leaves by train for San Sebastián, where he goes to the beach. After a pleasant walk about town Jake returns to his hotel, where French and Belgian cyclists are stopping for the night. The next day he receives a telegram from Brett asking him to come to the Hotel Montana in Madrid, so he takes the evening express train and arrives at the hotel the following morning. She feels very small when she greets him with a kiss and trembles in his arms. She has sent Romero away despite his wanting to marry her. She will return to Mike, she claims, who is "nice" and "awful," "my sort of thing" (247). The two decide to lunch at Botin's; Brett scarcely eats, but Jake consumes an enormous lunch and three bottles of wine. When he orders two more bottles of wine, Brett warns him against getting drunk; he suggests that they take a taxi through town. In the circle of his arm, Brett says, "Oh Jake . . . we could have had such a damned good time together." When their taxi slows suddenly and she is pressed against him, he ambiguously replies, "Yes . . . Isn't it pretty to think so?" (251).

PEOPLE OF *THE SUN ALSO RISES*

Jacob Barnes (Jake). From Kansas City but living alone on the Left Bank in Paris, Jake is the narrator. His wound in World War I has left him impotent. He and Brett Ashley, a nurse whom he has met while recuperating from his wound, are therefore unable to consummate their love. He works as a journalist and tries to focus his passion on fishing and the bullfights, traveling to Spain each year for the annual running of the bulls. He is a keen observer, often speaking and thinking ironically as he attempts to come to terms with his injury and his love for Brett.

Barnes is based loosely on Hemingway, who was wounded in World War I (though not rendered impotent), fell in love with his nurse, worked as a journalist, and attended the bullfights in Pamplona in 1925.

Brett Ashley (Lady Ashley). A modern Englishwoman, Brett smokes, drinks, is promiscuous, keeps her own hours, and selects her own company. Her own "true love" died in the war, where she served as a V.A.D. (Voluntary Aid Detachment) nurse. She meets and falls in love with Jake while he is hospitalized but marries the drunken and abusive Lord Ashley, from whom she is seeking a divorce when the novel opens. Thirty-four years old and an alcoholic, she is engaged to Mike Campbell and in love with Jake Barnes. Despite her financial dependence on men, she insists on control over her own body and chooses her own lovers.

She is based upon the twice-married-and-divorced Duff Twysden (1892–1938), an attractive alcoholic who had an affair with Harold Loeb (Robert Cohn), was engaged to Pat Guthrie (Michael Campbell), and was among the expatriates who attended the fiesta in Pamplona in 1925.[4]

Robert Cohn. A Jewish American expatriate living in Paris, the thirty-four-year-old Robert is the divorced father of three, living with Frances Clyne as the novel opens. He abandons her, however, before his tryst with Brett in San Sebastián. In many ways, he is the opposite of the expatriate crowd: idealistic and romantic where they are cynical; asleep for beautiful scenery or high frivolity while others are observant and engaged; public in his displays of emotion where others are private; sober while they are drunk; serious when they are ironic.

The model for Cohn is Harold Loeb (1891–1974), progeny of the multimillionaire Loeb and Guggenheim families and graduate of Princeton. Loeb edited *Broom*, an avant-garde magazine; published a novel; had an affair with Duff Twysden; and caused dissension among her male friends in Pamplona in 1925.[5]

Michael Campbell (Mike). Brett's bankrupt Scottish fiancé, Mike, will allegedly inherit his mother's substantial wealth. He is usually tolerant of Brett's promiscuous behavior, but her affair with Cohn rankles him. He makes light of his status as a bankrupt and relies on his friends to pay his bills. Although Mike is an alcoholic and completely irresponsible with money, Brett tells Jake that she will return to him at the end of the novel.

Campbell is based on the alcoholic Scotsman Pat Guthrie, the fiancé of Duff Twysden whom some thought to be her cousin and others thought to be a latent homosexual.[6]

Frances Clyne. The live-in fiancée of Robert Cohn, whom he sends to England when his infatuation with Brett begins, Frances has forgone alimony from her previous husband in an effort to get a divorce quickly and marry Cohn. She becomes vindictive when Robert decides that he cannot marry her. While her choices to live with Cohn and divorce her previous husband suggest her modern sensibilities, she ultimately seems focused on the traditional pursuits of marriage and children. Her nature reveals itself when she humiliates Robert at an outdoor café. She disappears in chapter VI and is not mentioned again until chapter XVIII, when Jake tells Bill that Robert will probably resume his relationship with Frances when he returns to Paris (226). Her character is based upon Kathleen "Kitty" Cannell, whose romantic involvement with Harold Loeb ended just prior to his affair with Duff Twysden.[7]

Bill Gorton. A good friend of Jake, he is a writer from Chicago. Visiting Europe on holiday from America and Prohibition, Bill is consequently intoxicated much of the time. Like other men, he finds Brett very attractive but halts his inquiries when he learns that she is engaged to be married. He likes Mike as well, but he soon learns that Mike's irresponsibility with money is a matter for reproach. Bill is the chief source of humor in the novel.

Bill is based in part on Donald Ogden Stewart (1894–1980), an American friend of Hemingway and companion at the fiesta in Pamplona in 1925. He was a successful humorist and parodist in the 1920s and later became an Academy Award–winning screenwriter.[8] Bill is also modeled upon William ("Bill") Smith, a childhood friend and fishing companion of Hemingway who joined him for the fiesta in 1925.

Juanito Montoya. Proprietor of the Hotel Montoya in Pamplona and, for a while, a friend of Jake for whom he saves rooms while Jake and Bill travel to Burguete to fish. Montoya can forgive anything of one who has *afición* for bullfights; consequently, he forgives Jake his friends. Montoya trusts Jake and comes to him when the American ambassador, who is accompanied by a predatory female, invites the young Pedro Romero to his hotel.

Jake encourages Montoya to refrain from extending the invitation, a gesture which Montoya admires. But shortly thereafter, Jake betrays Montoya and his *afición* when he introduces Brett to Romero.

Juanito Quintana is the model for Montoya. Quintana owned a hotel in Pamplona and was a great aficionado who remained friends with Hemingway throughout his life.[9]

Pedro Romero. The nineteen-year-old matador who exhibits a purity of line, grace, and courage that identify him as the real thing among the rising generation of bullfighters. Despite his many heroic qualities, he is mesmerized, like several other males in the novel, by Brett. Badly beaten by Robert Cohn, he nonetheless performs spectacularly, killing his bulls *recibiendo,* by having them charge at him and impale themselves on his killing sword. Pedro Romero is also the name of a renowned Spanish matador (1754–1839).

Romero's character is based upon Cayetano Ordóñez (1904–1961), who fought skillfully under the name of "Niño de la Palma" in the 1920s and was the father of Antonio Ordóñez, whom Hemingway befriended and wrote about in *The Dangerous Summer* (1985).

Georgette Hobin. A *poule* (prostitute) with bad teeth, she is Jake's companion for dinner at the Nègre de Toulouse and dancing at the *bal musette* in the richly ironic third chapter. Her sexual overture to Jake during their taxi ride provides the occasion for Jake's first mention of his injury, which he attributes to a war wound. She, too, claims to be sick. Like Cohn, she does not enjoy Paris. Jake finds dining with her dull until, after a second bottle of wine, the conversation comes more easily, and she announces that Jake is "not a bad type" (24). Jake returns the compliment by leaving money for her with the proprietor of the *bal musette* before leaving with Brett.

Count Mippipopolous. Enormously wealthy and fat, the Greek count owns a chain of sweet shops in the United States and is introduced to Brett and Jake by Zizi, a portrait painter. He likes the quiet life and conversation and offers Brett money to go away with him. Brett describes him as "one of us," perhaps referring to his use of irony, his wit, or his war wounds. His insistence on getting good value for his money links him to Jake, as do his acute observations.

Wilson-Harris. An Englishman whom Jake and Bill meet and fish with in Burguete. Sensitive and companionable, Wilson-Harris is genuinely pained when Jake and Bill return to Pamplona, claiming that he has "not had much fun since the war" (134). He gives them fishing

Poster announcing the July 1923 Fiesta of San Fermín

flies that he has tied himself as a token of his affection.

Edna. An attractive friend of Bill's from Biarritz, Edna accompanies Bill and Mike to the Bar Milano, where they encounter men from whom Mike has previously borrowed money. Fighting ensues and they are removed by the police. Edna finds the ordeal hilarious. She disappears when Brett rejoins the gang.

Henry Braddocks. Robert Cohn's "literary friend," Henry is an expatriate writer and organizer of the "dancings" where Jake and Brett first meet in the novel. His character is based upon Ford Madox Ford (1873–1939), the English novelist best known for *The Good Soldier* (1927) and influential editor of the *transatlantic review,* for which Hemingway worked as a subeditor.

Mrs. Braddocks. Jake mocks her slow-wittedness at failing to grasp his comic intention when he introduces Georgette Hobin, a common *poule,* as his fiancée. Her first name may be "Jo," although the text is unclear. Her character may be based upon Ford Madox Ford's companion, Stella Bowen, an Australian painter.

Harvey Stone. A friend of Jake's whom he meets at the Café Select, the drunken Harvey is friendly toward Jake but hostile toward Cohn. Modeled after Harold Edmund Stearns (1891–1943), a Harvard graduate and editor of *Civilization in the United States: An Inquiry by Thirty Americans* (1922), which criticized American materialism and puritanism, and author of *Liberalism in America* (1919) and *America and the Young Intellectual* (1921).[10] A resident of Paris during the 1920s, he also wrote a column on horse racing for the *Chicago Tribune.*[11]

ABOUT ERNEST HEMINGWAY

Ernest Hemingway (1899–1961) was reared in Oak Park, Illinois, a conservative, upper-middle-class suburb of Chicago. Preferring a career in journalism to college, he began working as a reporter for *The Kansas City Star* after high school. He participated in World War I as an ambulance driver and was seriously wounded while delivering chocolate and cigarettes to Italians in the trenches. During his recuperation, he fell in love with his nurse, but upon his return to America, she ended the romance. Determined to become a writer, Hemingway returned to journalism, married Hadley Richardson, and in the fall of 1921 traveled to Paris, where many of the greatest writers and artists of the day were residing. While working as a correspondent for *The Toronto Star,* he studied the craft of writing, learning from such writers as Sherwood Anderson, Ezra Pound, and Gertrude Stein. His first two books, *Three Stories and Ten Poems* (1923) and *in our time* (1924), were small but managed to announce him as a serious artist. Although he had not published much, he was known by fellow artists and critics on both sides of the Atlantic. His first novel, which many believe to be his best, brought him international fame and forever changed his life.[12]

"When I saw my wife again standing by the tracks as the train came in by the piled logs at the station, I wished I had died before I ever loved anyone but her. She was smiling, the sun on her lovely face tanned by the snow and sun, beautifully built, her hair red gold in the sun, grown out all winter awkwardly and beautifully, and Mr. Bumby standing with her, blond and chunky and with winter cheeks looking like a good Vorarlberg boy."

Ernest Hemingway

From *A Moveable Feast* (New York: Scribners, 1964), p. 210.

Growing up in the first decades of the twentieth century, young Ernest witnessed the automobile replace the carriage and social clubs supplant church activities. As a teenager, he saw the streets paved, gas- lights replaced by electric ones, and silent movies arrive. The cows and chickens gradually left Oak Park and the surrounding prairie began filling with houses. Hemingway's life must have struck him as mundanely suburban and nearly devoid of opportunity for distinction, let alone heroism. So, with adolescent enthusiasm, he was quick to join the Red Cross at age eighteen as an ambulance driver; later he would recall "just thinking that we [the Allies] were the home team and the Austrians were the visiting team."[13] But his severe wounding on 8 July 1918 by an Austrian mortar shell—essentially a five-gallon canister filled with explosives and steel fragments—gave him a shock that woke him to the realization of his own mortality. Suffering more than two hundred shrapnel wounds in addition to a pair of wounds from machine-gun fire, he was the first American to be

"Saturday—The Scribners (father and son) are publishing The Sun Also Rises. It is a treatise on basic loneliness and the inadequacy of promiscuity. Perkins the Scribners editor is enthused. Not as much for the moral content but what he naively calls the dialogue. I must study how to eliminate this as well as the overlong description of the Spanish country side."

Ernest Hemingway

From "Ernest von Hemingstein's Journal," item 407a, John F. Kennedy Library; reprinted in *Hemingway: Essays of Reassessment,* edited by Frank Scafella (New York: Oxford University Press, 1991), p. 52.

wounded on the Italian front and survive. The story of his near-fatal encounter was dramatic enough, but Hemingway embellished it further in the retelling.

Still recuperating, Hemingway attempted to write commercial fiction for popular magazines such as *The Saturday Evening Post* and took a job writing feature stories with *The Toronto Star Weekly* in 1920. That summer he returned to the family cottage at Walloon Lake in Michigan, where he had summered throughout his life, but a conflict with his mother sent him packing to Chicago. There he wrote for *The Cooperative Commonwealth* and continued to work on his own fiction in the evenings. In Chicago he met Hadley Richardson, and they married in September of 1921; by December they were in Paris. Between Hadley's modest trust fund and his own income from selling news stories, the young couple lived comfortably. Before leaving Chicago, Ernest had also secured letters of introduction from Sherwood Anderson, an established author who had recently traveled to France. The letters, addressed to prominent expatriates, eased the Hemingways' transition to Paris and introduced Ernest to influential writers. Although he kept busy covering economic conferences, the Greco-Turkish War, and the Lausanne Peace Conference, he still found time to write serious fiction, having abandoned his attempts to write slick, formulaic stories before voyaging overseas. Hadley packed nearly all of his manuscripts, intending to deliver them to Ernest at the conclusion of the conference in Lausanne, but the suitcase was stolen.

In the following year, 1923, the Hemingways witnessed their first bullfights and Hemingway's first book, *Three Stories and Ten Poems,* was published. They returned to Canada in August for the birth of Ernest's only child by Hadley, John Hadley Nicanor Hemingway, in October. Hemingway's first book was followed the next year by a collection of short prose sketches titled *in our time.* The Hemingways returned to Paris in January of 1924, this time to a flat over a sawmill near the Luxembourg Gardens. Working as an unpaid editor for Ford Madox Ford's *transatlantic review,* Hemingway found time to produce his own short stories. In 1925 he published *In Our Time,* which featured short stories alternating with the sketches that had appeared in the previous year's volume.

Harold Loeb, the original for Robert Cohn, astride a bull in Pamplona

Hemingway recast much of that year's summer vacation in Pamplona as roman à clef, pleasing some and offending others, prompting memoirs and refutations, and introducing himself to his international public. The Hemingways joined Bill Smith (one of the models for Bill Gorton), a boyhood friend of Ernest, for fishing on the Irati River in Spain. Returning to Pamplona, they rejoined their friends from Paris, Duff Twysden (Brett Ashley), Pat Guthrie (Mike Campbell), and Harold Loeb (Robert Cohn), as well as the accomplished humorist Donald Ogden Stewart (another model for Bill Gorton). Tensions were high between Guthrie and Loeb because Duff and Loeb had recently had an affair. This undercurrent of ill feelings colored the week's festivities, and on one occasion, Hemingway and Loeb nearly came to blows. The highlight of the fiesta was the performance of the bullfighter Cayetano Ordóñez (Pedro Romero), who shone brightly next to the aging Juan Belmonte.

Hemingway began drafting his novel following the fiesta and completed the task two months later. The handwritten draft required extensive revision, so he allowed it to remain dormant through the fall and turned his energies to a parody of Sherwood Anderson titled *The Tor-*

"How simple the writing of literature would be if it were only necessary to write in another way what has been well written. It is because we have had such great writers in the past that a writer is driven far out past where he can go, out to where no one can help him."

Ernest Hemingway

From Hemingway's Nobel Prize acceptance speech, read by John C. Cabot, U.S. ambassador to Sweden, on 10 December 1954.

rents of Spring (1926). Because Hemingway and Anderson shared Boni and Liveright as their publisher, there was little chance that the firm would publish a parody of one of their leading authors. Knowing this, Hemingway offered them the work. Their refusal of it released Hemingway from his contract, and he was free to act on the advice of his new friend, F. Scott Fitzgerald, who was encouraging him to sign with Charles Scribner's Sons. The publishing firm's famous editor, Maxwell Perkins, was eager to have Hemingway aboard, so he agreed to publish *The Torrents of Spring* as well as *The Sun Also Rises*, although he had not yet read the roman à clef.

Revising the book in Shruns, Austria, Hemingway produced a typescript that satisfied him and mailed it off to Perkins. In the meantime he allowed his friend Fitzgerald to read a copy, and the more established and successful author recommended substantial revisions to the opening chapters. Instead of making the piecemeal changes, Hemingway deleted everything up to the introduction of Robert Cohn. Maxwell Perkins requested and was granted further, minor revisions, and the book appeared in October of 1926.

That fall, Hemingway's relationship with Hadley fell apart. In the spring of 1927, he married Pauline Pfeiffer. Her wealth allowed them to travel, purchase a home in Key West, and go on safari in Africa. They had two sons and their marriage, lasting from May 1927 to November 1940, spanned Hemingway's most productive period, which included the short-story collection *Men without Women* (1927); the novels *A Farewell to Arms* (1929), *To Have and Have Not* (1935), and *For Whom the Bell Tolls* (1940); *Death in the Afternoon* (1932), a nonfiction work on bullfighting; and numerous short stories.

In 1940 Hemingway married the writer and journalist Martha Gellhorn and purchased the Finca Vigía (Lookout Farm) in Cuba. They traveled to China together as war correspondents, but two writers in the family soon proved one too many, and they were divorced in 1945. The following year Ernest married Mary Welsh, whom he had met while covering World War II for *Collier's* magazine. He worked on the novel *The Garden of Eden* (published posthumously in 1986) but abandoned it to write *Across the River and into the Trees* (1950), which was poorly received. He recovered his prestige with critical and popular audiences in

1952 when he published *The Old Man and the Sea. Life* magazine featured the entire novella in a single issue that sold more than five million copies in two days.

The winter of 1953–1954 was especially damaging. While on safari, Mary, Ernest, and their pilot crashed in their small plane. The plane that rescued them crashed as well, leaving Hemingway with several serious injuries, including a crushed vertebra and a severe concussion. The erroneous news of his death was published throughout the world, and Hemingway had the opportunity to read his own premature obituaries.[14]

For nearly his entire adult life, he enjoyed an enormous reputation as both a literary artist and a public personality. Without the aid of either a press or literary agent, Hemingway became the "architect of his public reputation" by facilitating his own publicity and by generating a persona in his nonfiction works that became one of his most famous creations.[15] By the 1950s he was a well-entrenched American icon, the subject of sixteen major feature articles in *Life* between 1941 and 1961.[16] He was as popular as the celebrities, athletes, and military leaders of his day; and posthumously he remains in the public domain, his face on a postage stamp, his papers housed at the John F. Kennedy Library.[17]

No longer a young man in 1954, Hemingway's recuperation was slow. In October his brief acceptance speech for the Nobel Prize mentions loneliness three times in four sentences and demonstrates his consciousness of the dual life—public man and private writer—that he had been living for nearly thirty years:

> Writing, at its best, is a lonely life. Organizations for writers palliate the writer's loneliness but I doubt if they improve his writing. He grows in public stature as he sheds his loneliness and often his work deteriorates. For he does his work alone and if he is a good enough writer he must face eternity, or the lack of it, each day.[18]

He continued writing about his most recent trip to Africa (posthumously published in 1999 as *True at First Light*), participated in the filming of *The Old Man and the Sea,* worked on sketches for a memoir of his Paris years (posthumously published in 1964 as *A Moveable Feast*), and returned to Spain in 1956 to see the bullfights. This experience rekindled his love for Spain and the bulls, and he agreed in 1959 to write an article for *Life* on the *mano-a-mano* (competitive bullfighting) between Antonio Ordóñez (son of Cayetano Ordóñez) and Luis Miguel Dominguín, the country's leading matadors.

The piece swelled to 120,000 words, and Hemingway required help in cutting it for serialization. Excerpts of the work were posthumously published as *The Dangerous Summer* in 1985. He struggled too, to revise and arrange his memoirs of Paris. Hemingway left Cuba in July of 1960, following Fidel Castro's rise to power, and settled in Idaho, where he and Mary had purchased a large house.[19] Ernest remained lonely and depressed. When he became suicidal, he entered the Mayo Clinic in November of 1960, where he received electroshock therapy. Released two months later, he remained unwell and was hospitalized again in the spring. Upon returning from the hospital in July of 1961, he committed suicide. Few personalities were as commanding as Hemingway's, and few artists have been as influential.

MAJOR THEMES, METAPHORS, AND ALLUSIONS

Without an omniscient narrator in *The Sun Also Rises* to make his points for him, Hemingway often reveals his themes by presenting contrasts.[20] This method, like his use of irony, requires much of readers: they must first perceive the contrast and then interpret it. Some contrasts, such as the Parisian city versus the Spanish countryside, are easily noticed, but others are more subtle. For example, Hemingway prefaces his novel with contrasting epigraphs. The second is from Ecclesiastes 1, verses 4–7:

> One generation passeth away, and another generation cometh; but the earth abideth forever. . . . The sun also ariseth, and the sun goeth down, and hasteth to the place where he arose. . . . The wind goeth toward the south, and turneth about unto the north; it whirleth about continually, and the wind returneth again according to his circuits. . . . All the rivers run into the sea; yet the sea is not full; unto the place from whence the rivers come, thither they return again.

Some readers initially inferred that the epigraph was meant to suggest "motion which goes no place."[21] Applying this reading to the novel, they asserted that the characters eventually settle, like the sun, wind, and river, where they began. This pessimistic reading was reinforced by typical interpretations of the first epigraph, "You are all a lost generation," attributed to "Gertrude Stein in conversation." In combination, the epigraphs seemed to suggest that the novel is about a bunch of ne'er-do-wells who go no place.

When Hemingway discovered that readers perceived the epigraphs as complementary rather than contradictory, he immediately asked his editor, Maxwell Perkins, to excise a portion of the second epigraph as originally quoted so that his counterpoint would be unambiguous. Cut was the second verse from chapter 1 of Ecclesiastes, "Vanity of vanities, saith the Preacher, vanity of vanities; all is vanity. . . ."[22] His intention was to "play off against that splendid bombast" from Stein "the quotation from Eccles." because "Nobody knows about the generation that follows them and certainly has no right to Judge." He added that

> The point of the book to me was that the earth abideth forever—having a great deal of fondness and admiration for the earth and not a hell of a lot for my generation and caring little about Vanities. . . . I didn't mean the book to be a hollow or bitter satire but a damn tragedy with the earth abiding for ever as the hero.[23]

Even perceptive readers such as Perkins, who admitted that he had "misunderstood the relations of these two quotations," failed to see that Hemingway meant to reject what he called "the Gertrude Stein thing" and to embrace the idea that generations may come and go, but the earth abides forever.[24] The "Stein thing" stuck, however, and Hemingway was henceforth known as the chronicler of the "lost generation" as if he had sought to glamorize café sitting.

Few readers, however, failed to notice that the generation depicted in the novel was the walking wounded, physical or psychological casualties of World War I. Mike Campbell has been to war, and whereas the extent to which his wartime experiences have contributed to his alcoholism and irresponsibility is impossible to determine, he certainly attributes no value to the medals he has won (he does not even send away for them). Brett has lost her "true love" to dysentery during the war, and it has apparently unhinged her current husband, Lord Ashley, an abusive alcoholic who sleeps with a loaded gun under his pillow. Wilson-Harris confesses to Bill and Jake that he has not had much fun in the nine years that have elapsed since the armistice. Jake, of course, comes away from his war experience suffering from impotence.

Jake's sturdy work ethic, his financial responsibility, and his serious reflection upon his spiritual life serve as a clear contrast to the lives of most of his friends. Bill Gorton jokingly tallies the common criticisms, although they seem to apply less to Jake than to his friends:

> "You're an expatriate. You've lost touch with the soil. You get precious. Fake European standards have ruined you. You drink yourself to death. You become obsessed by sex. You spend all your time talking, not working. You are an expatriate, see? You hang around cafés. . . . One group claims women support you. Another group claims you're impotent." (120)

The generation of young Americans who participated in the war embraced serious responsibilities in service to their country. Even noncombatants like Hemingway dealt regularly with life and death; in fact, one of Hemingway's first duties as a Red Cross worker was to collect the body fragments of workers who had been blown up in a munitions fac-

Harold Loeb

tory in Italy.[25] When such veterans returned home, they often found America stifling. F. Scott Fitzgerald's Nick Carraway, the narrator of *The Great Gatsby* (1925), recalls that he "enjoyed the counter-raid so thoroughly that I came back restless, instead of being the warm center of the world the middle-west now seemed like the ragged edge of the universe."[26] Harold Krebs, a veteran of considerable action who appears in Hemingway's story "Soldier's Home," is made to feel beholden to his mother for persuading his father to allow him to use the family car. He is warned against mussing the morning paper because his "father can't read his *Star* if it's been mussed," and is accused of having no ambition and failing to be a credit to his community.[27] Suffocating at home, in a country that prohibited alcohol and censored art, many Americans went abroad, taking advantage of the favorable exchange rate, and enjoyed life in Europe, where jazz filled the clubs, liquor ran freely in the cafés, and the moral strictures of the Midwest did not apply.

Having been through the war, this generation developed a distrust for political rhetoric. Oral communication had become suspect, and often the characters speak elliptically, hinting at their meaning in such a way as to communicate effectively with initiates but to baffle outsiders. Jake and Brett illustrate this in their initial conversation at the *bal musette,* leaving Cohn, an outsider, baffled. The aficionados, too, eschew excessive verbiage like Frances Clyne's diatribe against Robert, and substitute the succinct "buen hombre" (137). The preference for authentic touch rather than inauthentic rhetoric is echoed in the scene where Jake purchases leather wine bottles in Pamplona. When the merchants learn that Jake intends to use them rather than sell them, they give him "the lowest price" and slap him on the back (160).

The novel offers geographical contrasts as well. France is modern and urban; Spain is primitive and rural. The French waiters are materialistic and the meal tickets on the train are doled out at the "office of the company" in an impersonal way that infuriates Jake and Bill. In Spain, conversely, the woman in the *posada* (inn) where Jake, Bill, and the

Basques stop for wine, returns his tip to him, thinking he has overpaid by mistake. The Basques on the bus share their wine bags freely, and the *riau-riau* dancers insist that the expatriates eat from their large bowl of tuna fish, onions, and vinegar: "Eat," says one of the natives, "What do you think it's here for?" (161).[28]

Hemingway also contrasts his heroes with their tutors. This contrast is more clearly seen in Hemingway's short stories, but it is found in *The Sun Also Rises* as well.[29] If readers assume that Jake Barnes is the hero who has a conflict to resolve, then they should be able to identify those characters who teach him to act or think in a new way. Candidates for the role as the novel's tutors include Pedro Romero, who exhibits purity of line and grace under pressure; to a lesser extent, Count Mippipopolous, who has developed a personal philosophy that enables him to enjoy life; and Juan Belmonte, who endures physical pain and adverse criticism.

Hemingway's use of allusion in the novel also invites comparison with mythical, biblical, and historical people and incidents. Brett Ashley is associated with Homeric myth. Robert Cohn calls her Circe because of her ability to turn men into swine, and she is sometimes viewed as the pagan goddess of the novel. She provides an image for the Basques to dance around, and when she is turned away from the Catholic Church, she comfortably fits in at the gypsy camp where she has her fortune told. Some critics view the entire novel as Hemingway's version of T. S. Eliot's *The Waste Land* (1922). That poem, a lament of the postwar world, is filled with epigraphs, ironies, juxtapositions, crisp images, and mythical allusions. Hemingway's version alludes to the myth of the ailing Fisher King, who appears in Chrétien de Troyes's *Conte du Graal* (ca. 1100), one of the earliest versions of the legend of search for the Holy Grail (the chalice used by Jesus at the Last Supper). The Fisher King's sexual wound is mirrored by the barrenness of his entire kingdom. Jake's Paris, like the wounded Fisher King's dominion and Eliot's London in *The Waste Land,* is sterile and unproductive. In Thomas Malory's *Le Morte Darthur* (1485), Galahad returns to the Fisher King's castle and experiences a vision of the grail, whereupon the Fisher King's wounds are healed and his lands restored. In Eliot's poem, the waters necessary to restore the dry land are hinted at in the sound of thunder; but in Hemingway's novel, Jake cannot make the water run into the great stone bath in Pamplona.

A pair of allusions to military heroes may also lend insight into Jake's self-perception. Following the initial meeting of Jake and

Brett in the novel, Jake walks past the statue of Marshal Michel Ney (1769–1815), a man of uncommon bravery who led Napoleon's rear guard. Ney was remembered not for achieving an impressive victory, but for retreating with skill and dignity. Although the battle was lost, he demonstrated grace and courage in a losing cause. The same is true of Roland's actions at the Battle of Roncesvalles in Spain, fought on 15 August 778. Jake, Bill, and Wilson-Harris visit the monastery there on the last day of their fishing vacation. Roland chose to die waging a rear-guard battle against insurmountable odds rather than summon Charlemagne because the king could have lost his own life in attempting to rescue him. Roland endured his defeat bravely and may be seen as a model for Jake: "victory" may be beyond the grasp of Hemingway's hero, but he may still establish and maintain standards of conduct for himself.

In 1963 Earl Rovit observed of *The Sun Also Rises* that "there is a surprising lack of unanimity among critics on what would seem to be basic non-controversial issues."[30] Some of the diversity of interpretation is attributable to Hemingway's use of ambiguity, of saying neither precisely what he means nor its opposite. And some of it, no doubt, results from his contrapuntal method that contrasts people, places, and groups, requiring that the reader not only notice the contrast but also interpret the contrasting statements in some consistent fashion. One or two contrasted items, taken out of context, might be easily aligned; but a novel filled with them presents the reader with an interpretive challenge. Since Rovit's observation, two generations of critics have written a considerable number of books and articles on *The Sun Also Rises*. The result is that the novel continues to yield rich and diverse readings, and the surprising lack of unanimity continues.

NOTES

1. Audre Hanneman, *Ernest Hemingway: A Comprehensive Bibliography* (Princeton: Princeton University Press, 1967; corrected, 1969), p. 6.

2. The precise nature of Jake's wound is unclear. In the novel, Jake tells Georgette that he "got hurt in the war" (24) and tells Bill that he "just had an accident" (120). Neither the manuscript nor the typescript shed further light. Searching beyond the text for explanation, readers find Hemingway's comment to Perkins that the sketch of him on the cover of the novel "looks very much like a writer who had been saddened by the loss or atrophy of certain non replaceable parts" (*The Only Thing that Counts: The Ernest Hemingway/Maxwell Perkins Correspondence,* edited by Matthew J. Bruccoli [New York: Scribners, 1996], p. 48). Nearly thirty years later he objected when George Plimpton commented that Jake was "emasculated precisely as is a steer." "Actually," asserted Hemingway, "he had been wounded in quite a different way and his testicles were intact and not dam-

aged. Thus he was capable of all normal feelings as a *man* but incapable of consummating them. The important distinction is that his wound was physical and not psychological and that he was not emasculated" ("Ernest Hemingway," in *Writers At Work: The Paris Review Interviews, Second Series,* edited by Plimpton [New York: Viking, 1963], p. 230). Most commentators have concluded that the shaft of Jake's penis is missing; however, nerve or vascular damage, rather than amputation, may account for Jake's impotence. Jake's penis is apparently functional enough for urination without special accommodations such as a catheter.

3. Ernest Hemingway, *The Sun Also Rises* (New York: Scribner Paperback Fiction, [1995]), p. 251. All subsequent page citations are from this edition.

4. Michael Reynolds, *Hemingway: The Paris Years* (Oxford: Blackwell, 1989), pp. 288–289.

5. Bertram D. Sarason, *Hemingway and the Sun Set* (Washington, D.C.: NCR Microcard Editions, 1972), p. 7.

6. *Hemingway: The Paris Years,* pp. 289, 301.

7. *Hemingway and the Sun Set,* p. 11.

8. Matthew J. Bruccoli and Robert Trogdon, eds., "They All Came to Paris (And Most of Them Wrote About It)," in *American Expatriate Writers: Paris in the Twenties, Dictionary of Literary Biography, Documentary Series,* volume 15 (Detroit: Gale, 1997), p. 197.

9. Charles M. Oliver, *Ernest Hemingway A to Z: The Essential Reference to the Life and Work* (New York: Facts on File, 1999), p. 274.

10. "They All Came to Paris," p. 195.

11. *Ernest Hemingway A to Z,* p. 312.

12. The best single-volume Hemingway biographies are Carlos Baker's *Ernest Hemingway: A Life Story* (New York: Scribners, 1969) and James R. Mellow's *Hemingway: A Life Without Consequences* (Boston: Houghton Mifflin, 1992). The best multivolume biography is by Michael Reynolds: *The Young Hemingway* (Oxford: Blackwell, 1986); *Hemingway: The Paris Years* (Oxford: Blackwell, 1989); *Hemingway: The American Homecoming* (Cambridge, Mass.: Blackwell, 1992); *Hemingway: The 1930s* (New York: Norton, 1997); and *Hemingway: The Final Years* (New York: Norton, 1999).

13. *Ernest Hemingway: A Life Story,* p. 38.

14. See John Raeburn, *Fame Became of Him: Hemingway as Public Writer* (Bloomington: University of Indiana Press, 1984), pp. 145–146; and Leonard J. Leff, *Hemingway and His Conspirators: Hollywood, Scribners, and the Making of American Celebrity Culture* (Lanham, Md.: Rowman & Littlefield, 1997).

15. *Fame Became of Him,* p. 7.

16. Ibid., p. 131.

17. Michael Reynolds, "Hemingway as American Icon," in *Picturing Hemingway: A Writer in His Time*, by Frederick Voss (New Haven: Yale University Press, 1999), pp. 1–9.

18. *Ernest Hemingway: A Life Story,* pp. 528–529.

19. *Hemingway: A Life Without Consequences,* p. 599.

20. See Carlos Baker, "The Wastelanders," in his *Hemingway: The Writer as Artist* (Princeton: Princeton University Press, 1952), pp. 75–93.

21. Philip Young, *Ernest Hemingway: A Reconsideration* (University Park: Pennsylvania State University Press, 1966), p. 86.

22. *Ernest Hemingway: A Comprehensive Bibliography,* p. 14.

23. Matthew J. Bruccoli, ed., *The Only Thing that Counts: The Ernest Hemingway/Maxwell Perkins Correspondence* (New York: Scribners, 1996), p. 51.

24. Ibid., pp. 51, 52.

25. *Ernest Hemingway: A Life Story,* p. 41.

26. F. Scott Fitzgerald, *The Great Gatsby,* edited by Matthew J. Bruccoli, Cambridge Edition of the Works of F. Scott Fitzgerald (Cambridge & New York: Cambridge University Press, 1991), p. 6; *The Great Gatsby,* edited by Bruccoli (New York: Collier, 1992), p. 7.

27. Ernest Hemingway, *The Complete Short Stories of Ernest Hemingway: The Finca Vigía Edition* (New York: Collier, 1987), p. 114.

28. See Delbert Wylder, *Hemingway's Heroes* (Albuquerque: University of New Mexico Press, 1969), pp. 31–65; and Scott Donaldson, "Hemingway's Morality of Compensation," in Harold Bloom, ed., *Hemingway's The Sun Also Rises* (New York: Chelsea House, 1987), pp. 71–90.

29. See *Ernest Hemingway: A Reconsideration,* pp. 55–78; and Earl Rovit and Gerry Brenner, *Ernest Hemingway,* revised edition (Boston: Twayne, 1986), pp. 37–61.

30. Earl Rovit, *Ernest Hemingway* (New York: Twayne, 1963), p. 146.

THE EVOLUTION OF *THE SUN ALSO RISES*

The final draft of a work that an author approves, for better or for worse, for reasons artistic or economic, is usually taken to represent his final intentions. By studying the evolution of a work, readers can learn about how and why an author reaches editorial decisions. Some of these decisions are entirely his own, while others he shares with his editor, publisher, and friends. Authors occasionally make mistakes: in one instance, Hemingway apparently forgot to change Bill's last name from "Grundy," as it appeared in the manuscript, to "Gorton."[1] Publishers introduce errors or fail to correct obvious ones: the word "stopped" appears as "stoppped" in the first edition (181). Editors argue for the deletion of objectionable words or references for commercial reasons. And a friend, especially one who is himself a successful writer with the same publisher and editor, may contribute significantly to an author's final decisions about his art.

To examine the progress of Hemingway's manuscript of *The Sun Also Rises* through the publication process is to learn about the decisions that a young artist makes as he composes, revises, and negotiates with a savvy editor at one of America's major publishing houses. It is to learn, as well, about the evolution of Hemingway's thematic concerns. The manuscript, which for the first month of writing had no outline, begins with one set of thematic issues and concludes with another; it is contradictory regarding its hero. The typescript abandons the presentation in the manuscript of events in medias res (opening the story in the middle of the action and then supplying background information) in favor of a chronological rendition that eliminates many of Jake's interior monologues. Initially, the narrative commenced with the meeting between Jake, Bill, and Romero at the Montoya, and the conflict concerned a predatory American woman's desire to become acquainted with the young matador. The first edition excludes the typescript's opening chapters and includes a half-dozen other alterations made at the behest of Hemingway's friend, F. Scott Fitzgerald, and his new editor, Maxwell Perkins.

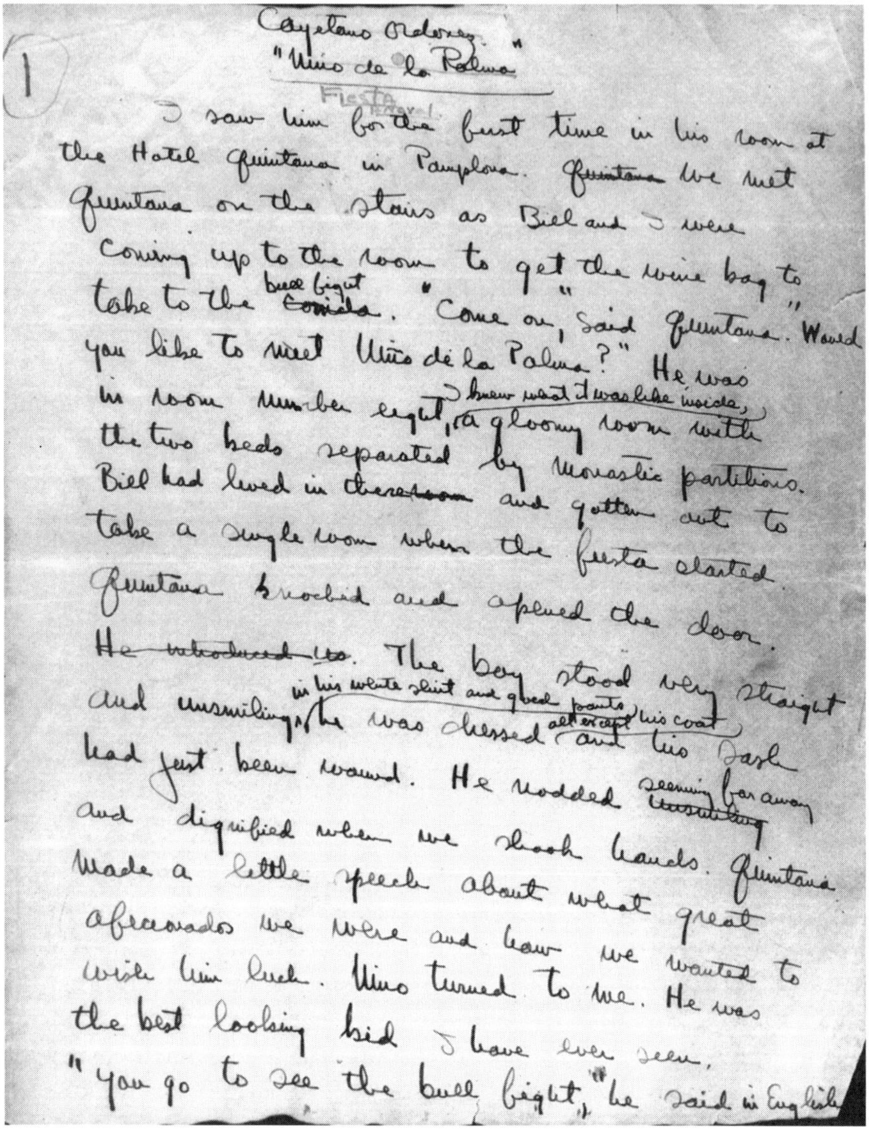

Cayetano Ordonez
"Niño de la Palma"
Fiesta

I saw him for the first time in his room at the Hotel Quintana in Pamplona. ~~Quintana~~ We met Quintana on the stairs as Bill and I were coming up to the room to get the wine bag to take to the bull fight ~~comida~~. "Come on," said Quintana. "Would you like to meet Niño de la Palma?" He was in room number eight, I knew what it was like inside, a gloomy room with the two beds separated by monastic partitions. Bill had lived in ~~there room~~ and gotten out to take a single room when the fiesta started. Quintana knocked and opened the door. ~~He introduced us~~. The boy stood very straight and unsmiling, in his white shirt and glued pants he was dressed all except his coat and his sash had just been wound. He nodded seeming far away ~~unsmiling~~ and dignified when we shook hands. Quintana made a little speech about what great aficionados we were and how we wanted to wish him luck. Nino turned to me. He was the best looking kid I have ever seen. "You go to see the bull fight," he said in English

Draft for the discarded opening of *The Sun Also Rises*

Perhaps the most surprising fact is that the famous Hemingway style, with its dialogue and objective descriptions, seems to spring wholly formed onto the page and survives in the novel essentially unchanged from its appearance in the manuscript.[2] That document, which is housed at the John F. Kennedy Library in Boston, begins on thirty-two loose pages and continues in seven numbered and two unnumbered composition notebooks.[3] The typescript is at the University of Virginia.

THE CREATION OF THE MANUSCRIPT

Confident in his ability to write stories, Hemingway knew that being a writer meant being a novelist, too, and that he must parlay his strengths beyond the scope of the short story. He began writing *The Sun Also Rises* in Madrid in July 1925, following his visit to Pamplona. The vacation had ended in a shambles: the fishing was unsuccessful; the male members of the gang had vied for the beautiful Lady Duff Twysden's favors; and the squabbling nearly degenerated into fistfights. But after a soothing train ride to Valencia and a little warming up by way of reading the proofs for the story collection *In Our Time* (1925), Hemingway titled his work-in-progress first, "Cayetano Ordóñez / Niño de la Palma," then "Fiesta: A Novel," before finally settling on *The Sun Also Rises,* derived from the verses of Ecclesiastes used as one of the novel's epigraphs.

Hemingway commenced using the real names of the people on whom the characters were based but having, apparently, no real direction. The opening scene in the manuscript, for which the reader is given no background, is something exotic, a brief meeting at the Hotel Quintana (Montoya in the final version), arranged by the proprietor, between the narrator Hem (Jake), his friend Bill, and the rising young matador Niño de la Palma (later called Guerrita, then Pedro Romero in the typescript) twenty minutes before the afternoon's bullfight. The young matador is "dignified," "the best looking kid" the narrator has ever seen, and "the essence of torero" who performs extraordinarily in the ring that afternoon.[4] Hemingway began filling unlined sheets with his looping, upright handwriting:

> I saw him for the first time in his room at the Hotel Quintana in Pamplona. We met Quintana on the stairs as Bill and I were coming up to the room to get the wine bag to take to the bull fight. "Come on," said Quintana. "Would you like to meet Niño de la Palma?" (5)

After the bullfights, Hem and Quintana agree that the teenager "was the best torero we had seen, the finest and purest style and the most authority in the ring." He is "a great one," not flashy or vulgar, not one who kills so quickly that the spectator's eye is deceived into perceiving danger where none existed (8).

Having established the novelty of this extraordinary new fighter, Hemingway then introduces what appears to be the complication: the American ambassador and his wife arrive in the plaza with another

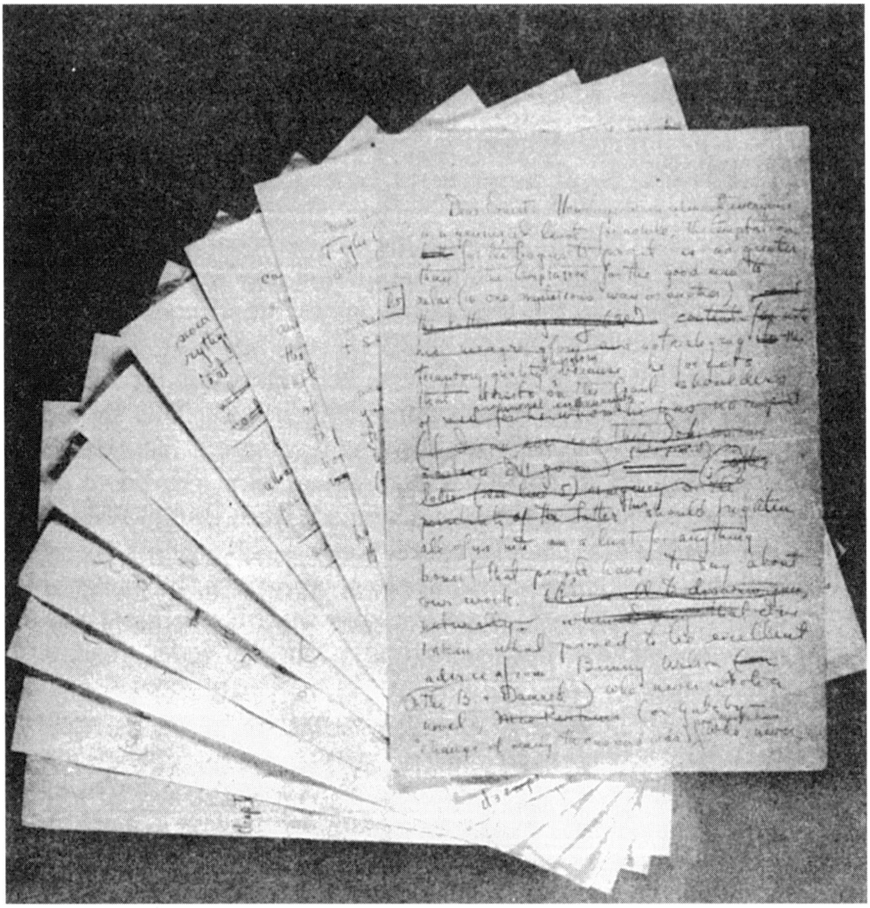

F. Scott Fitzgerald's letter of June 1926 to Hemingway offering criticism of *The Sun Also Rises*

attractive woman. When no one rises to greet the dignitary and his entourage, friends of Hem encourage him, as a fellow American, to welcome the ambassador and present him with the keys to the city. The narrator, Hem, eventually becomes Jacob Barnes, and his friends include a titled English Lady, Duff Anthony (Brett Ashley); her Scottish fiancé, Pat Guthrie (Mike Campbell); American friends of the narrator Donald Ogden Stewart and Bill Smith (Bill Gorton); fellow expatriate Harold (Gerald, then Robert Cohn); and Hadley (Hemingway's first wife), who was later eliminated from the manuscript. In greeting the ambassador, Hem discovers that the attractive woman is interested in meeting the matadors and poses the threat of corrupting them. Her desire is revealed shortly thereafter when a troubled Quintana informs Hem that the ambassador has invited Niño de la Palma out for the evening. The two aficionados agree that no one has any business keeping a young matador out late before his bullfights, so they decide not to relay the invitation to him (22).

Thus, Quintana and Hem squelch the initial complication of Niño de la Palma's involvement with the predatory American woman. But only an hour later, Hem betrays Quintana and the matador when he accedes to Duff's request that he introduce her to the bullfighter. No sooner does Duff, whose potential for destructiveness is as great as the American woman's, manage to win a seat next to the matador than Quintana walks into the room:

> "Cayetano Ordonez, Nino de la Palma, in his first season as a matador, promoted in the spring after some beautiful performances as a novillero in Sevilla, Malago and some incomplete ones in Madrid, looked like the messiah who had come to save bullfighting if ever any one did. . . . Bullfighting is the only art in which the artist is in danger of death and in which the degree of brilliance in the performance is life to the fighter's honor."
>
> *Ernest Hemingway*
>
> From *Death in the Afternoon* (New York: Scribners, 1932), pp. 88, 91.

> You ought to have seen his face. He started to smile at me then he saw Niño with a big glass of cognac in his hand, sitting laughing between me and two women one with bare shoulders and a table full of drunks. He did not even nod. All of a sudden I realized how funny it was. (32)

There is, of course, nothing remotely "funny" about Hem's betrayal. In this moment he has exchanged his hard-earned place among the aficionados for the privilege of appeasing a thirty-four-year-old woman who desires a nineteen-year-old boy. Her alcoholic fiancé is angry at the flirtation, as well, and he explosively turns his anger on Harold, berating him for not knowing when he is not wanted (34).

Thus ends the opening chapter, and exchanging the loose sheets for the first of seven composition notebooks, Hemingway began chapter two in Valencia by describing the "gang" in a series of critical character sketches, remarking disdainfully, "That was the kind of crowd we were, a fine lot" (38). They had no business mingling with a "great one" such as the young matador. Thus far, Hemingway had a dramatic moment and some unique characters, but at this point in the manuscript his narrator realizes that the direction of the narrative is ambiguous: "I don't know why I have put all this down. It may mix up the story but I wanted to show you what a fine crowd we were; what a good crowd for a nineteen year old kid to get in with" (46–47).

Just when the narrator seems poised to tell a story about the corruption of the young bullfighter by immoral expatriates, he suddenly recounts the details of an uncle's funeral. The uncle had dabbled in drinking and gambling, and Hem's mother had told her son that she would prefer to see him in his grave rather than engaging in such vices. Hem finds this attitude bizarre and resolves not to "judge the gang who were at Pamplona" and not to "say that it would be better for Niño de la Palma to be in his grave than to train with a crowd like that . . ." (50).

> "I always worked until I had something done and I always stopped when I knew what was going to happen next. That way I could be sure of going on the next day. But sometimes when I was starting a new story and I could not get it going, I would sit in front of the fire and squeeze the peel of the little oranges into the edge of the flame and watch the sputter of blue that they made. I would stand and look out over the roofs of Paris and think, 'Do not worry. You have always written before and you will write now. All you have to do is write one true sentence. Write the truest sentence that you know.' So finally I would write one true sentence, and then go on from there."
>
> *Ernest Hemingway*
>
> From *A Moveable Feast* (New York: Scribners, 1964), p. 12.

Having sketched his attitude toward the expatriate crowd, Hem notes that in order to understand that crowd, the reader would first have to understand its home base, the Latin Quarter in Paris. He describes the state of mind of the Quarterites as one of "contempt," relates an unfavorable anecdote about an English writer named Braddocks (Ford Madox Ford), and suddenly announces that Gerald Cohn, a friend of Braddocks, is the "hero" of the story. Here, sixty-four pages into the manuscript, can be found the opening lines of the novel as published: "Gerald Cohn was middleweight boxing champion of Princeton" (64). Hemingway continued writing in Valencia, Madrid, San Sebastián, and Hendaye. Having filled a third notebook shortly after returning to Paris, Hemingway outlined the upcoming chapters:

> Chap XIII—Finishes work Gerald [Cohn] not going
>
> Chap XIV Ride to Burgettte [*sic*] Fishing return to Pamplona.
>
> Chap XV Duff Gerald and Mike thru the party out at the wine shop. Desencajonda when we get in. Mike's first out burst.
>
> Chap XVI Encierro, first corrida brings back to point where book starts.
>
> Goes on with that night—the South American—the dancing place. Noel Murphy. Count shows up.
>
> XVII Duff sleeps with Niño de la Palma. Gerald fights with Niño
>
> XVIII Corrida. Duff goes off with Niño. Count refuses Mike job. Bill goes to Paris. Mike talks, goes to St. jean de luz to wait for Duff. Gerald talks, goes to San Sebastian afterwards Paris. I go on down into Spain to bring Duff back. Get her letter. (316)

At last, a structure began to appear. Having opened by introducing the marked contrast between Niño de la Palma and the expatriate gang, Hemingway would flash back, provide the necessary background information, and then bring the narrative forward, chronologically, until it rejoined the opening chapter. The novel as published would deviate from this plan, but the outline provided banks between which Hemingway's words would flow.

He had gained control of the plot, but the point of his story remained elusive. On at least two occasions, Hemingway brings the action to a halt as his narrator indulges in curious interior monologue regarding the "hero" of the tale:

> Now you can see it looked as though I were trying to get to be the hero of this story. But that was all wrong. Gerald Cohn is the hero. When I bring myself in it is only to clear up something. Or maybe Duff is the hero. Or Niño de la Palma. He never really had a chance to be the hero. Or maybe there is not any hero at all. Maybe a story is better without any hero. (143)

Much later he adds: "Well this is not the story. The story is Guerrita [Romero]. For a time Guerrita is the hero. Mr. Gerald Cohn is not the hero. He was the hero for a time but he has been dropped" (447).

Only three weeks from completing the manuscript, Hemingway had no clearly defined hero, and he had not yet settled upon the characters' names. Niño de la Palma became Guerrita, a still-living but retired legend, before becoming, in the revision, Pedro Romero, a still more legendary performer from the eighteenth century whose killing style, *recibiendo,* featured a stationary matador who enticed the charging animal to impale himself on the curved killing sword. At the moment when the bull's reach and grasp seem to become one, he dies in what is touted as the most emotional way to kill.

By the third week in September, Hemingway's plot had run its course, filling seven blue notebooks; he used another notebook to list tentative titles. Before him lay the tasks of identifying his hero and crystallizing his theme. These he would accomplish through revision. Publication was still more than a year away. In the meantime, Hemingway dashed off a slim volume titled *The Torrents of Spring* (1926) that facilitated a break with his publisher, Boni and Liveright, and allowed him, with the help of his good friend Fitzgerald, to pursue a new editor, Max-

"A writer's job is to tell the truth. His standard of fidelity to the truth should be so high that his invention, out of his experience, should produce a truer account than anything factual can be. For facts can be observed badly; but when a good writer is creating something, he has time and scope to make it of an absolute truth."

Ernest Hemingway

From the introduction to *Men at War* (New York: Crown, 1942), an anthology of war stories edited by Hemingway.

well Perkins, and a new publishing house, Scribners.[5]

HEMINGWAY ON REVISING

Interviewer: "How much rewriting do you do?"

Hemingway: "It depends. I rewrote the ending to *Farewell to Arms,* the last page of it, thirty-nine times before I was satisfied."

Interviewer: "Was there some technical problem there? What was it that had stumped you?

Hemingway: "Getting the words right."

From "Ernest Hemingway," *Writers at Work: The Paris Review Interviews, Second Series* (New York: Viking, 1963), p. 222.

HEMINGWAY'S REVISIONS

After a false start in December of 1925, Hemingway found his rhythm with the new year, revising in the mornings and skiing the slopes of Schruns, Austria, in the afternoons. By mid January he was trying to push the narrative away from the first-person mode of Jake Barnes: he did not want to fall into the trap of so many first-time novelists and write something that appeared to be too autobiographical; and he was well aware that the newest writers were rendering their stories objectively. T. S. Eliot, whose poem *The Waste Land* (1922) was much heralded, urged modern writers to think of their art as "not a turning loose of emotion, but an escape from emotion," and not as "the expression of personality, but an escape from personality."[6] Hemingway had been absorbing the tutelage of Sherwood Anderson, Ezra Pound, Gertrude Stein, and Ford Madox Ford, and while he may have seemed humble and receptive in their presence, he had his own ideas about how fiction ought to be written. Very early in his draft he had begun to articulate his own theory of composition:

> Probably any amount of this does not seem to have anything to do with the story and perhaps it has not. I am sick of these ones with their clear restrained writing and I am going to try to get in the whole business and to do that there has to be things that seem as though they had nothing to do with it just as in life. In life people are not conscious of these special moments that novelists build their whole structures on. That is most people are not. That surely has nothing to do with the story but you can not tell until you finish it because none of the significant things are going to have any literary signs marking them. You have to figure them out by yourself. (51)

This clumsy prose was eventually excised, but the message was clear: this narrative would not be filled with literary signposts; if readers really wanted to grasp the "special moments," then they would have to work hard to discover them.

And Hemingway would have to work hard to revise the structure of the novel, to excise the self-conscious patches of the manuscript, to clarify the point of the story, and to identify the hero. The opening in medias res had led to a series of digressions in the manuscript as well as a clear contradiction. The narrator claims that he will "not judge the gang," but his disdain for their lax morality, alcoholism, and various weaknesses is clearly palpable (50). By opening with the conflict, Hemingway seemed to be leading the reader on a faultfinding tour. So he relocated Jake's betrayal of his *afición* to its proper chronological place; he cut Hem's reflection on his mother's morality and both trimmed and refocused the background information on the characters and the Quarter. In the Taube Inn in Austria, he revisited the vexing issue of his novel's hero, beginning his revised typescript:

> This is a novel about a lady. Her name is Lady Ashley and when the story begins she is living in Paris and it is Spring. That should be a good setting for a romantic but highly moral story. As everyone knows, Paris is a very romantic place. Spring in Paris is a very happy and romantic time.[7]

This observation would seem to indicate that Brett will be the hero, since the novel is "about" her; but the typescript states at the end of chapter two that "Cohn is the hero."[8] And as the preponderance of background information concerns Cohn, and not Brett, Mike, or Jake, first-time readers, as yet unacquainted with Jake's ironic tone, would have little cause to question the validity of Jake's assessment.

Hemingway's selection of straight chronology allows his narrator to reserve judgment and forces his readers to determine for themselves what the significant moments in the narrative are and then judge the characters' actions accordingly. The major conflicts in the typescript and manuscript are consistent: how one derives meaning from experience and how one determines one's values continue to be the focus of Jake's interior monologues and much of the action. The question of the novel's hero or heroine remains unresolved in the typescript. Jake cannot seem to determine if the novel is Brett's or Robert's, and he seems curiously unaware that it is as much his as anyone's.

FINAL CHANGES

Perkins received Hemingway's typescript in May, and he knew immediately that he had an excellent property; but he also knew that he could not publish all of the particulars of the typescript. Charles Scribner would not publish a book containing offensive language; neither was he likely to allow passages to stand that poked fun at one of the firm's authors, Henry James (1843–1916). In fact, there was a short list of things that would have to go, but Perkins apparently thought it best to

Bill Smith, a childhood friend of Hemingway; Smith and Donald Ogden Stewart served as models for Bill Gorton in *The Sun Also Rises*

begin this new round of negotiations with the reference to James's obscure hurt, which apparently left him, like Jake, sexually incapacitated. Hemingway's response could not have been heartening to Perkins: he found nothing wrong with the reference to James, who was "as dead as he will ever be"; what is more, Hemingway was working on some short stories and didn't even want to think about the novel until the galleys arrived.

In the same letter Hemingway informed Perkins that he wanted to "start the book at what is now page 16," eliminating the introduction and background to Brett and the Parisian crowd.[9] He coyly added, "Scott agrees with me"; but, in fact, Fitzgerald had read the typescript and argued persuasively that much of the opening needed extensive revision. Rather than do it piecemeal, Hemingway simply lopped off the original opening, leaving the book to commence with the statement, "Robert Cohn was once middleweight boxing champion of Princeton." How, then, were readers to learn that the novel was "about a lady" named Brett Ashley, as the revised typescript began? They would have to figure that out for themselves.

Having been instrumental in securing Hemingway for Scribners, Fitzgerald naturally was anxious to read Hemingway's typescript to verify that his assumptions had been correct. He did so, early in June 1926, after Hemingway had mailed his typescript to Scribners. Fitzgerald, knowing the volatility of his friend, tried to be gentle but unambiguous: "there are about 24 sneers, superiorities, and nose-thumbings-at-nothing that mar the whole narrative up to p. 29 where (after a false start on the introduction of Cohn) it really gets going." The letter forged on for ten pages, and includes advice that Hemingway found unforgivably good:

> I can't imagine how you could have done these first 20 pps. so casually. You can't play with peoples attention. . . . I can't tell you the sense of disappointment that beginning with its elephantine facetiousness gave me. Please do what you can about it in proof. Its 7500 words—you could reduce it to

5000. And my advice is not to do it by mere pareing but to take out the worst of the scenes.[10]

The measure of Hemingway's respect for Fitzgerald's judgment was clear: he lopped off the opening. Gone, now, was an accounting of Jake's life since the war, his Catholicism, Brett's background, and the narrator's critical opening assertion, "This is a novel about a lady."

Despite Hemingway's directive that he wanted the novel to begin with the description of Cohn, Perkins included the entire opening of the typescript in the galleys. When they were completed, the editor sent a carefully worded letter that questioned Hemingway's desire to excise the opening and included "two points to consider that bear on this publication: the danger of trouble from referring to real people in a way to reflect upon them, and the danger of suppression." Roger Prescott, who appeared in the *bal musette,* was too easily recognized as Glenway Wescott: "why not call him Prentiss. You don't want to harm him."[11] Other references—to Hillaire Belloc, Joseph Hergesheimer (the "garter snapper"), Henry James—needed to be disguised. Mike Campbell's reference to "a particular adjunct of the Bulls" (i.e., their testicles) should be "not spelled out, but covered by a blank"; and Hemingway should "not so plainly" indicate the second line to a song Bill sings about irony and pity—which perceptive readers would understand to be "When you're feeling shitty."[12]

Perkins artfully made the case that Hemingway was inviting trouble from authorities outside the publishing house—censors and conservatives who would label the book obscene. Not insensitive to these concerns, Hemingway was quick to trade Mike's "balls" for "horns," a reading that stood until Hemingway was able to have his original intention restored in the 1953 Uniform Edition.[13] He maintained, however, that "Bitch," as the word is used by Brett at the close of the novel, is "absolutely necessary" and "must stand."[14] In the end, Hemingway made all of the changes that Perkins requested and, by lopping off the opening, addressed Fitzgerald's complaints as well. He wrote Perkins:

> 1st—I have commenced with Cohn—I believe that the book loses by eliminating this first part but it would have been pointless to include it with the Belloc eliminated—and I think that would be altogether pointless with Belloc's name out.
>
> 2nd—Roger Prescott is now Roger Prentiss. I believe I went to school with a Roger Prentiss but at least he was not Glenway.
>
> 3rd—Hergesheimer now changed to something else.
>
> 4th—Henry James now called either Henry or Whatsisname—whichever seems best to you.
>
> 5th—I do not believe that the blanks left in the Irony and pity song can be objectionable—anybody knowing what words to put in might as well put them in. In case they are offensive the word "pretty" can be inserted.

6th—The bulls now without appendages.[15]

Five days later, he seems to have changed his mind about the detrimental impact of deleting the opening:

> I believe that the book is really better starting as it does now directly with Cohn and omitting any preliminary warming up. After all if I'm trying to write books without any extra words I might as well stick to it. Now that it is finally out of my hands and there is no chance of doing anything to make it any better I feel rather cheerful now about The Sun. Hope you feel the same way.

In this amiable mood, Hemingway even allowed that Perkins could "reduce the size of the dashes and omit the periods" in the irony and pity section, further disguising the already absent word "shitty."

After the book came out, Perkins returned to the subject of the excised chapters and suggested that Hemingway review the cut portion and, culling from it the best material, include it henceforth as a foreword or prologue.[16] Hemingway demurred. He did foreshorten the quotation from Ecclesiastes to accentuate its contrast with Gertrude Stein's "splendid bombast" about the "lost generation"; and he made one more attempt to identify his hero, denying that the book was "a hollow or bitter satire" and insisting that it was "a damn tragedy with the earth abiding forever as the hero."[17]

One could see how the beautiful and enduring earth might be a "hero" of the piece. However, having tried out Brett, Cohn, and Romero for the part, and having seen where readers might even think that Jake might be vying for the honor, it is strange that Hemingway never mentioned that the "earth" might be his hero in earlier drafts or typescripts. In the thirty-five years that Hemingway lived after publishing *The Sun Also Rises,* he would occasionally revisit the novel, commenting on the nature of Jake's wound or the lostness of his generation. Such retrospective assessments, even Hemingway's, should not be confused with the facts delivered by the novel itself.

NOTES

1. Michael Reynolds, "Words Killed, Wounded, Missing in Action," *Hemingway Review,* 6, no. 2 (1981): 5. "Grundy" appears in the first issue of the first edition (New York: Charles Scribner's Sons, 1926), p. 91, line 13.
2. Excellent discussions of compositional history include the following: Frederic Joseph Svoboda, *Hemingway & The Sun Also Rises: The Crafting of a Style* (Lawrence: University Press of Kansas, 1983); William Balassi, "The Writing of the Manuscript of *The Sun Also Rises,* with a Chart of Its Session-by-Session Development," *Hemingway Review,* 6, no. 1 (1986): 65–78; Balassi, "The Trail to *The Sun Also Rises:* The First Week of Writing," in *Hemingway: Essays of Reassessment,* edited by Frank Scafella (New York: Oxford University Press, 1991), pp. 33–51; Michael Reynolds, "False Dawn: *The Sun Also Rises* Manuscript," in *A Fair Day in the Affections: Literary Essays in Honor of Robert B. White, Jr.,* edited by Jack D. Durant and M. Thomas Hester (Raleigh, N.C.: Winston Press, 1980), pp. 171–186; Reynolds, *Hemingway: The Paris Years* (Oxford: Basil Blackwell, 1989), pp.

306–355; Reynolds, *Hemingway: The American Homecoming* (Oxford: Basil Blackwell, 1992), pp. 1–63; Carlos Baker, *Hemingway: The Writer as Artist,* fourth edition (Princeton: Princeton University Press, 1972), pp. 75–93; and James Hinkle, "'Dear Mr. Scribner'—About the Published Text of *The Sun Also Rises,*" *Hemingway Review,* 6, no. 1 (1986): 43–64. For an introduction to editorial cruxes, see Herschel Parker, "Textual Criticism and Hemingway," in *Hemingway: Essays of Reassessment,* pp. 17–31; and Parker, "The Determinacy of the Creative Process and the Authority of the Author's Belated Textual Decisions," in his *Flawed Texts and Verbal Icons* (Evanston, Ill.: Northwestern University Press, 1984), pp. 17–51. The manuscript of the novel is housed at the John F. Kennedy Library in Boston; a more accessible source is Matthew J. Bruccoli, ed., *Ernest Hemingway: The Sun Also Rises. A Facsimile Edition,* 2 volumes (Detroit: Omnigraphics, 1990).

3. For fuller descriptions of the manuscript, see *Ernest Hemingway: The Sun Also Rises. A Facsimile Edition,* p. iii; and *Catalog of the Ernest Hemingway Collection of the John F. Kennedy Library,* 2 volumes (Boston: G.K. Hall, 1982).

4. *The Sun Also Rises: A Facsimile Edition,* pp. 5–6; following citations in discussion of manuscript are from this edition.

5. For an account of Fitzgerald's role in bringing Hemingway to Scribners and in encouraging him to revise the novel, see Matthew J. Bruccoli, *Fitzgerald and Hemingway: A Dangerous Friendship* (New York: Carroll & Graf, 1994).

6. T. S. Eliot, "Tradition and the Individual Talent," in *Critical Theory Since Plato,* edited by Hazard Adams (New York: Harcourt Brace Jovanovich, 1971), p 787.

7. Ernest Hemingway, "The Unpublished Opening of *The Sun Also Rises,*" *Antaeus,* 33 (Spring 1979): 7.

8. Ibid., p. 14.

9. Matthew J. Bruccoli, ed., *The Only Thing that Counts: The Ernest Hemingway/Maxwell Perkins Correspondence* (New York: Scribners, 1996), p. 40.

10. Bruccoli, ed., *F. Scott Fitzgerald: A Life in Letters* (New York: Simon & Schuster, 1994), pp. 142, 144.

11. *The Only Thing that Counts,* p. 41.

12. Ibid., p. 42.

13. Audre Hanneman, *Ernest Hemingway: A Comprehensive Bibliography* (Princeton: Princeton University Press, 1967; corrected, 1969), pp. 18–19.

14. *The Only Thing that Counts,* p. 43.

15. Ibid., p. 44.

16. Ibid., p. 47.

17. Ibid., p. 51.

THEMES IN *THE SUN ALSO RISES*

The Sun Also Rises resists conclusive readings about its themes. Its subjects are clear enough—drinking, traveling, fishing, loving, and bullfighting—but its themes, the abstract ideas made concrete through their representation in these subjects, are less clearly defined. With the omniscient narrator of the nineteenth century gone, readers are forced to rely upon the first-person narrator for help in discovering the theme of the story. But Hemingway's narrator, Jake Barnes, does not even clearly identify the hero of his story. He confesses that "maybe there is not any hero at all. Maybe a story is better without any hero."[1] What is more, while he occasionally relates information—about the archivist of Pamplona, for example—and then explains, "That has nothing to do with the story" (102), Jake never clearly explains what, precisely, his story is about. Perhaps, instead of a single, predominant theme, the book has a series of themes, and the relative scrutiny that readers accord to particular themes depends upon other questions in the novel that they discover and resolve.

Individual readers have a great deal of latitude in their interpretation of the novel, because Hemingway so often employs irony. Often an ironic statement is one that declares the opposite of what it actually means: a character says *on* but he clearly means *off*. Jake uses such verbal irony when he observes that "Georgette smiled that wonderful smile" (26), meaning she showed her bad teeth. Because Hemingway has already explained to readers that "With her mouth closed she was a rather pretty girl" (23), they know to read the word *wonderful* as its opposite. But the ironic statements of the novel are not always so easily understood. When Georgette demands to see the patronne's daughter's yellow card, she does not mean the *opposite* of what she said; rather, she means to insult the patronne by suggesting that his daughter is a prostitute. Later, when Brett Ashley asks, "I've never let you down, have I?" Jake's response "Heard from Mike?" (37) goes a step beyond the traditional definition of verbal irony. Had Jake said "Oh, no, never," readers attuned to

Pamplona, 1924: Hemingway, on right in white pants, attempting a pass with a bull

his ironic mode might quickly have inferred that, yes, Brett has let Jake down. But Jake's query "Heard from Mike?" does not allow the reader to grasp Jake's irony immediately. In fact, the full significance of Jake's line is not apparent to first-time readers until subsequent actions unfold—Brett's failure to meet Jake at the Hotel Crillon and Jake's explanation to Robert Cohn that Brett "is in love with Mike Campbell, and she's going to marry him" (46). Only then do readers grasp the depth of Jake's ironic reply: yes, Brett has let him down, not only by missing dates but also by marrying Lord Ashley, engaging herself to Mike Campbell, and sleeping with Jake's friends and acquaintances.

Despite the ambiguity of the novel, most readers perceive a few important themes. While no single interpretation dominates the critical response, readers generally agree that the book explores values, the changing role of the *New Woman,* and the natures of the *narrator* and the *hero*.

VALUES

Values of all sorts appear in the story—monetary values, professional values, spiritual values, and moral values, to name a few. The word *value* rolls off the tongue of several characters, and it occupies their thoughts. As Jake contemplates Brett's side of their relationship, he realizes that he has "been getting something for nothing" (152). The give and take between humans, he surmises, is just an "exchange of values. You gave up something and you got something else" (152). This philosophy works well enough for financial matters. For fifty francs, Jake can salve his loneliness by dining with Georgette (31). That transaction is an equitable exchange of money for company. Yet, later, when Jake asks the chauffeur how much he will charge to drive him from Bayonne to San Sebastian, the man asks for fifty pesatas, then thirty-five. But Jake will not agree to the exchange, saying "It's not worth it" (235).

Jake's theory helps him to make financial decisions, but it does not help him to balance his life. He suspects that in five years this "fine philosophy" (152) will appear silly to him, but he seems to grasp its inadequacy much sooner than that. During the course of the novel, he discovers that human relations—such as the pleasant experiences he shares with the count, Wilson-Harris, and the Basques en route to Burguete—are not reducible to financial formulae, to debits and credits. Nonetheless, the language of finance provides useful metaphors for describing the condition of some characters. Mike is both literally and spiritually bankrupt; by continuing to roll dice with Bill and Jake after his funds are exhausted, he perpetuates a fraud against his friends. Brett's carelessness in financial matters—giving Jake's concierge two hundred francs belonging to the count and stranding herself without a sous in the Hotel Montaña in Madrid—is childlike in its selfishness. Frances Clyne reveals her grasping nature when she describes her relationship with Robert as a waste of time—"two years and a half"—and money—"I could have had alimony, but I got the divorce the quickest way" (54). It is not that her heart is broken but that her purse is empty. Robert's attempt to purchase Jake's companionship for a trip to South America suggests that Robert does not understand that friendship is not a commodity to be purchased like the services of a chauffeur, an escort, or an interpreter.

Commentary regarding Count Mippipopolous's values is divided. Detractors call him the "high priest of materialism," one who exchanges money for pleasure.[2] Even his obesity suggests that he is accustomed to satisfying his sensual appetites. His offer to Brett of $10,000 to go to Biarritz with him is not only extraordinary but also links him in an unflattering way with Robert: Robert has just bought himself out of a relationship with Frances for £200; the count attempts to buy himself into a relationship with Brett. Detractors agree with Brett, who says that he has no values, that he is "dead" (67). His claim that he is always in love is false, for he is never emotionally involved.

The count, however, so his advocates have observed, seems genuinely happy and well adjusted: he enjoys food and wine, the bustle of the café and the relative quiet at closing time, his antiquities, and the company he has chosen to keep. That he chooses not to become emotionally involved with women he "loves" is perhaps a useful survival mechanism. His interest in Brett, similar to the Pamplona *riau-riau* dancers' interest in her, is as an object—something that he can procure and admire. Brett has told the count that she is in love with Jake, a statement that may account for his propensity to wax philosophical during their only extended meeting. Jake is strangely reticent during this scene. True, he has just gone through a rocky time, indulging in a bit of self-pity while the count makes a trip for champagne. But from the time that the count returns with the champagne until they head to Montmartre, Jake contributes only six lines of dialogue. Even some questions that are put to him directly—such as the count's "Where should I have him put it [the champagne], sir?" (63)—are answered by Brett. Jake sits like a dutiful pupil and listens as the count counsels Brett. The count warns her that if she makes jokes about people, she will "make enemies" (65); he encourages her to finish her sentences, presumably so that he can more fully understand her meaning (65); and he insists that she drink one glass of champagne slowly, so that she may enjoy it before getting drunk (66). Finally, he objects to her characterization of him as "dead" merely because he can be in love without losing control of either his head or his heart. The count is a connoisseur of fine wines, a good judge of feminine beauty, a successful entrepreneur, a seasoned traveler, and a wounded veteran. He apparently has learned to like many things—including wine, business, women, travel, antiquities, and conversation—and learned to apportion his interests and passions carefully so that no single one dominates. Everything has a place in his values, and his interests are democratic: one is not permitted more status than another. Perhaps his message to Jake is that if you want peace of mind, you must control your passions, especially those passions that will never be entirely satisfied.

One explanation for Jake's reticence during the count's discussion is that Jake already understands most of the count's point. Jake has immersed himself in a challenging professional life. His leisure pursuits, following the bullfights and fishing, also require a fair amount of reading, study, and practice. Were he to speak, Jake no doubt would agree with the count, for Jake follows the count's advice in all but one way: Jake cannot be in love with Brett without his feelings adversely affecting the rest of his values. The count may be sufficiently emotionally detached (or incapacitated) so that love becomes something for which he may write a check; but for Jake, the francs that are adequate compensation for Georgette do not begin to represent the value that he places on Brett, who seems to be the impetus for Jake's writing his story.

In Paris, Bill Gorton's humorous discourse on finances anticipates the language of Jake's interior monologue in Pamplona. As Bill and Jake drunkenly ramble past a taxidermist's shop, Bill comically insists that Jake buy "just one stuffed dog . . . Mean everything in the world to you after you bought it. Simple exchange of values. You give them money. They give you a stuffed dog" (78). Bill inverts the logic typically employed by consumers who purchase things that are valuable *before* they have exchanged money for them. Bill's suggestion that the stuffed dog will come to mean something to Jake *after* or perhaps *because* he had purchased it is reminiscent of Frances's naive and potentially tragic conception of parenthood: "have them and then like them" (54).

Bill gets his money by working for it; he even writes in his room in Pamplona before the fiesta begins (154). He knows the value of things: the first anecdote that he relates in the novel focuses upon financial and social injustice and human dignity. Although he is a foreigner who does not speak the language, Bill attempts to help the "wonderful nigger" recover the money that was due him, as well as his clothes and watch. Although the money is not forthcoming and the watch has been stolen, Bill is still able to do several kind things: lend the man his coat, provide him with a ride home, and lend him some money. This anecdote is not about a "simple exchange of values" (78), such as a few francs to a waiter for hailing a taxi. This story details a complex exchange of values: a vacationing man gives up his time and money in an effort to correct an injustice. Bill knows that one cannot affix a price tag to such actions any more than he can measure in dollars and cents his affection for Jake.

Neither can Wilson-Harris reduce his feelings for Bill and Jake to debits and credits. When Wilson-Harris learns that they are to return to Pamplona, he stays with Bill and Jake for the rest of the day and buys several rounds of drinks at the pub across from the monastery at Roncesvalles, insisting that buying the drinks gives him "pleasure" (134). Finally, Wilson-Harris gives Bill and Jake fishing flies that he has tied himself. These flies represent not dollars and cents but time and affection, as Wilson-Harris makes clear in his final words to his friends: "I only thought if you fished them some time it might remind you of what a good time we had" (135). The value of such good times is hard to quantify.

Duff Twysden, the original for Brett Ashley in *The Sun Also Rises*

The same is true of the pleasant experiences that Bill and Jake have with the Basques on their bus ride to Burguete. The day is "baking hot" (109), and the passengers are wedged in among the baggage and the boxes. Yet, in this setting ripe for irritable outbursts, a convivial atmosphere dominates. The Basques seated on the roof of the bus lean back against Bill's and Jake's legs, for the two are fortunate enough to have seats on the bench. The Basques offer their wine, humorously startle Jake by imitating a motor horn and causing him to misdirect the wine streaming from the leather bottle, and, as if they understood how glad Jake and Bill were to be temporarily rid of Robert, in unison they wave good-bye to him as the bus pulls away (110).

Several critics point to the geographical dichotomy between France and Spain as a metaphor for some of Jake's conflicting values. The narrator commutes between the two in the final book and assesses the differences: France is sterile and materialistic; Spain is virile, primitive, perhaps more romantic. French transactions are predictable and allow for less-complicated interactions with people; French waiters predictably respond in accordance with how they are tipped. Spanish waiters, on the other hand, are not "on a clear financial basis" (237) and sometimes speak their minds quite freely—for example, denouncing the running of the bulls as "*muy flamenco*" (flashy; 202). The sports of the two countries differ as well: the Spaniards have their *afición* (passion), the French, their

"The writer who cannot leave his country, who must stay in the middle of that which he writes, is the local color writer with his characters who must have their Wessex, their Cumberland Mountains, their old New Orleans, their dialect and all the rest of it. But if he is a writer who deals with the human heart, with the human mind and with the presence or absence of the human soul then if he can make a heart break for you, or even beat, make the mind function, and show you what passes for the soul then you may be sure he does not have to stay in Wessex for fear that he will lose it. He can make the country not merely describe it, and he can make it five thousand miles away from it looking at the white washed wall of a cheap room in any land you name and make it truer than anyone can who lives in it."

Ernest Hemingway

From "Ernest von Hemingstein's Journal," item 407a, John F. Kennedy Library; reprinted in *Hemingway: Essays of Reassessment*, edited by Frank Scafella (New York: Oxford University Press, 1991), p. 91.

bicycle racing—a sport for which the money can be "arranged" (240) by the competitors, who simply agree beforehand to split the spoils. France is modern and more progressive than Spain—but in achieving its modernity, it has assumed sterility. Spain is known for its beech woods, the mark of mature forests, and of long and uninterrupted natural processes. On the Quai d'Orléans side of the Ile St. Louis, the French are tearing down old houses to accommodate a new street. That symbol of modernity, the automobile, is beginning to dominate the urban landscape.[3] Jake, like the contrasting landscapes, is divided: he has the passions of a virile man but the capacities of an impotent one; he has a romantic imagination but is faced with a realistic predicament. Just as Jake has learned to mediate between the contrasting landscapes and value systems of France and Spain, perhaps he will learn to deal with his inner conflicts.

Jake's careful observation of his financial exchanges is indicative of his overriding desire to discover what is meaningful in life. Perhaps Jake thinks that if he exercises care in the simpler exchanges of value—money for goods or services—then the more complex exchanges of value, such as deciding to forego one's idyllic vacation in San Sebastian in exchange for bailing a friend out of a hotel in Madrid, will take care of themselves. But Jake's attempt to view human relationships as if they were financial exchanges is no more successful than Robert's attempts to solve his problems by knocking people about. Robert attaches value to his physical prowess. But as a medium of exchange, Robert's value (power) is useless: neither Harvey Stone nor Pedro Romero is intimidated by it. Jake encounters a similar difficulty in his dealings with Brett. Unlike Jake, she does not care a whit for money, and it does not reliably predict her actions—a fact made clear by her inability to convert to pounds the count's offer of $10,000. She does not appreciate or understand people in terms of financial metaphors. If the love between Jake and Brett is going to prosper, they will have to communicate it to one another in terms neither sexual nor financial. In the end

Jake seems to solve the problem by acting as Brett's friend without thought of recompense and without revisiting the illusion that they might go off to the country together.

Jake's concern for value also extends beyond financial matters; he seeks to attain the maximum meaning and pleasure from experience. In Pamplona, after Mike accuses Robert of following Brett around like a steer and the gang convenes for a dinner filled with "ignored tension" (150), Jake cannot fall asleep. Hearing Mike and Brett laughing in the room next door angers him, and he begins reflecting on his personal philosophy. Initially, he conveys it in financial terms:

> I thought I had paid for everything. Not like the woman pays and pays and pays. No idea of retribution or punishment. Just exchange of values. You gave up something and you got something else. Or you worked for something. You paid some way for everything that was any good. I paid my way into enough things I liked, so that I had a good time. Either you paid by learning about them, or by experience, or by taking chances, or by money. Enjoying living was learning to get your money's worth and knowing when you had it. You could get your money's worth. The world was a good place to buy in. It seemed like a fine philosophy. In five years, I thought, it would seem just as silly as all the other fine philosophies I've had. (152)

Jake does not have to wait five years to perceive the fallacy of this thinking. He has learned from experience that the world is more than "a good place to buy in."

> Perhaps that wasn't true, though. Perhaps as you went along you did learn something. I did not care what it was all about. All I wanted to know was how to live in it. Maybe if you found out how to live in it you learned from that what it was about. (152)

In most situations, Jake knows from the start of the novel that the world is more than a place in which to trade cash for pleasures; it is a place to live. When Robert complains that "in about thirty-five years more we'll be dead," Jake retorts, "Why don't you start living your life in Paris?" (19). For Jake, an important part of living one's life means experiencing the sensual pleasures that are available to him. He *sees* the blooming horse-chestnut trees in the Luxembourg Gardens and the Spanish countryside. He *feels* the "good breeze" generated by the bus as it moves toward Burguete, the cold and wind at the inn, and the warm sand under his feet in San Sebastian. He *tastes* the count's "amazing champagne" and contrasts French and Spanish cuisine. He *hears* the pretentious accent of Robert Prentiss. For Jake, living one's life "all the way up" (18) also means understanding things such as traveling or bullfighting as thoroughly as possible. In order to derive the maximum value from travel, Jake learns the requisite languages, transportation schedules, and customs. Unlike Robert, Jake admires the genuine friendliness of the

Basques and tries to experience the land and the people as a native rather than as a tourist. Living a full life means becoming a keen observer and immersing oneself so entirely that one is able to discern the authentic experience from the sham.

In *Death in the Afternoon* (1932) Hemingway writes, "all stories, if continued far enough, end in death, and he is not a true-story teller who would keep that from you."[4] Since death is the inevitable end of things, Jake needs to embrace a code of living that lends meaning and value to his existence. In *The Sun Also Rises,* Jake learns lessons in "how to live" from Count Mippipopolous, who urges him to get to know the value of things, and from Pedro Romero, who in the midst of his performance "did not look up to ask if it pleased" because "he did it all for himself inside" (220). Jake also has negative examples. Robert's public displays of emotion are anathema to Jake, who prefers not to talk about his troubles, even with Bill, who inquires about his relationship with Brett. Mike's and Brett's displays of financial irresponsibility are also characteristics that Jake avoids: his personal independence, linked to his financial independence, is important to him, and he will not sell his companionship to Robert, who offers to pay Jake's expenses for a vacation to South America. Living, then, for Jake becomes not a matter of understanding the end of the game but an exercise in playing the game well.

NEW WOMAN

"She wore a slipover jersey sweater and a tweed skirt, and her hair was brushed back like a boy's. She started all that" (30). Brett saunters into the novel looking lovely, wearing a man's hat, and socializing with homosexuals. She smokes, drinks, enjoys her physical relationships with men, and casually explains to Jake her need for other men by saying "It's the way I'm made" (62).

Iconoclastic women can be found throughout literary history, but Brett's immediate predecessors had been evolving for more than half a century.[5] Since the Civil War, American girls had been cultivating their independence, socializing unchaperoned in their neighborhoods. They had entered the work force with males and begun to adopt mannish habits of dress. The boldest among them lived alone and accounted for the rise and dissemination of birth control. The conception of feminine beauty moved away from the hourglass buxomness of the Victorian era and toward the image of young women who were both seductive and athletic and who dressed the part. As she evolved into the "flapper" prior to World War I, the differences between her behavior and that of her male counterparts dwindled: she drove, drank, slept around, and earned a living. She met resistance, of course, from a patriarchal society that wanted women in the home and men in the work force.

But evolving social and professional arrangements soon led to a demand for new emotional arrangements between the sexes. No longer defined as domestic beings, women had careers, insisted on reproductive freedom, and rebelled against patriarchal marriage. This behavior is the point of contact between the New Woman and Brett.[6] As the New Woman ventured out of the private spaces traditionally accorded women, her visibility increased as well. No longer a housebound nurturer, she could take her new look and attitude to bars and bullfights.

JAKE BARNES ON THE MEANING OF LIFE

"Perhaps as you went along you did learn something, I did not care what it was all about. All I wanted to know was how to live in it. Maybe if you found out how to live in it you learned from that what it was all about."

Ernest Hemingway

From *The Sun Also Rises* (New York: Simon & Schuster, 1995), p. 152.

Brett is a New Woman in many respects, although she was not reared to be one. While one can scarcely imagine Brett as a dutiful housewife, she certainly has an inclination toward nurturing. Trained in the stereotypically feminine role of nurse, she meets Jake during his recuperation. After Robert has pummeled Romero, Mike reports that Brett "loves looking after people. That's how we came to go off together" (206). She may be incapable of taking care of herself, as her disordered room at the Hotel Montaña suggests (245), but she feels compelled to nurture Jake, Mike, and Pedro. While she enjoys the New Woman's freedom of movement, she has no financial stability. Without money she is as disenfranchised as Frances Clyne and just as dependent upon men and marriage. She may be a New Woman, but she has not managed the transition to "free woman." Two more generations had to pass before women achieved the economic empowerment they needed in order to enjoy fully their status as New Women.

While much has been written about Hemingway's "men without women," particularly in reference to the Burguete episode, the closing note of *The Sun Also Rises* is of a man *with* a woman, endeavoring to sustain a friendship in the face of their realization that they will never be lovers tucked away in the country somewhere. Jake and Brett have, for a moment at least, switched roles at the end of the novel. When he hastens to her call in Madrid, instead of *thinking* as he is wont to do, he *feels* that she is preoccupied, trembling, and small (245), an occurrence that

> "All modern American literature comes from one book by Mark Twain called *Huckleberry Finn*. . . . it's the best book we've had. All American writing comes from that. There was nothing before. There has been nothing as good since."
>
> *Ernest Hemingway*
>
> From *Green Hills of Africa* (New York: Scribners, 1935), p. 22.

reminds readers of Brett's and Jake's first moments alone in the novel, when Jake observes that Brett is "afraid of so many things" (26). After he greets her in the Hotel Montaña, he reports three times that he can *feel* her crying or shaking (245, 247). His focus, at last, is on Brett's side of things, and he gives her what she needs from him: comforting arms, a sympathetic ear, financial support, and a nonjudgmental friend. The dense irony that characterizes their previous conversations is gone. For her part, the New Woman Brett Ashley has finally begun analyzing her actions, reckoning with the new responsibility that accompanies her new freedom. She is trying to determine what she values—a preoccupation familiar to Jake. In the end, the New Woman, not entirely free, chooses marriage to Mike Campbell, exchanging her liberty for the financial security that Mike's inheritance will bring.

THE HERO AND THE NARRATOR

Storybook heroes were no match for mustard gas, and no soldier's physical prowess could thwart machine-gun or mortar fire. The new century's literature required new heroes, or, perhaps, an "antihero." Several characters are candidates to be the hero of *The Sun Also Rises*. Robert leaves the book much as he entered it—refusing to believe that the modern world does not embrace nineteenth-century standards of conduct. Despite being an accomplished fighter, writer, and ladies' man, Robert is doomed because he refuses to see things as they are and conduct himself accordingly. Romero displays heroic qualities—but he is consistently heroic and changes no more than Robert. Brett's decision to send Romero back to his vocation has long been viewed with skepticism among critics who believe that her basic nature is insincere and that "there is little prospect that her future will be any different from her past."[7] Despite her physical beauty, Brett displays some unattractive qualities: she flicks ashes on Jake's rugs, interrupts his sleep, and is promiscuous and alcoholic. But none of these behaviors disqualifies her as the hero (heroine)—the character who is the focal point of the readers' interest and who engages their sympathies.

Jake may be the hero, because he eventually accepts the limitations of his relationship with Brett, something Robert refuses to realize.

Cayetano Ordóñez, called Niño de la Palma, the original for the bullfighter Pedro Romero in *The Sun Also Rises*

While the result of Jake's physical wound seems clear enough—he is unable to consummate his relationship with Brett—he also suffers from acute obtuseness when it comes to Brett and fails to notice when the love-struck Robert and the accommodating Lady Ashley are absent, together. Jake is not slow thinking about all things; in fact, Jake, with Bill as a distant second, is without a doubt the most observant and perceptive character in the novel—just not when it comes to Brett. In matters regarding her, he is, if not an utterly romantic fool like Robert, then at least temporarily blinded by her beauty or the beautiful illusion that they might one day live in the country.

Neither Brett's promiscuity nor Jake's obtuseness disqualifies either of them as heroine or hero. By the end of the novel Brett has changed (as a hero or heroine must), and she has helped others to change as well. The major conflict in the novel appears like the exposed tip of an iceberg in the tearful conversation between Jake and Brett when she informs him that she is "going away" to San Sebastian. When Jake asks why, she informs him, "Better for you. Better for me" (62). The explanation for her leaving, the submerged portion of the iceberg, seems to have escaped Jake. She has told him that she *must* see him, but as her seeing him prompts dreadful scenes, she must cure him of his illusion that they will eventually live together. They cannot live together, explains Brett, and until Jake realizes this fact, Brett will not be able to have him "for a friend" (152). He realizes that he has been getting something for nothing from her: she is the object of his affections and, as long as she is out of sight, he may imaginatively court her. But when she is present, which is to say when she is trying to get what she needs from the relationship, then Jake goes to pieces.

Brett tells Jake "I've always done just what I wanted" (188), and in choosing to go off to San Sebastian, she is not being buffeted about by cosmic forces; she is exercising her will. In sleeping with Robert, Brett is readjusting her relationship with Jake. She is, in fact, doing Jake a service. Her tryst with Robert will either cure Jake and facilitate their friendship without the annoying distraction of Jake's romantic illusions, or it will kill their relationship. Brett is ready to take the risk, because the impossibility of Jake and her living together "in the country" (62) or anywhere has been clear to her for some time—perhaps years—and she desperately needs a change.

She achieves her desire: her going to bed with Robert cures Jake, although it embitters him toward Robert, and she is unable to reveal her motives to Jake. But it also produces an unexpected result: Robert shadows her and eventually makes her lose her self-respect by reminding her that she has traded her body to one man in an attempt to win the mind of another. The consequence of the cure, her loss of self-respect, is remedied by her affair with Romero, which allows her, once again, to do just what she wants with her body. The proof of the cure is Jake's response to her telegram from the Hotel Montaña in Madrid. Jake, in the midst of securing his own much-needed peace of mind in San Sebastian, is exercising, observing, and enjoying his retreat away from intimate contact with both men and women when Brett's cable arrives. Who but a friend would retrieve an irresponsible thirty-four-year-old woman after her short-lived affair with a nineteen-year-old boy?

Jake does not misinterpret Brett's plea for help as a romantic overture. He is "over" his romantic infatuation with Brett. He loves her, but her escapade with Robert has finally forced him to come to terms with the knowledge that he can have her only as a friend. So, as a friend, he takes the Sud Express to Madrid to retrieve her. When she had solicited his help in meeting Romero, he had told her five times that she "oughtn't to do it" (187–188). But when she makes clear to him that she has no choice, that she needs Romero to help regain her self-respect, he obliges her—at a tremendous personal sacrifice. But when he helps her, he is not, as Robert suggests, acting as her pimp—for a pimp usually reaps a share of the proceeds, and Jake is not acting from self-interest. He is helping her to regain her self-respect, although ironically, he does not understand that he was at least partially responsible for her loss of it. In this ironic novel, no reader should be surprised that the heroine, who has lost her self-respect in a successful bid to rid Jake of his romantic illusions, regains it when he facilitates a relationship between her and a man nearly half her age.

Hemingway's narrator never makes up his mind about who the hero of the story is—not in the draft, the typescript, or the published novel. The heroic action of book 1, Brett's ridding Jake of his romantic illusion, remains hidden to Jake, the controlling consciousness of the novel. Likewise, when his love for Brett prompts him to introduce her to Romero and then to retrieve her in Madrid, he understands his own heroic action no better than does Huckleberry Finn, who tears up his note to Miss Watson and declares he will go to hell. Huck and Jake both follow their hearts and do the right thing, but neither understands why.

NOTES

1. Matthew J. Bruccoli, ed., *Ernest Hemingway: The Sun Also Rises. A Facsimile Edition,* 2 volumes (Detroit: Omnigraphics, 1990), p. 143. Subsequent references are parenthetical.

2. See Delbert E. Wylder, *Hemingway's Heroes* (Albuquerque: University of New Mexico Press, 1969), p. 40.

3. See Wylder's "The Wounded Anti-Hero" and Scott Donaldson's "Hemingway's Morality of Compensation," in *Modern Critical Interpretations of Hemingway's The Sun Also Rises,* edited by Harold Bloom (New York: Chelsea House, 1987), pp. 31–65, 71–90.

4. Ernest Hemingway, *Death in the Afternoon* (New York: Scribners, 1932), p. 122.

5. This description of the cultural milieu is drawn from Sibbie O'Sullivan's "Love and Friendship/Man and Woman in The Sun Also Rises," in *Hemingway: Seven Decades of Criticism,* edited by Linda Wagner-Martin (East Lansing: Michigan State University Press, 1998), pp. 61–79. See also Linda Paterson Miller, "Brett Ashley: The Beauty of It All," in *Critical Essays on Ernest Hemingway's The Sun Also Rises,* edited by James Nagel (New York: G. K. Hall, 1995), pp. 170–184.

6. This information drawn from Wendy Martin's fuller discussion of the New Woman in "Brett Ashley as New Woman in The Sun Also Rises," in *New Essays on The Sun Also Rises,* edited by Wagner-Martin (New York: Cambridge University Press, 1987), pp. 65–82. Martin also discusses the role-switching between Brett and Jake at the end of the novel.

7. Michael Reynolds, *The Sun Also Rises: A Novel of the Twenties* (Boston: Twayne, 1988), p. 23.

CRITICAL RESPONSE TO *THE SUN ALSO RISES*

CRITICAL SUMMARY

Before *The Sun Also Rises*, Hemingway published *Three Stories & Ten Poems* (1923); *in our time* (1924), a collection of vignettes to which he added fifteen short stories for his next collection, *In Our Time* (1925); and a satirical work, *The Torrents of Spring* (1926). The first two slim volumes appeared in meager quantities: 300 copies for the first; 170 for the second. But Boni and Liveright published *In Our Time* in an edition of 1,335 copies, and the collection was enthusiastically endorsed by contemporary writers and reviewers.[1] Early and influential reviewers linked the new young writer with such established successes as Gertrude Stein, Sherwood Anderson, and F. Scott Fitzgerald. Hemingway's first publications showed promise not only to well-known literary critics such as Edmund Wilson but also to anonymous reviewers such as one from Kansas City who called the new author "one of the most promising young writers in the English Language."[2] Only H. L. Mencken seemed unimpressed by Hemingway's earliest efforts, and his disparaging review of *In Our Time* won him the author's special scorn in his next two published works.

Initial commentary on *The Sun Also Rises* was mixed but generally positive; the sales of the novel were brisk, its influence substantial. Critics observed that the novel was a roman à clef, that it seemed to capture the essence of the "lost generation," and that its style was new but accessible. Naysayers such as Allen Tate seemed perplexed by Hemingway's "singularly oblique" method of presenting character; Herbert Gorman disapproved of his "plotless incidents"; and Edwin Muir found that the story "tells us nothing of importance about human life."[3] After all the promise of his earlier writing, how could he focus on such drunkenness and sordidness? Why would he record such tiresome conversations and engage in such an unsuccessful experiment? Tate, who had much admired *In Our Time*, conceded that the author had produced a "successful novel, but not without returning some violence upon the integrity

Dust jacket for the first edition of Hemingway's 1926 novel

achieved in his first book."[4] Virginia Woolf accused Hemingway of cheating in his presentation of character by leaning "against the flanks of that particular bull after the horns have passed."[5] But the book's sales and positive reviews kept growing, and the few dissenting opinions have come to represent historical curiosities. Singled out for praise most often was Hemingway's dialogue. Others found the action exciting, the verisimilitude riveting. Intriguing was the fact that the characters were drawn from life, their prototypes to be found at cafés in the Latin Quarter. The wandering and drunken expatriates comprised for these early reviewers a "lost generation," cut adrift by World War I, cynical, hard-boiled, and doomed. Just as detractors engaged in ad hominem attacks, friendly critics tipped the scales with unequivocal praise, calling the twenty-seven-year-old author "the most interesting figure in American letters in the past ten years."[6]

A roman à clef, in which the originals of thinly veiled characters are easily recognized by their contemporaries, typically attracts the interest of the general reader. Hemingway's roman à clef was even more interesting for its stylistic innovation and cultural relevance. Newspapers, both mirroring and creating public interest, kept track of divorces, suicides, and scandals among the expatriate crowd. When newspaper reviews announced that "practically all of these characters are directly based on actual people," readers wanted to know *which* real people and how accurately the prototypes had been portrayed. According to the gossip in Paris, a more apt title for the book would have been *Six Characters in Search of an Author—With a Gun Apiece.*[7] Usually such short-lived biographical interest boosts initial sales but is soon relegated to a footnote. Not so with Hemingway's novel.

Nearly fifty years after the publication of *The Sun Also Rises,* readers were treated to Bertram D. Sarason's *Hemingway and The Sun Set* (1972), an entire volume of reminiscences, interviews, and a lengthy essay that tries to distinguish the facts from the fiction. Juanito Quintana, owner of Quintana Hotel and basis for the hotel proprietor Montoya, recounts the drunken antics of "Brett," Lady Duff Twysden, and "Mike," Pat Guthrie, and insists that the friendship between him and Hemingway was uninterrupted by the escapades of the expatriates.[8] Twysden's death and cremation are documented, exploding the myth that her pallbearers "had all been her lovers" and "slipped on the church steps and the casket dropped and split open."[9] The most sustained explanation surely comes from Harold Loeb, the prototype for Robert Cohn, who was hurt by Hemingway's portrayal of him as a romantic buffoon. His effort to set the record straight prompted an entire memoir, titled *The Way it Was* (1959).

The Sun Also Rises was much more than a best-seller that evolved into a literary classic. It sprung from Hemingway's most productive decade, launched his international acclaim, and came to be a representative work of "modernism." This literary movement broke with traditional forms and techniques; its themes include alienation, loss, and despair. Because of the pivotal place of the novel in Hemingway's canon, no biographer fails to investigate Hemingway's several excursions to Pamplona in the 1920s, to extol the physical charms of Duff Twysden, enchanter of all men whom she encountered, and to describe the evolution of the manuscript whose narrator went by the name of "Hem" and whose other characters bore the names of the author's acquaintances in Paris and Pamplona.[10] Of course, such investigations of the "real" events that inspired those depicted in the novel are principally biographical inquiries. And while they might satisfy historical curiosity, they do not typically generate the depth of analytical commentary needed to sustain critical interest in the novel.

Fortunately for Hemingway, his first novel was known not only as a roman à clef but also as "the definitive account of a war-wearied lost generation."[11] Many readers found the novel's suggestive epigraph from Gertrude Stein—"You are all a lost generation"—was borne out by the story, which was "a tale of great spiritual debacle, of a generation that has lost its guiding purpose and has been driven by time, fate or nerves (whatever one desired to call it) into the feverish atmosphere of strained passions."[12] The "lost generation" refers to those such as Jake, Mike, Brett, and Wilson-Harris who participated in World War I. They were more easily identified as a group than other generations because their defining experiences were national, not regional. The war thinned their ranks, encouraged their political consciousness, and introduced provincial teenagers to cosmopolitan cities in Europe. Like the members of many other generations, those born at the turn of the century defined some of their values in opposition to the values of their parents. Their parents had voted for prohibition; they chose to imbibe. Their mothers were bound and padded Victorian matrons; so daughters raised their hemlines, bobbed their hair, and wore drop-waisted and loose-fitting garments. Their fathers perpetuated the Protestant work ethic; but sons, having seen Paris, would not be content down on the farm. The old world of the nineteenth century was gone: the war and well-publicized political corruption, such as the Teapot Dome scandal, undermined faith in political rhetoric. Just as Charles Darwin's theories of natural selection

"Hemingway's words strike you, each one, as if they were pebbles fetched fresh from a brook. They live and shine, each in its place. So one of his pages has the effect of a brook-bottom into which you look down through the flowing water. The words form a tessellation, each in order beside the other."

Ford Madox Ford

From the introduction to *A Farewell to Arms* (New York: Modern Library, 1932), p. xvi.

had prompted reconsiderations of the biblical account of creation in Genesis, Sigmund Freud's psychoanalytical theories caused reexamination of the motivations for human behavior and reflections on subconscious desires. The American economy was changing, cities were growing, and transportation and technology were quickening life's pace.

Hemingway's characters depict the members of this "lost generation" at thirty-something, devoid of their moral and spiritual moorings, grappling with the newness of their new century. They have affairs—in Robert Cohn's case, shamelessly ending a romance with his secretary so that he can begin another with Frances Clyne, only to end that affair so that he can start one with Brett. The characters drink to excess. With few exceptions, none of them seems to embrace much of a work ethic or hold a job, yet they all enjoy travel and socializing; the result is that Mike is bankrupt and Brett is penniless in the last chapter of the novel. Just as their morality has lapsed, so has their spirituality. Although Jake and Romero are exceptions, most of the characters seem to have lost touch with traditional faith. Brett illustrates this best with her remark that not being a bitch is sort of what we have "instead of God" (249).

The Sun Also Rises became the showcase for the "lost generation" because its characters embodied the mood of disillusionment following the war and parlayed it into "a way of feeling and acting." People who had been "morally unhinged or physically maimed during the war" went through a period of readjustment. During this time, they expressed "their bitterness, their feeling of disenchantment, with calculated bravado."[13] They avoided discussing the past, as Jake does when Georgette mentions "that dirty war" (24), or when Bill inquires about Jake's relationship with Brett: "I'd a hell of a lot rather not talk about it," says Jake (128). They "live for the present, constantly searching for new and fresh sensations."[14] They are quick to mock institutions and ideas and seem not to embrace any core set of beliefs that might guide them through personal crises.

The third great initial attraction of *The Sun Also Rises* was its style. Malcolm Cowley notes that within a decade of the publication of the novel, Hemingway's influence had spread far beyond the circle of those who had known him in Paris: "The Smith College girls in New

York were modeling themselves after Lady Brett in *The Sun Also Rises*. Hundreds of bright young men from the Middle West were trying to be Hemingway Heroes, talking in tough understatements from the sides of their mouths. . . ."[15] But while a character's personal style, his expressions or mannerisms, are easily mimicked, Hemingway's seemingly simple style is much more complex than most readers imagine.

What exactly comprises the "Hemingway style"? Most assessments are impressionistic: it is simple, spare, or direct. Despite near-universal agreement that Hemingway's style may be the most influential literary style of the century, surprisingly little has been written about it. A few perceptive critics have taken the time to catalogue Hemingway's stylistic attributes, and it behooves readers to acquaint themselves with these discussions because in order to understand the *what* of his prose, one must appreciate the *how*. Hemingway's diction is simple and economic. His frequent use of expletives ("it is" or "there are/is") emphasizes his nouns; modifiers are used sparingly. His syntax tends toward simple sentences, often coordinated with the conjunction *and* (polysyndeton) or simply abutted without coordination (parataxis). Subordination is rare, and causative connectors (therefore, thus) are infrequent. Combine these stylistic features with a narrator who often reports what he sees without commentary, and the result is a narrative that seems to catalogue sensations objectively. Gone is the omniscient narrator of the nineteenth century who would address the "gentle readers" and explain how they should interpret the text. Modern readers are on their own: they have to read between the lines, to *hear* the dialogue, to be attuned to nuance and subtlety. They must become readers upon whom nothing is lost so that they can join the ranks of "one of us" and become interpreters of Hemingway's prose.

Joseph Warren Beach ventured an assessment in 1941 that deserves quoting for its perceptive observations about Hemingway's coordination and simplicity, which Beach identified as intentional, designed to record the lives of characters who have rejected the facade of intellectual sophistication:

> All the English teachers in the country are trying to get their pupils to discover the varied relationships of ideas, and to range their ideas in the proper order of subordination. Hemingway is just as strenuously working to reduce all ideas to a single order of relationship, the conjunctive coordinate relationship, in which no one item is subordinated to any other. It is the great leveling democracy of the *and*. . . . The simple-minded reader may be grateful to Hemingway for putting up so few obstacles to his understanding. But the simple-minded reader does not understand the half of what the man is driving at. The point is that Hemingway has set out to record the behaviour of people not precisely sim-

ple-minded, but who have not learned, or who have deliberately unlearned, the language of intellectual sophistication.[16]

Writing in the same era, Robert Penn Warren further refined some of Beach's distinctions. He too noted the simplicity and coordination in Hemingway's writing, but he attributed them to a different cause. For Warren, the discrete units of data placed side by side represent the author's fragmented world:

> The style is characteristically simple, even to the point of monotony. The characteristic sentence is simple, or compound, and if compound, there is no implied subtlety in the coordination of the clauses. The paragraph structure is, characteristically, based on the simple sentence. There is an obvious relation between this style and the characters and situations with which the author is concerned—a question of dramatic decorum. . . . But there is a more fundamental aspect of the question, an aspect which involves not the sensibility of characters but the sensibility of the author. The short, simple rhythms, the succession of coordinate clauses, the general lack of subordination—all suggest a dislocated and ununified world. The figures which live in this world live a sort of hand-to-mouth existence perceptually, and conceptually, they hardly live at all.[17]

Harry Levin's significant expansion of Warren's analysis addresses Hemingway's diction. He notes "understatement," the "restricted use of adjectives," and "the heavy load of subjective implications carried by such words as 'fine' and 'nice.'" Levin suggests that Hemingway packs these monosyllables (*good* and *fine*) with an emotional charge, projecting the "narrator's euphoria in a given situation." The effect, writes Levin, is prose that sends a message to the reader: "Having a wonderful time. Wish you were here."[18] Levin also documents Hemingway's tendency to employ expletives, which leaves his diction thin, his syntax weak, his adjectives rather bland, and his verbs not particularly energetic.[19] While this hardly seems a complimentary assessment of one of the most innovative literary styles of the century, Levin explains how Hemingway makes it work: the expletives, which many writing instructors would consider weak constructions, "take the place of the observer and his observations are registered one by one." The expletives shift the burden of communication to the nouns, which are especially important to Hemingway because they come closest to things, and, as Levin observes, when Hemingway "string[s] them along by means of conjunction, he approximates the actual flow of experience."[20]

What keeps the noun-heavy style rolling along? Richard Bridgman suggests that Hemingway mastered the use of the preposition, which "points a direction or locates an object. At times Hemingway's prose became a series of arrows rhythmically pointing now this way, now that. He relied especially upon prepositional intensity for the difficult job of describing movement through towns and across landscapes."[21] Bridgman cites an excellent example from *The Sun Also Rises:*

> Down below there were grassy plains and clear streams, and then we crossed a stream and went through a gloomy little village, and started to climb again. We climbed up and up and crossed another high Col and turned along it, and the road ran down to the right. (99)

In addition to deftly using prepositions, Hemingway also designs his dialogue to help him diversify his prose. "Unlike the highly specific narrative," Bridgman observes, "his dialogue is often vague, ambiguous, indirect. It is even more truncated and narrowed than the prose. Indeed, the epitome of inexpressiveness between quotation marks is reached in the account of a Montmartre dance in *The Sun Also Rises:*"[22]

> "A writer's problem does not change. He himself changes, but his problem remains the same. It is always how to write truly and, having found what is true, to project it in such a way that it becomes a part of the experience of the person who reads it."
>
> *Ernest Hemingway*
>
> From a speech to the American Writers' Congress, New York, 4 June 1937.

> The drummer shouted: "You can't two time—"
>
> "It's all gone."
>
> "What's the matter?"
>
> "I don't know. I just feel terribly."
>
> ". . . . . ." the drummer chanted. Then turned to his sticks.
>
> "Want to go?"
>
> I had the terrible feeling as in a nightmare of it all being something repeated, something I had been through and now I must go through again.
>
> ". . . . . ." the drummer sang softly.
>
> "Let's go," said Brett. "You don't mind."
>
> ". . . . . ." the drummer shouted and grinned at Brett.
>
> "All right," I said. (70–71)

Here the drummer's words are more than ambiguous; they are entirely absent. This leaves the reader to assume that, whatever the words actually were, they served only to deepen Brett's dejection and her longing for what is "all gone" (70). A similarly ambiguous exchange of dialogue occurs when Brett asks Jake "I've never let you down, have I?" to which Jake replies "Heard from Mike?" which indirectly answers her question in the affirmative (37).

Once critics had had a few years to digest the novel as well as some other works by Hemingway, they began to think of *The Sun Also Rises* as more than a period piece or a roman à clef whose primary attraction was that it was based on real people. The new round of criticism pursued the mythical allusions in the novel; provided two new critical terms, the Hemingway Hero and the Hemingway Code; and focused on Jake's attempt to establish a meaningful life.

Hemingway was very much aware of T. S. Eliot, whose poetry and criticism were enormously influential, particularly in the 1910s and 1920s, when Hemingway was shaping his own theory of literature. Following the publication of his poem *The Waste Land* in 1922, Eliot wrote a review of James Joyce's novel *Ulysses,* "*Ulysses,* Order, and Myth," which used the phrase "mythical method." This method was "a continuous parallel between contemporaneity and antiquity" or "a way of controlling, of ordering, of giving shape and significance to the immense panorama of futility and anarchy which is contemporary history".[23] Joyce superimposed his *Ulysses* upon the skeleton of Homer's epic; Eliot's *The Waste Land* drew upon the Grail Legend; William Faulkner draped the tale of the Compson family in *The Sound and the Fury* (1929) over the darkest and brightest days in the Christian calendar. And Hemingway's first novel pursued analogies to the Grail legend and to Eliot's poem.

Malcolm Cowley was among the first to write about the parallel between Hemingway's novel and Eliot's poem, and he broached the subject gingerly, for Hemingway was particularly sensitive about the discovery of his literary debts. Cowley observed the parallel between Jessie L. Weston's description of the legend of the Fisher King (the King, wounded in the loins, lay wasting abed while in his kingdom nothing was fruitful or multiplied) and Hemingway's depiction of the postwar expatriates in Paris. But Cowley was quick to add, "I don't mean to imply that Hemingway owes a debt to *The Waste Land*"; he had merely "dealt with the same legend that Eliot had discovered by scholarship[,] recovering it or himself, I think, by a sort of instinct for literary situations."[24]

Other critics, however, were less shy about associating Hemingway's novel with Eliot's poem. In *Hemingway: The Writer as Artist* (1952) Carlos Baker titled his chapter on *The Sun Also Rises* "The Wastelanders," explicated a few of its allusions, and proposed that the novel employed a "mythological" method that was different from Eliot's or Joyce's by virtue of its being less literary. Richard P. Adams more fully explicated the parallels between Hemingway's novel and both *The Waste Land* and the legend of the Fisher King.[25] Eliot's "Unreal City" and Hemingway's Paris, the City of Lights, are chaotic and spiritually dead. Sexual relations are meaningless, both in part 2 of *The Waste Land,* "A Game of Chess," and in the short-lived affair between Robert Cohn and Brett Ashley. And hope is dissipated: in part 5 of Eliot's poem, "What the Thunder Said," the thunder brings no rain, and Jake realizes, as Adams observes, that "not even the illusion of physical potency would have permitted him felicity" with

Brett. Brett has her own links to fertility myths: excluded from the Catholic Church, with its confessions in a language that she does not know, she joins the gypsies in their fortune-telling, becomes an image for the revelers to dance around, and, like Circe, turns men into swine. One of these men, Cohn, makes a feeble attempt at being a Grail knight: but his naive infatuation with Brett earns him nothing but alienation—separation from the herd.

Hemingway in Paris, 1924

These parallels support Adams's claim that Hemingway's mythical method was as literary and complex as Eliot's and Joyce's. In emphasizing the structural parity, Adams suggests that just as in Eliot's poem it "remained uncertain whether any renewal of cultural fertility or creative power was possible," so too is Jake's final sarcasm an attempt to shore up fragments against the ruin of his own life.[26] The novel leaves Jake, as Philip Young observes, "returned to Brett as before, and we discover that we have come full circle, like all the rivers, the winds, and the sun, to the place where we began. This is motion which goes no place."[27] Love is impossible. The structure, echoing the second epigraph of the novel, is circular and rife with allusion. This allusiveness does not refute Baker's observation that Hemingway's prose did "not require special literary equipment to be interpreted."[28] It merely suggests that the plot and themes readily grasped by contemporary audiences were enough to generate and sustain interest in the novel for three quarters of a century. Hemingway's "mythical method" has proven to be an interesting, if ancillary, avenue of inquiry into the text.

In fact, the far more influential critical approach to the novel has been readings that focus on the "Hemingway Hero" and the "Hemingway Code." In 1952, the same year that Baker published his *Hemingway: The Writer as Artist,* with its "Wastelanders" chapter, Young produced *Ernest Hemingway,* with a chapter titled "The Hero and the Code."[29] Young took a wide view of the Hemingway canon and observed similarities among many of the protagonists, as well as experiences common to the heroes and Hemingway himself. The most significant shared experience is the "wound." Before his nineteenth birthday, Hemingway had been injured by an Austrian trench-mortar shell and had had the opportunity to contemplate his own mortality. Similarly, Nick Adams in the Chapter IV vignette of *In Our Time* has been wounded in the spine and, by way of withdrawing from the war, makes a "separate peace" with the enemy.[30] Young notes that "it would be quite impossible to exaggerate the importance of this short scene, which is to be duplicated by a new protagonist named Frederic Henry in *A Farewell to Arms,* and to serve as the climax for all of Hemingway's heroes for at least the next twenty-five years."[31] The physical and psychological wounds that the protagonists suffer vary: sometimes it is the shock of witnessing a jackknife Cesarian section and a nearly decapitated Indian, as in "Indian Camp," or being struck by a deceptive brakeman, as in "The Battler." For Jake Barnes, it is clearly his emasculation.

Having been wounded, the sensitive and reticent Hemingway hero must find some way of "holding tight against pain." In order to accomplish this, Young observes, the protagonist adopts

> the Hemingway "code"—a "grace under pressure." It is made of the controls of honor and courage which in a life of tension and pain make a man a man and distinguish him from the people who follow random impulses, let down their hair, and are generally messy, perhaps cowardly, and without inviolable rules for how to live holding tight.[32]

The protagonist, sometimes called the "tyro," grows by emulating a tutor who possesses the heroic code. The tyro,

> faced with the overwhelming confusion and hurt (*nada*) inherent in an attempt to live an active sensual life, admires the deliberate self-containment of the tutor (a much "simpler man") who is seemingly not beset with inner uncertainties. Accordingly, the tyro tries to model his behavior on the pattern he discerns.[33]

But the tyro is not a simple man, and at best he learns to project the appearance of contentment in the face of the pressures that besiege him.

Several critics have persuasively argued that Count Mippipopolous and Pedro Romero act as tutors for Jake. The count, bearer of arrow wounds and apparently at peace with himself, encourages Jake to "get to know the values" (67) that will guide his actions and perhaps lead to his contentment. The matador's wounds, too, are visible during the last bullfights of the fiesta. Jake explains that "[t]he fight with Cohn had not touched his spirit but his face had been smashed and his body hurt" (223). Without tricks or mystifications, Romero demonstrates skill, control, and grace under pressure.

The notions of the hero and the code provided an interesting reading of the Hemingway canon, but like all readings, they were partial, limited. The hero/code readings did help to redirect interest in the novel away from the author and roman à clef readings and toward the narrator, prompting assessments of Jake's dynamic or static qualities. The hero/code readings were meant to offer a new avenue into the texts, and they suffered by virtue of their success. The critical terminology was so accessible and the critical theory was so logical that thousands of undergraduates and hundreds of academics applied code readings to their favorite stories. They forced the reader's eye onto what was soon to be a well-traveled path. Hemingway's stories or characters that could not be made to "fit" into the rubric of code/hero readings were marginalized. The luster seemed to be fading from critical inquiry, but *The Sun Also Rises,* and indeed the whole of Hemingway's canon, is far too sophisticated to be reduced to formulaic readings, and the next critical movement—a revisionist one—was soon under way.

Just when the idea that *The Sun Also Rises* was Hemingway's *Waste Land* approached the status of critical cliché, readers began to remark different parallels and structural principles and to champion them as primary. The structural analogy for the novel, so revisionists such as Dewey Ganzel and Donald T. Torchiana claim, is not Eliot's poem or the Grail legend, but the bullfight.[34] The first attempt at such a reading placed Jake, "the human punching bag," in the role of steer and both Cohn and Brett in the role of fighting bulls (203). But subsequent rereadings are more expansive, finding the novel to be "an unrelieved attack on America," whose tourists are ruining Paris, whose pilgrims are clogging the dining cars, and whose contradictory morality produces prohibition on the one hand and women who collect bullfighters on the other.[35] The new readings emphasize Jake's love of the earth and pursue the allusion to Jake's biblical namesake, Jacob the fighter. Jake's sensitivity to injustice, which can be seen by his interest in the Negro boxer in Vienna, belies his propensity as a newsman to discover and reveal the true story, whether it be about the war or about Brett's past.

Cowley had suggested years earlier that the novel "is a less despairing book than the critics like to think; at times it is gay, friendly, even exuberant," and the new readings began to articulate the affirmative qualities.[36] The earth is celebrated: the wine, jazz, stifling heat, and cool breezes; the barges, bridges, promenading couples, and sun bathing lovers; and the cols, vistas, and quiet solitude that allow for reading, reflection, and mending. In the middle of this celebration and very much in touch with the earth is Jake, the only one among the expatriates who ruminates upon the passing of Vincente Girones, who is killed during the running of the bulls in Pamplona. Jake is in search, perhaps, of an explanation for the young man's "muy flemenco" (foolish, daring) behavior (202).

How does the bullfight serve as an analogy for the novel? In Book I, notes Torchiana, "animalism seems to triumph on all sides": Robert is successful at cards, publishes a bad book, and woos a titled lady. In her affair with Cohn, Brett two-times Jake, or perhaps it is Mike, depending upon whether one views her as owing allegiance to the man she loves or to the man she is engaged to marry. In Book II, Jake begins by quietly dominating his circle of friends, keeping them "off each other and himself by a combination of skillful dodges, compassionate understanding, as with Brett and Harvey Stone, and iron determination to get on with his own work."[37] But soon the actions of Jake's friends come to resemble the dangerous unloading and then running of the bulls; the chaotic action leaves Jake wounded by Cohn, Mike disgraced, and Brett gone off with her bullfighter. Book III places Jake the fighter alone with the most dangerous and beguiling of his friends, Brett; he handles himself admirably and will probably continue to come to her rescue again and again.

Not only did critics spy a new structure in the novel, but they also began to see Jake as a dynamic character, a man who undergoes a profound change after he witnesses Romero's masculinity, which sharply contrasts with his own shameful behavior that differs only a little from Robert Cohn's.[38] In the end, he has "bartered reasonably well. He has traded off false hope and empty illusion and salvaged integrity." Soon the critical consensus was that Jake had changed, and if this was true, then it called into question the critical commonplace that the structure of the novel was circular: if Jake does not end where he began, then the circular model for the structure of the novel needed to be replaced with a linear one.

And if Jake could learn about himself, was it possible for Brett and Jake to learn about each other? Early critics had equated the impossibility of sex between Brett and Jake with the impossibility of their love; in fact, one of the most influential readings of the novel detailed the ways in which it was an allegory about the death of love.[39] But revisionists viewed Brett as something more than a nymphomaniac alcoholic. They called her a "new woman" and dubbed Hemingway's novel a "goodbye kiss to the Victorian ethos."[40] Far from viewing the characters as emotionally sterile, their friendships now seemed more obvious; the warmth between Bill and Jake profound; the comradeship with Wilson-Harris in Burguete healthy. And what of Jake and Brett in Madrid at the close of the novel? There Jake takes Brett into his arms and adds to this physical solace the earnest desire that she "tell [him] about it" (245). Her easy confidence gone, her shapely curves trembling, she cries in Jake's arms. They have been there for one another not as lovers but as friends, and the novel "exhibits the cyclical nature of friendship, its rhythm of disintegration and renewal."[41]

Following this healthy round of revisionist readings of *The Sun Also Rises,* which included more than a thousand books and articles during the 1980s, the Hemingway archive became available at the John F. Kennedy Library, spurring yet another line of inquiry and causing a resurgence of biographical interest that had abated since the publication of Baker's *Ernest Hemingway: A Life Story* in 1969.[42] Soon *The Sun Also Rises* became known nearly as much for what Hemingway excised as for what he had included. Having claimed status as a "classic" with the popular audience by virtue of its continued sales and adaptations for the screen, its merit in scholarly circles earned it the distinction of having a facsimile edition of the manuscript.[43] One of the most celebrated excisions to appear subsequently in print was the opening. Fitzgerald had counseled extensive revisions for this section, but Hemingway chose a wholesale cut over piecemeal editing. The result was that he eliminated background information about Brett Ashley, Mike Campbell, and Jake Barnes. Lost, too, was Jake's accounting of the years between the war, when he met Brett, and the present time of the novel. The three best treatments of the manuscript are by Michael Reynolds, whose *Hemingway: The American Homecoming* (1992) covers the stages of revision; William Balassi; and Frederic Joseph Svoboda.

Critics also attempted to bridge gaps caused by the passage of time, explicating the allusions, the jokes, and the historical references and continuing to revise received notions about the novel. A pair of lengthy articles explored Hemingway's use of humor—his verbal slips, puns, and double entendres. Some sixty embedded jokes are identified, as are several kinds of humor: Mike's self-deprecation; Bill's jibes at ideas and institutions; Bill and Jake's allusive banter; and amusing dramatic irony in the *bal musette* episode, in which Braddocks blithely informs his obtuse wife that he has known Georgette, a common prostitute, for a long time. There is humor in the most unexpected places: *zizi,* French slang for *penis,* certainly adds a new twist to Brett's query to the Count "How's your little friend, Zizi?" Nothing wrings the humor from a joke like scholarly analysis, but these inquiries into Hemingway's comic strain are typical of the heightened level of scrutiny that revisionist critics were bringing to the text. These new inquiries involved irony, mood, tone, and ambiguity. Suddenly *The Sun Also Rises* was being treated as if it were a prose poem, which, of course, it is.[44]

While much of the humor in the novel hinged on incongruity, some of the narrative depended upon knowledge shared by Hemingway and his audience. Three generations after the novel was written, it had lost most of its original audience. President Warren G. Harding and the Teapot Dome Scandal, the inception of the Ku Klux Klan, Charlie Chaplin, Jack Dempsey, and Babe Ruth—these were the stuff of history, and by now the novel itself had become a part not only of literary history but also of American culture. So critics began to recover Hemingway's history in general and the history of the novel in particular. Reynolds, the most tenacious archeologist to turn his attentions to Hemingway, spent more than twenty years crafting a five-volume biography.[45] Viewing *The Sun Also Rises* as an historical artifact, he asserts that "historically blind readers see only the timeless qualities of the work, and even these they are reading at a discount."[46] So Reynolds revisits the era, reminding readers of the predominant value system and morality, explaining the decline of nineteenth-century standards. In doing so, he provides the kinds of historical context that, one day, will be found in critical editions of Hemingway's works. Interest in Hemingway's female characters surged in the revisionist period. Brett Ashley, initially perceived as a nymphomaniac alcoholic, attracted enough interest to warrant her own collection of essays. Through the lens of contemporary reviews of the novel, which were none too favorable, Brett could be viewed as a Circe figure, as dominated by self-pity, as a pagan fertility goddess, as an emblem of "the Bought Generation," as a stoic heroine, as an allegorical figure, and as a quester for what cannot be found. She was seen in contemporary reviews as the "new woman," caught between the roles of the traditional, idealized woman and the self-reliant, modern woman.[47]

After compiling the critical response to Hemingway's canon in his invaluable *Hemingway: The Critical Heritage,* Jeffrey Meyers concluded, "Unless new discoveries are made among the unpublished material, the books that inevitably follow at the fag-end of literary criticism will vary existing ideas, repeat what has already been said or offer madcap theories. Except for archival research, the essential work on Hemingway has already been done."[48] Meyers rightly condemns the worst work of the 1960s and 1970s for recycling ideas from the first thirty years of Hemingway criticism; but he is premature in condemning all criticism from the last twenty years as inevitably repetitious or madcap. True, Cowley's mythological reading, Young's "wound theory," and Wilson's notion of the Hemingway "code" were trotted out ad nauseam; but this repetition was due in large part to the sheer accessibility of the critical ideas. Once these ideas took root in the fertile fields of Hemingway criticism, they seemed without a natural predator and, for a time, threatened to propagate unchecked, choking out new readings.

But the new readings came, many of them assuredly prompted by the posthumous publication in 1986 of Hemingway's *The Garden of Eden,* which pursued themes of androgyny and lesbianism. This provocative text was followed by a revisionist biography by Kenneth S. Lynn, *Hemingway* (1987), which pursued the theme of androgyny in Hemingway's own life, focusing particularly on the mixed gender signals that young Ernest received from his mother. Mark Spilka suggests that androgyny was a childhood condition that initially promised great happiness, but it was soon resisted and repressed and became a "wounding condition . . . that could be overcome only through strenuous male activities."[49] In her man's felt hat, the hard-drinking "chap," Brett Ashley, "represents the arrival of the liberated woman of the 1920s, a type whose assumption of equality with men makes her much too difficult for Hemingway's heroes to handle even while it makes her more attractive."[50] Other gender studies contemplate neglected questions: why is Brett introduced along with a "garland of gay young men" during the time that impotent Jake has chosen to take up with a *poule*? Why does Jake become angry? Is it because he views the men synechdochically, as fragments, noting their "white hands, wavy hair, white faces" (28), and is reminded of his own fragmented (impotent) being? To what degree do Brett's mannish attire and iconoclastic behavior contribute to her allure? What relation has Brett's close-cropped hair with Hemingway's own fetishism?[51] The effect of these new investigations is to release Hemingway from the stereotypical readings that consign him exclusively to the "cult of masculinity."

Despite the loss of the historical and cultural contexts, which yearly retreat farther into the past, *The Sun Also Rises* has survived. For many of today's students, who operate without knowledge of the historical context of the novel, it has simply become a book about character. *The Sun Also Rises* is unique in that it will not disclose its hero, and it compels readers to determine which characters they like and why. The novel lacks an omniscient narrator to interpret the action and a coda to explain the resolution. And once readers have all of the variables in place and return to the text to confirm their reading, they discover that they are a little older, have a little more sympathy for some characters, or are less inclined to judge others. Just as the novel accommodates readers by insisting that they bridge the gaps in the text and that they resolve the narrative's ambiguities, so too does it comply with the critics' needs, providing them with a story that can be read on as many levels as they can establish.

CRITICAL SURVEY

Initial reviews of *The Sun Also Rises* were predominantly favorable. A few American commentators objected to the subject matter and were perturbed by the "utterly degraded people" who were "as shallow as the saucers in which they stack their daily emotions." English reviewers of *Fiesta*, as the book was titled by Hemingway's London publisher, cared little for the novel. One found that it gave "neither people nor atmosphere" and complained that the characters were merely shadows rather than flesh and blood. Another called it an "unsuccessful experiment" that was "frankly tedious to read." A third reviewer applauded the dialogue of *Fiesta* but condemned the novel for its "lack of artistic significance."[52]

But most readers of the 1920s sensed that they had read something extraordinary—an old story of impossible love told in a new way. Many of their critical observations were surprisingly accurate, considering that they were conceived with little pause for reflection. The more exuberant reviewers, such as Conrad Aiken, labeled the author "the most exciting of contemporary American writers of fiction."[53] Edwin Muir wrote that Hemingway "simply states; he even, as a general rule, can be said to understate. . . . The action, he seems to say, must speak wholly for itself," and found the realism "so exact that it has the effect of imagination; it evokes scenes, conversations, characters."[54] André Maurois wrote that the plot was "practically non-existent. . . . But any plot will do when a novelist knows how to create live human beings and Hemingway's characters are alive."[55] Herbert Gorman thought the structure of the novel was easily outlined and wrote that "all of these characters are directly based on actual people."[56] Burton Rascoe noted that "[s]ome Americans familiar around the Dome and the Rotondo [*sic*] in Paris appear in the novel in the thinnest of disguises, and remarkably true to character."[57] Aiken declared that Hemingway had "learned something from Mr. [Sherwood] Anderson, and something, perhaps, from Mr. Fitzgerald's 'Great Gatsby'; he may even have extracted a grain or two of ore from Miss Gertrude Stein—which is itself no inconsiderable feat."[58] Gorman called *The Sun Also Rises* "a tale of a great spiritual debacle, of a generation that has lost its guiding purpose and has been driven by time, fate or nerves (whatever one desires to call it) into the feverish atmosphere of strained passions."[59] Aiken praised the technical accomplishment of Hemingway's dialogue: "More than any other talk I can call to mind, it is alive with the rhythms and idioms, the pauses and suspensions and innuendoes and shorthands, of living speech. It is in the dialogue, almost entirely, that Mr. Hemingway tells his story and makes his people come alive and act. This is the dramatist's gift."[60]

Hemingway was much talked about and widely read in the 1920s and 1930s, and by the time of the publication of *For Whom the Bell Tolls* in 1940, he had already attracted considerable attention from critics. In the mid 1920s, he was widely considered a young man of much promise, and both his stories and novels of that decade were well received. An early admirer of Hemingway's short stories, Edmund Wilson, viewed the theme of *The Sun Also Rises* as the attempt of the hero and heroine to "find some way of living" in the world. Life was clearly a losing game, but the characters' responsibility was to "stick to the code of the sportsman and lose in a sportsman-like way."[61] Wilson grew weary of Hemingway and less enamored of his work in the late 1930s, explaining his dissatisfaction in an influential article that expanded on his previously stated idea of "the code" and anticipated the type and tenor of much of the criticism that followed.[62] First, he presents the idea of a composite hero, suggesting that Hemingway's male protagonists are different versions of the same man: Nick Adams of the early short stories is taken by Wilson to be the "American boy" who reappears as "the young American," Jake Barnes, in *The Sun Also Rises*. Others concurred, labeling the "Hemingway hero" a "composite exaggeration of all the Hemingway heroes, yet nothing in himself."[63]

Second, Wilson elaborates on the idea of "a code" existing amid all the drunkenness and social chaos. If Hemingway's characters were soulless and his novels Godless, then at least the code "supplies a dependable moral backbone" and helps Jake to withstand the hostile environment of the novel, in which "all the things that are wrong with human life are there on the holiday, too." This code "is usually some principle of courage, of honor, of pity—that is, some principle of sportsmanship in its largest sense—upon which the drama hinges."[64] The notion that Hemingway's heroes establish and live by a code that lends meaning to their lives permeated Hemingway scholarship for nearly half a century. Refining Wilson's notion of the "code" a decade later, Robert Penn Warren saw Hemingway's characters as doomed to defeat, "and when they confront defeat they realize that the stance they take, the stoic endurance, the stiff upper lip mean a kind of victory."

> It is the discipline of the code which makes man human, a sense of style or good form. . . . the code and the discipline are important because they can give meaning to life which otherwise seems to have no meaning or justification. In other words, in a world without supernatural sanctions, in the God-abandoned world of modernity, man can realize an ideal meaning only in so far as he can define and maintain the code. The effort to define and maintain the code, however limited and imperfect it may be, is the characteristically human effort and provides the tragic or pitiful human story.[65]

Café du Dôme, Paris, 1924

The third trend that Wilson initiated was the blending of critical estimations of Hemingway's work with biographical excursions into his private life and public persona. Already in 1927, scarcely a year after the novel had been published, Wilson observed that the "reputation of Ernest Hemingway has, in a very short time, reached such proportions that it has already become fashionable to disparage him."[66] He liked the early Hemingway—both man and work. But he loathed the author of the 1930s, "of the handsome photographs with the sportsman's tan and the outdoor grin, with the ominous resemblance to Clark Gable." Wilson found this Hemingway to be "arrogant, belligerent and boastful . . . certainly the worst-invented character to be found in the author's work." His justification for treating both the man and the work? The "heroic Hemingway legend has at this point invaded his fiction and, in claiming and inflating his symbols, has produced an implausible hybrid, half Hemingway character, half nature myth."[67] Other critics concurred and blamed "American criticism for the illegitimate emergence of Hemingway the 'man' and the resultant inferiority of his two recent major works" (*Green Hills of Africa* and the play *The Fifth Column*).[68] The tension between Hemingway and the critical establishment brought about by the author's sudden success, his outspoken views, and his popularity with general readers would last a lifetime.

Finally, Wilson addresses a common complaint against Hemingway in the 1930s, that "he shows no interest in political problems." In a decade of Hoovervilles, dustbowls, and migrant despair, Hemingway wrote about safaris, bullfights, and smugglers. Where was his social conscience? It was always there, replied Wilson in Hemingway's defense, and "we can clearly see what an error of the politicos it was to accuse him of an indifference to society" because his "whole work is a criticism of society." He responded to the moral pressure of his time "as it is felt at the roots of human relations, with a sensitivity almost unrivaled."[69] The notion of Hemingway as a social critic, concerned to teach the self-reliant individual how to survive in the twentieth century, would not reach full blossom until the 1950s, when Philip Young compared Hemingway to Mark Twain.

"From things that have happened and from things as they exist and from all things that you know and all those you cannot know, you make something through your invention that is not a representation but a whole new thing truer than anything true and alive, and you make it alive, and if you make it well enough, you give it immortality. That is why you write and for no other reason that you know of. But what about all the reasons that no one knows?"

Ernest Hemingway

From "Ernest Hemingway," in *Writers at Work: The Paris Review Interviews, Second Series* (New York: Viking, 1963), p. 239.

The important critical works of the 1940s, by which time Hemingway was already a permanent part of the landscape of the American literature, were articles, chapters, and introductions. Perhaps the most original ideas set forth in this decade were Malcolm Cowley's. He relished the timeless allure, particularly the concrete details of Hemingway's prose. But *The Sun Also Rises,* a novel of the Roaring Twenties, which had been followed by a decade of economic depression, now came to be viewed in light of World War II. The critical focus on stylistic innovation and moral dissipation was now widened to include violence and despair and fuller explanations of the now-famous "Hemingway code." From the vantage point of 1945, Cowley could see not an alliance with Theodore Dreiser or Jack London but a kinship with Edgar Allan Poe, Nathaniel Hawthorne, and Herman Melville, "the haunted and nocturnal writers, the men who dealt in images that were symbols of the inner world."[70] Hemingway's canon was filled with a profusion of corpses, suffering animals, and morally wounded people—all nightmares at noonday.

Cowley also noticed that sometimes Hemingway's stories "come close to being adaptations of ancient myths." *The Sun Also Rises,* noted Cowley, "deals in different terms with the same legend that T. S. Eliot was not so much presenting as concealing in *The Waste Land.*" That myth "is largely based on the legend of the Fisher King":

> The legend tells how the king was wounded in the loins and how he lay wasting in his bed while his whole kingdom became unfruitful; there was thunder but no rain; the rivers dried up, the flocks had no increase, and the woman bore no children. *The Sun Also Rises* presents the same situation in terms of Paris after the First World War. It is a less despairing book than critics like to think; sometimes it is gay, friendly, even exuberant; but the hero has been wounded like the Fisher King, and he lives in a world that is absolutely sterile . . . he dealt with the same legend that Eliot had discovered by scholarship, recovering it for himself, I think, by a sort of instinct for legendary situations.
>
> And it is this instinct for legends, for sacraments, for rituals, for symbols, appealing to the buried hopes and fears, that helps to explain the power of Hemingway's work and his vast superiority over his imitators.[71]

By the 1950s Hemingway had attracted his first anthology of criticism, *Ernest Hemingway: The Man and his Work* (1950), edited by John K. M. McCaffery, and important full-length studies that offered the accepted readings for the next twenty years. McCaffery's anthology brought into focus the principal themes that readers of the World War II era found in Hemingway and his work: studies of death; explorations of the composite hero; considerations of the antagonism between Hemingway and his critics; reflections on his intellectual development and his literary influences; and assessments of his influence on the "hard-boiled" novels of the previous two decades. The views of *The Sun Also Rises* propounded in this anthology were elaborations, not radical revisions, of the ideas that Wilson and Cowley had forged in the 1920s and 1930s.

Carlos Baker and Philip Young produced the first of what were to be many book-length studies on Hemingway. Baker believed that Hemingway's first novel derived its power from "its sturdy moral backbone," "memorably drawn" characters, and "still-fresh representation" of Paris and Spain in the mid 1920s. Baker praised "the subtle operative contrast between vanity and sanity, between paganism and orthodoxy, between the health and the humor of Burguete and the sick neuroses of the Montparnassian ne'er-do-wells." He also cited the "complicated interplay" between two common readings of the novel—one that sees it as "a romantic study in sexual and ultimately in spiritual frustration," and another that perceives the book as a "qualitative study of varying degrees of physical and spiritual manhood, projected against a background of ennui and emotional exhaustion which is everywhere implicitly condemned."[72] Baker noted that, like Joyce in *Ulysses* and Eliot in *The Waste*

Land, Hemingway employed his own "mythological method"; but rather than employing a "literary kind of myth-adaptation," he engaged in "psychological symbol-building." This becomes apparent when one considers Hemingway's use of counterpoint, his technique of emphasizing or clarifying something by contrasting it with something else, as in his depiction of France and Spain.[73]

Young's *Ernest Hemingway* offers his influential reading of the Hemingway "hero," his wound, and the "code." The "hero," Jake, should be read as an aging version of Nick Adams, a character who appears in many of Hemingway's short stories (like George Willard in Anderson's *Winesburg, Ohio* stories and Stephen Dedalus in Joyce's *Dubliners* stories). The notion of a composite "hero" is drawn from perceived similarities among the male protagonist in stories and novels. More specifically, Hemingway's adult protagonists are sometimes read as aged versions of Nick Adams, whose experiences Hemingway traces from the Michigan woods to European battlefields, from adolescent trysts in the woods to poignant conversations between father and son, when Nick has grown to become a father himself. As a soldier, Nick is gravely wounded, and this "wounding" recurs in Jake Barnes's emasculation. All of Hemingway's heroes, argues Young, "have had Nick's childhood, Nick's adolescence, and Nick's young manhood."[74] What is more, "Nick Adams has much in common with Ernest Hemingway. This is not to say that he 'is' Hemingway. He is, rather, a projection of certain kinds of problems Hemingway was deeply concerned to write out. Nick is a special kind of mask." This composite hero, often mistaken for a thinly disguised author, adopted a "code" to help him cope. Young labels this code "grace under pressure":

> It is made of the controls of honor and courage which in a life of tension and pain make a man a man and distinguish him from the people who follow random impulses, let down their hair, and are generally messy, perhaps cowardly, and without inviolable rules for how to live holding tight.[75]

While Young focuses on the code, the wound, and the hero, he also agrees with Baker regarding the use of myth in the novel, calling *The Sun Also Rises* Hemingway's *Waste Land* and Jake his Fisher King. In the wasteland of *The Sun Also Rises* there is fun "but no hope," and in the end, when Jake returns to Brett, "we discover that we have come full circle, like all the rivers, the winds, and the sun, to the place where we began."[76]

Neither is there much love, argues Mark Spilka in "The Death of Love in *The Sun Also Rises*." Spilka cites the death of love as one of the most persistent themes following World War I, and he reads the novel as an extensive parable whose characters are allegorical figures: Jake and

Brett, lovers desexed by war; Cohn, the romantic false knight; Romero, the code hero and personification of the good life which will survive.[77] The climax of the parable occurs when the code hero, Romero, outlasts the romantic false knight, Cohn; but Jake, too, experiences a "total disillusionment" when he realizes that even "without his wound, he would still be unmanly, and Brett unable to let her hair grow long." The war and the society that made it "robs them of their normal sexual roles. As Barnes now sees, love itself is dead for their generation." Pedro is "the real hero of the parable, the final moral touchstone, the man whose code gives meaning to a world where love and religion are defunct, where the proofs of manhood are difficult and scarce, and where every man must learn to define his own moral conditions and then live up to them."[78]

The decade of the 1960s opened with news of Hemingway's suicide and closed following the publication of the first full-length study of Hemingway's life, Baker's *Ernest Hemingway: A Life Story* (1969). Wedged between these biographical bookends were studies of the narrator of the novel, its symbolism, its sources, and its hero. Earl Rovit included a cogent chapter on the novel in his *Ernest Hemingway* (1963), a general introduction to the life and works. In it, Rovit observes the "surprising lack of unanimity among critics on what would seem to be basic non-controversial issues." For example, critics "have divided handsomely on determining where the moral center of the book rests." Is it with Romero? Jake? Or could it be Cohn? The novel resists quick closure to this and other questions because it rests "on a special base of ambiguity." That ambiguity results from "the use of a particularly opaque first person narrator," which generates questions about his reliability, as well as from Jake's wound, which "forces him to be a spectator rather than a participator in the events of the novel." Rovit's analysis focuses on Jake, who "must be *mostly* reliable and *mostly* sympathetic," as the one who must "accept the absurd meaninglessness of his fate and somehow wrest meaning from it."[79] His challenge is to recover from his wound and learn how to live with it.

The novel, according to Rovit, "will be a recording of Jake's painful lessons in learning how to live in the world while getting his money's worth of enjoyment for the price that it has extracted from him." Jake learns the value of becoming an "unillusioned connoisseur" from Count Mippipopolous, whose experience has taught him to distinguish between life and its varied imitations. The count is willing to exchange money for the very-much-alive Brett, whereas others are willing to settle for imitations—Bill for his stuffed animals, Woolsey and Krum for lifestyles that deny them the ephemeral pleasures of tennis on Sunday or conversation at the cafés.[80] Jake learns the importance of shedding his illusions when he is confronted with a "double" in Robert Cohn. Both men are tennis players and writers, both love Brett and are superior to the hedonists who surround them. But Robert holds tight to his illusions and is accorded the unenviable fate of alienation. Jake, conversely, gives up his illusion of living with Brett, admits his failures, and secures his own forgiveness. His story, while also being a polemic against the war, which fostered the hedonistic environment of Paris, asserts that "individual man is the puny maker of his meanings in life."[81] He learns and grows.

While Baker's criticism encouraged investigations of Hemingway's mythical method, his biography seemed to rekindle interest in the sources for Hemingway's characters and story. In the 1920s, many readers of *The Sun Also Rises* delighted in guessing at the identity of the characters. Now, in the long-awaited biography, they had a scholarly source by which to gauge their accuracy. Bertram D. Sarason's *Hemingway and the Sun Set* (1972) pursues this vein of inquiry in seventeen studies that address the background of individual characters and provide commentary from friends and experts. The prototypes for Robert Cohn, Frances Clyne, and Bill Gorton provide their recollections; other memoirists recount tales about Duff Twysden and others. Harold Loeb (Cohn), and Kitty Cannell (Clyne) record their recollections, and Sarason's sorting out of the "real" versus the fictional events occupies a third of the text. The book, largely a collection of backgrounds and sources, is a fascinating biographical resource, but it also highlights one of the difficulties that Hemingway criticism has encountered over the decades: the line between criticism and biography often blurs.

Critical interest kept pace with biographical inquiry, and in 1969 William White edited a small collection of reviews and reprinted essays, *The Merrill Studies in The Sun Also Rises*. Perhaps the best original essay of the year was Donald T. Torchiana's "*The Sun Also Rises:* A Reconsideration." Torchiana quarrels with Young and Baker's assessment of the novel, identifying them as "equally explicit in deeming the drift of the book a journey to nowhere, a study in futility, and a picture of the Lost Generation."[82] The proper analogy for the book is not Eliot's *The Waste Land* but the bullfight, which provides an analogy for the structure of the novel. The novel, writes Torchiana, is an unrelieved attack on America, its recent war, its racial injustice, its critical establishment, and its mores. But its central thrust is affirmative because its protagonist strives to learn how to live in a world that is alive and vibrant—not sterile and dead like that of *The Waste Land*. This thrust can been seen once we recognize that "the tripartite structure of the bullfight match[es] up imaginatively with the three sections of the novel[.]" In the first book, "animalism seems to triumph on all sides": Cohn wins card games and a titled lady; Brett "stands Jake up . . . runs off with Cohn, and returns with Mike in tow"; and even minor characters such as the concierge and Harvey Stone cause the "matador," Jake, discomfort. In the second book he tries to "bring out the best in his friends" and subtly dominates them. In the final book he returns to Spain to gather Brett, having quelled "the beast in himself."[83] While Torchiana's attempt to equate the three books of the novel with the three stages of the bullfight is not entirely convincing, his overriding contention that the novel should not be read merely as Hemingway's rendition of Eliot's wasteland theme is provocative.

The 1970s brought a new intensity to Hemingway studies: both the *Fitzgerald/Hemingway Annual* and *Hemingway Notes* provided ample venues for scholarly articles. Dozens of important articles appeared, and an excellent volume of criticism, Arthur Waldhorn's *A Reader's Guide to Ernest Hemingway* (1972), advanced some compelling new arguments about the novel.

Jake's values are the subject of Scott Donaldson's inquiry into "Hemingway's Morality of Compensation." Observing the more than thirty instances in the novel where the cost of things is mentioned, Donaldson surmises that Hemingway's rationale for including the price of everything was not only to enhance the verisimilitude of the novel but also to illustrate the "moral conviction that you must pay for what you get." Money, in fact, is the "metaphor by which the moral responsibility of Jake, Bill, and Pedro is measured against the carelessness of Brett, Mike, and Robert."[84] Robert, who has inherited money rather than earned it and who is apparently quite tightfisted, uses it to pay off women with whom he is finished. Mike and Brett are completely irresponsible with funds: Mike cannot even write checks, and Brett is likely to register at a hotel without enough money to pay for her stay. Jake's financial responsibility, argues Donaldson, is a measure of his morality. He earns his money and pays his way in all things—hotels, tips, prostitutes, cabs, and bars. In fact, Jake measures the cultures that he encounters by the way that they handle financial matters. The French, epitomized by Jake's landlady, are easily "bought" with tips or bribes. Conversely, the Spanish, particularly the Basques, are financially disinterested and share their wine without thought of recompense. In Pamplona, Jake is able to purchase a wine bag at the lowest price because he intends it for personal use and not for commercial profit. Earlier in the novel Count Mippipopolous has modeled the morality of compensation for Jake, for he too is willing and in fact gratified to pay for the things he desires.

Jake's ability to act on the models that he sees, to observe and grow, is the focus of Carole Gottlieb Vopat's "The End of *The Sun Also Rises:* A New Beginning." The most influential prior criticism of the novel had focused on what was perceived to be its circular structure that leaves the characters where they began—in a sterile wasteland. Vopat objects to such readings and insists that Jake undergoes a profound change that culminates in Book III. He realizes, after witnessing Romero, that "he is in his romantic dreaming little different, although quieter, than Robert Cohn." He has learned to control his actions, to live with his wound. He is no longer compelled by Brett and learns to take care of his own appetites.[85] Donald A. Daiker, in "The Affirmative Conclusion of *The Sun Also Rises,*" argues that the events Jake describes teach him how to live—despite his wound and his inability to marry Brett.[86] These two readings signal an important shift in critical thinking about the conclusion of the novel.

Further exploring Jake's growth is Arthur Waldhorn's outstanding book-length study. While he still appreciates the novel as commentary on the times, agreeing with Baker and Young that it "echoes the hollow ache of Ecclesiastes" and that "Jake is Hemingway's Fisher King without T. S. Eliot's hint of rejuvenation," he also believes that *The Sun Also Rises* is a novel of character and that Jake is "an apprentice slowly and painfully absorbing the lessons he must master to achieve rank as an exemplary hero."[87] Jake's self-proclaimed objective is to learn "how to live," and he does so by observing the principle exemplary hero, Romero, as well as lesser lights, including Montoya and Count Mippipopolous. His apprenticeship ends, writes Waldhorn, when Brett leaves the fiesta with Romero, and in the final book of the novel Jake gains his maturity. This maturity manifests itself in his final encounter with Brett, where Jake, for the first time, controls an encounter with her: "He has traded off false hope and empty illusion and salvaged integrity, discipline, and control. Scarcely a 'simple exchange of values,' it might, in a marketplace where moral bankruptcy destroys most traders, be accounted a margin of profit."[88]

The original opening of the typescript of *The Sun Also Rises* was published in the spring 1979 issue of *Antaeus*. It commences with the sentence "This is a novel about a lady," provides background information on Brett, Jake, and Mike, ruminates aloud about how the novel should be narrated and read, and characterizes the tale as a "romantic but highly moral story."[89] The role that this "primary" material should play in the criticism of the novel sparked the usual discussions: should excised portions of the text be considered as the novel is assessed? In the 1980s this question was answered during a renaissance in Hemingway studies, prompted by three key events: the founding of the Hemingway Society, opening of the Hemingway collection at the John F. Kennedy Library in Boston, and the commencement of *The Hemingway Review.* Delving into the recently opened archive, several scholars documented the evolution of *The Sun Also Rises*. The most thorough manuscript study is Frederic Svoboda's *Hemingway & The Sun Also Rises: The Crafting of a Style* (1983). Other examinations of compositional history include William Balassi's "The Writing of the Manuscript of *The Sun Also Rises,* with a Chart of Its Session-by-Session Development" (1986) and his "The Trail to *The Sun Also Rises:* The First Week of Writing" (1991), which describes the original opening and the effect of its excision. Michael Reynolds assessed the deleted material as well, in "False Dawn: *The Sun Also Rises* Manuscript" (1980). Two volumes of Reynolds's five-volume biography, *Hemingway: The Paris Years* (1989) and *Hemingway: The American Homecoming* (1992), provide the most detailed re-creation of creative process.

Archival research not only precipitated a surge in textual scholarship, it also set the wheels of the biographical industry churning; in the 1980s alone, more than a dozen biographies appeared. The best of the multivolume works is certainly Reynolds's, whose attention to detail, stamina for painstaking research, and inviting prose style have given readers their most circumspect view of a very complex artist. While Baker's *Ernest Hemingway: A Life Story* remains the best single-volume compendium, James R. Mellow provided an excellent alternative, *Hemingway: A Life Without Consequences* (1992). Many other biographical works appeared, some by admirers and some by detractors, most of them adding something of value to the record, all of them attesting to Hemingway's status as both a literary and popular icon.

The industry of Hemingway criticism in the 1980s produced a great number of articles and books.[90] Reynolds's *The Sun Also Rises, a Novel of the Twenties* (1988) is an excellent student's companion to the novel, stressing the historical context and providing readings of the narrator, themes, and techniques. Edward F. Stanton's *Hemingway and Spain: A Pursuit* (1989) revisits the terrain of the novel, explaining how the author discovered Spain and wrote about it for forty years. Linda Wagner-Martin edited *New Essays on The Sun Also Rises* (1987). Her introduction explores the backgrounds and compositional history of the novel and helps readers to appreciate the elements of *The Sun Also Rises* that make it a modern American novel: its "open, suggestive structure, built upon clusters of images and shaded descriptions as much as from plot, characters, and a linear progression of events."[91] Other essayists in Wagner-Martin's collection addressed new concerns or reassessed old ones: Donaldson examines humor; Reynolds recovers the historical context of the novel, concluding that the novel is a "moral indictment" of expatriates' self-indulgence; and Wendy Martin focuses on Brett Ashley as the New Woman. Taking up this same theme is Delbert E. Wylder's "The Two Faces of Brett: The Role of the New Woman in *The Sun Also Rises*," which puts Brett forward as the new woman, free of Victorian strictures.[92] Harold Bloom edited a pair of anthologies, *Modern Critical Views: Ernest Hemingway* (1985) and *Ernest Hemingway's The Sun Also Rises: Modern Critical Interpretations* (1987).

Harbor of San Sebastián, Spain

Critics also examined Hollywood's treatment of *The Sun Also Rises*. Gene D. Phillips's *Hemingway and Film* (1980) and Frank M. Laurence's *Hemingway and the Movies* (1981) provide comprehensive studies on adaptations of Hemingway's work for film and television. Charles M. Oliver edited an anthology, *A Moving Picture Feast: The Filmgoer's Hemingway* (1989), that includes an article on the 1984 television miniseries. Hemingway's own celebrity status is the subject of John Raeburn's *Fame Became of Him: Hemingway as Public Writer* (1984) and Leonard J. Leff's *Hemingway and His Conspirators: Hollywood, Scribners, and the Making of American Celebrity Culture* (1997), each of which includes substantial reference to *The Sun Also Rises*.[93]

A pair of articles expands upon the notions of Vopat and Daiker regarding the affirmative conclusion of *The Sun Also Rises* and Jake's character development: These new readings go beyond asserting that Jake learns to accept his plight and insist that not only does he accept his limitations, but he also learns that he can love Brett and have her for his friend without the prospect of romance. Jim Steinke's "Brett and Jake in Spain: Hemingway's Ending for *The Sun Also Rises*" argues that the novel leaves Jake and Brett as friends and not frustrated lovers.[94] Sibbie O'Sullivan's "Love Friendship/Man and Woman in *The Sun Also*

Rises" takes aim at Spilka's "Death of Love," identifying patterns of love and friendship in the novel that allow it to conclude on a note of affirmation. O'Sullivan's article is particularly helpful in tracing the rise of the modern or "new" woman, reaching back to 1860 to document the gradual enfranchisement of women. The novel was Hemingway's "goodbye kiss to the Victorian ethos under which he was raised" and his welcome to the new woman who was "a positive force, a determined yet vulnerable woman who makes an attempt to live honestly." In creating her, he "dismantled nineteenth century gender lines by uniting love with friendship" and lent credence to Jake's notion that "in the first place, you had to be in love with a woman to have the basis for a friendship."[95] Roger Whitlow's *Cassandra's Daughters: The Women in Hemingway's Fiction* forcefully attacks the notion first put forth by Wilson that Brett is "an exclusively destructive force" and suggests that Brett is self-destructive and that her nymphomania is a product of her self-doubt (successive sexual encounters convince her of her attractiveness).[96]

In honor of the sixtieth anniversary of *The Sun Also Rises, The Hemingway Review* produced a special issue. In it, H. R. Stoneback explored Jake's Catholic sensibility; William Balassi charted the session-by-session development of the manuscript; James Hinkle followed the changes in the work as it progressed from typescript through publication; Allen Josephs explained the significance of the bullfight and the matador to the novel; Frank Scafella examined Hemingway's correspondence with Owen Wister, particularly the older writer's admonitions about questionable language; and Robert A. Martin explicated the metaphor of the sun in the novel.[97]

Scholars in the 1990s contributed essential primary and critical texts, beginning with *Ernest Hemingway, The Sun Also Rises: A Facsimile Edition* (1990), edited by Matthew J. Bruccoli, which includes the manuscript first draft and related early material. Bruccoli, with Robert Trogdon, also edited *The Only Thing That Counts: The Ernest Hemingway/Maxwell Perkins Correspondence 1925–1947* (1996), which, coupled with Bruccoli's *Fitzgerald and Hemingway: A Dangerous Friendship* (1994), provides a wealth of primary material regarding Hemingway's composition and revision process and explains Fitzgerald's role as friend and mentor. Miriam B. Mandel's *Reading Hemingway: The Facts in the Fictions* (1995) annotates the people, characters, and cultural constructs in Hemingway novels and is an indispensable reference tool. Charles M. Oliver's *Ernest Hemingway A to Z* (1999) is a comprehensive reference to the life and work, with plot summaries to the novels and stories and descriptions of characters. Joining these reference works are critical studies that address gender and sexuality: Spilka examines androgyny in *Hemingway's Quarrel with Androgyny* (1990); Carl P. Eby explores Hemingway's fetishism in *Hemingway's Fetishism: Psychoanalysis and the Mirror of Manhood* (1999); and Nancy R. Comley and Robert Scholes in *Hemingway's Genders: Rereading the Hemingway Text* (1994) reread the Hemingway canon with an eye toward how characters are constructed along lines of gender and sexual behavior.

A pair of anthologies warrants special distinction. James Nagel's excellent *Critical Essays on Ernest Hemingway's The Sun Also Rises* (1995) offers a comprehensive overview of the initial reception and subsequent criticism. It includes eight contemporary reviews, nine reprinted essays, and three commissioned essays: Linda Patterson Miller's analysis of Brett, which places her in the center of the novel; Jane E. Wilson's assessment of Wilson-Harris as an affirmation of humane values in contrast to those on display in Pamplona; and Robert E. Fleming's consideration of an unpublished coda to the novel. Fleming's own book, *The Face in the Mirror: Hemingway's Writers* (1994), takes up the several writers who appear in *The Sun Also Rises* and examines Hemingway's attitude toward them. The second excellent anthology is Donaldson's *The Cambridge Companion to Hemingway* (1996). Only one essay, Nagel's "Brett and the Other Women in *The Sun Also Rises*," is devoted exclusively to the novel, but the collection includes substantial references to articles on Hemingway's treatment of gender, politics, and his Spanish sensibility.[98]

Bloom's *Major Literary Characters: Brett Ashley* (1991) is an anthology of articles and critical excerpts devoted entirely to Brett Ashley. J. Gerald Kennedy and Jackson R. Bryer's *French Connections: Hemingway and Fitzgerald Abroad* (1998) considers Hemingway and France, including the expatriates, prostitution, and the relationships that flourished between Hemingway and other writers. Kennedy makes the fullest examination of France as a place in Hemingway's life in *Imagining Paris: Exile, Writing, and American Identity* (1993). Monographs by Peter Hays (1990) and Peter Messent (1992), both titled *Ernest Hemingway,* include significant discussion of *The Sun Also Rises*. Hays provides a reading of the novel and a lucid discussion of the author's style; Messent focuses on the work as a response to modernity and its conditions. Marc D. Baldwin in *Reading The Sun Also Rises: Hemingway's Political Unconscious* (1997) assesses the "social totality" of the novel that "illuminates the economic, political, and cultural sectors that compose civilized society." At the close of the 1990s, Hemingway continued to make himself relevant to cultural and critical conversation, and his reputation continued to grow.[99]

CRITICAL EXCERPTS

PRE-PUBLICATION EDITORIAL ADVICE: F. Scott Fitzgerald to Ernest Hemingway, autograph letter, June 1926, critiquing *The Sun Also Rises.* From *F. Scott Fitzgerald: A Life in Letters,* edited by Matthew J. Bruccoli (New York: Simon & Schuster, 1995), pp. 142–145; idiosyncrasies in spelling and punctuation have been retained.

Drawing on the advice that Fitzgerald presented in this letter to his younger and less-established friend, Hemingway deleted the first two chapters from the typescript of *The Sun Also Rises,* which contained background information about Brett Ashley and Mike Campbell, as well as explanations about how the book came to be written in first person. Fitzgerald's advice is widely recognized as having been very good.

> Dear Ernest: Nowdays when almost everyone is a genius, at least for awhile, the temptation for the bogus to profit is no greater than the temptation for the good man to relax (in one mysterious way or another)—not realizing the transitory quality of his glory because he forgets that it rests on the frail shoulders of professional entheusiasts. This should frighten all of us into a lust for anything honest that people have to say about our work. I've taken what proved to be excellent advice (On the B. + Damned) from Bunny Wilson who never wrote a novel, (on Gatsby—change of many thousand wds) from Max Perkins who never considered writing one, and on T. S. of Paradise from Katherine Tighe (you don't know her) who had probably never read a novel before.
>
> [This is beginning to sound like my own current work which resolves itself into laborious + sententious preliminaries].
>
> Anyhow I think parts of <u>Sun Also</u> are careless + ineffectual. As I said yestiday (and, as I recollect, in trying to get you to cut the lst part of 50 Grand) I find in you the same tendency to envelope or (and as it usually turns out) to <u>embalm</u> in mere wordiness an anecdote or joke thats casually appealed to you, that I find in myself in trying to preserve a piece of Afine writing." Your first chapter contains about 10 such things and it gives a feeling of condescending <u>casuallness</u>
>
> P. 1. "highly moral story"

"Brett said" (O. Henry stuff)

"much too expensive

"something or other" (if you don't want to tell, why waste 3 wds. saying it. See P.23—"9 or 14" and "or how many years it was since 19XX" when it would take two words to say That's what youd kid in anyone else as mere "style"—mere horse-shit I can't find this latter but anyhow you've not only got to write well yourself but you've also got to scorn not-do what anyone can do and I think that there are about 24 sneers, superiorities, and nose-thumbings-at-nothing that mar the whole narrative up to p. 29 where (after a false start on the introduction of Cohn) it really gets going. And to preserve these perverse and willfull non-essentials you've done a lot of writing that honestly reminded me of Michael Arlen.

[You know the very fact that people have committed themselves to you will make them watch you like a cat. + if they don't like it creap away like one]

For example.

Pps. 1 + 2. Snobbish (not in itself but because the history of English Aristocrats in the war, set down so verbosely so uncritically, so exteriorly and yet so obviously inspired from within, is shopworn.) You had the same problem that I had with my Rich Boy, previously debauched by Chambers ect. Either bring more thot to it with the realization that that ground has already raised its wheat + weeds or cut it down to seven sentences. It hasn't even your rythym and the fact that may be "true" is utterly immaterial.

That biography from you, who allways believed in the superiority (the preferability) of the imagined to the seen not to say to the merely recounted.

P. 3. "Beautifully engraved shares" (Beautifully engraved 1886 irony) All this is O.K. but so glib when its glib + so profuse.

P. 5. Painters are no longer real in prose. They must be minimized. [This is not done by making them schlptors, backhouse wall-experts or miniature painters]

P. 8. "highly moral urges" "because I believe its a good story" If this paragraph isn't maladroit then I'm a rewrite man for Dr. Cadman.

P. 9. Somehow its not good. I can't quite put my hand on it—it has a ring of "This is a true story ect."

P. 10. "Quarter being a state of mind ect." This is in all guide books. I havn't read Basil Swoon's but I have fifty francs to lose.

[About this time I can hear you say "Jesus this guy thinks I'm lousy, + he can stick it up his ass for all I give a Gd Dm for his 'critisism.'" But remember this is a new departure for you, and that I think your stuff is great. You were the first American I wanted to meet in Europe—and the last. (This latter clause is simply to balance the sentence. It doesn't seem to make sense tho I have pawed at it for several minutes. Its like the age of the French women.

P. 14. (+ therabout) as I said yesterday I think this anecdote is flat as hell without naming Ford which would be cheap.

It's flat because you end with mention of Allister Crowly. If he's nobody its nothing. If he's somebody its cheap. This is a novel. Also I'd cut out actual mention of H. Stearns earlier.

Why not cut the inessentials in Cohens biography? His first marriage is of no importance. When so many people can write well + the competition is so heavy I can't imagine how you could have done these first 20 pps. so casually. You can't play with peoples attention—a good man who has the power of arresting attention at will must be especially careful.

From here Or rather from p. 30 I began to like the novel but Ernest I can't tell you the sense of disappointment that beginning with its elephantine facetiousness gave me. Please do what you can about it in proof. Its 7500 words—you could reduce it to 5000. And my advice is not to do it by mere pareing but to take out the worst of the scenes.

I've decided not to pick at anything else, because I wasn't at all inspired to pick when reading it. I was much too excited. Besides this is probably a heavy dose. The novel's damn good. The central theme is marred somewhere but hell! unless you're writing your life history where you have an inevitable pendulum to swing you true (Harding metaphor), who can bring it entirely off? And what critic can trace whether the fault lies in a possible insufficient thinking out, in the biteing off of more than you eventually cared to chew in the impotent theme or in the elusiveness of the lady character herself. My theory always was that she dramatized herself in terms of Arlens dramatatization of somebody's dramatizatatg of Stephen McKenna's dramatization of Diana Manner's dramatization of the last girl in Well's Tono Bungay—who's original probably liked more things about Beatrix Esmond than about Jane Austin's Elizibeth (to whom we owe the manners of so many of our wives.)

Appropos of your foreward about the Latin quarter—suppose you had begun your stories with phrases like: "Spain is a peculiar place—ect" or "Michigan is interesting to two classes—the fisherman + the drummer."

Pps 64 + 65 with a bit of work should tell all that need be known about Brett's past.

(Small point) "Dysemtry" instead of "killed" is a clichês to avoid a clichê. It stands out. I suppose it can't be helped. I suppose all the 75,000000 Europeans who died between 1914–1918 will always be among the 10,000,000 who were killed in the war.

God! The bottom of p. 77 Jusque the top p. 78 are wonderful, I go crazy when people aren't always at their best. This isn't picked out—I just happened on it.

The heart of my critisim beats somewhere apon p. 87. I think you can't change it, though. I felt the lack of some crazy torturing tentativeness or insecurity—horror, all at once, that she'd feel—and he'd feel—maybe I'm crazy. He isn't like an impotent man. He's like a man in a sort of moral chastity belt.

Oh, well. It's fine, from Chap V on, anyhow, in spite of that—which fact is merely a proof of its brilliance.

Station Z.W.X. square says good night. Good night all.

CONTEMPORARY REVIEWS OF *THE SUN ALSO RISES*

From poet and novelist Conrad Aiken's review in *New York Herald Tribune Books,* 31 October 1926, p. 4; reprinted in *Hemingway: The Critical Heritage,* edited by Jeffrey Meyers (London & New York: Routledge & Kegan Paul, 1982), pp. 89–91.

It has been apparent for some time that Mr. Hemingway is a writer of very unusual gifts; it has been merely a question as to what direction he would take. In "The Sun Also Rises" he takes a decided step forward and makes it possible for me to say of him, with entire conviction, that he is in many respects the most exciting of contemporary American writers of fiction. To say that his literary debts are obvious is not to mitigate this assertion in the slightest. He has learned something from Mr. Anderson, and something, perhaps, from Mr. Fitzgerald's "Great Gatsby"; he may even have extracted a grain or two of ore from Miss Gertrude Stein—which is in itself no inconsiderable feat.

But in the accomplished fact his work is not in the least like the work of any of these writers. If one thing is striking about it, furthermore, it is its extraordinary individuality of style. His publishers say of him, with a discernment unusual in publishers, that he has contrived, in his novel, to present his people and his actions not as perceptible through a literary medium but as if immediate, and that is true. If once or twice in his story he slips into something of Mr. Anderson's cumbersome and roundabout explanatory method, with its "what I mean to say" and its "the thing is this," these echoes are few and unimportant. His own method lies at the other extreme. He simply states; he even, as a general rule, can be said to understate. It almost appears that he goes out of his way, now and then, to avoid the descriptive or expressive methods—one has the feeling that he is a little afraid of being caught with any sort of purple on his palette, whether it be of rhetoric or of poetry. The action, he seems to say, must speak wholly for itself.

This results, as might be expected, in a quite extraordinary effect of honesty and reality. The half dozen characters, all of whom belong to the curious and sad little world of disillusioned and aimless expatriates who make what home they can in the cafés of Paris, are seen perfectly and unsentimentally by Mr. Hemingway and are put before us with a maximum of economy. In the case of the hero, through whose mind we meet the event, and again in the cases of Brett, the heroine, and Robert Cohn, the sub-hero, Mr. Hemingway accomplishes more than this—he achieves an understanding and revelation of character, which approaches the profound. When one reflects on the unattractiveness, not to say the sordidness of the scene, and the (on the whole) gracelessness of the people, one is all the more astonished at the fact that Mr. Hemingway should have made them so moving. These folk exist, that is all; and if their story is sordid, it is also, by virtue of the author's dignity and detachment in the telling, intensely tragic.

If one feature of "The Sun Also Rises" demands separate discussion, it is Mr. Hemingway's use of dialogue. The dialogue is brilliant. If there is better dialogue being written today I do not know where to find it. More than any other talk I can call to mind, it is alive with the rhythms and idioms, the pauses and suspensions and innuendoes and shorthands, of living speech. It is in the dialogue, almost entirely, that Mr. Hemingway tells his story and makes the people live and act. This is the dramatist's gift, and it reminds one of those novels of Henry James which were first projected as plays and then written, with something like an excess of talk, as fiction. Will Mr. Hemingway try his hand at a play? He clearly has the ability to make his story move, and move with intensity, through this medium. It is possible that he overuses this ability. One occasionally longs for a slowing down and expansion of the medium, a pause for more leisurely luxuriation in the instant, such as Mr. Hemingway only vouchsafes us in the fishing episode and in the account of the fiesta and the bull-fight. James himself, despite his sins in this regard, somewhere remarked that dialogue, the most trenchant of the novelists' weapons, should be used as sparely as possible, to be kept in reserve, its force and edge unimpaired, for those scenes in which the action took a definite and decisive turn; it is above all in dialogue that climax should flower. In a sense, therefore, Mr. Hemingway gives us the feeling of finality and climax a little too often and thus deprives himself and his reader of that long curve of crescendo without which a novel lacks final perfection of form. His spareness and economy, his objective detachment, would be only the more effective for an occasional offset, and his canvas greatly richer.

From English poet, critic, and translator Edwin Muir's review of *Fiesta* (the title used for the first British edition of *The Sun Also Rises*) in the *Nation and Athenaeum*, 41 (2 July 1927): 450, 452; reprinted in *Hemingway, the Critical Heritage*, p. 96.

Mr. Hemingway is a writer of quite unusual talent. His observation is so exact that it has the effect of imagination; it evokes scenes, conversations, characters. His dialogue is by turns extraordinarily natural and brilliant, and impossibly melodramatic; when he has to describe anything he has a sureness and economy which recall Maupassant; he neither turns away from unpleasant details, nor does he stress them. There is, however, a curious inequality among his characters. Brett, the heroine, might have stepped out of "The Green Hat"; she is the sentimen-

Schruns, Austria, 1926: Ernest and Hadley Hemingway with their son, John, called Bumby

tally regarded dare-devil, and she never becomes real. But most of the other characters, the majority of them American Bohemians living in Paris, are graphically drawn. The original merits of the book are striking; its fault, equally apparent after one's first pleasure, is a lack of artistic significance. We see the lives of a group of people laid bare, and we feel that it does not matter to us. Mr. Hemingway tells us a great deal about those people, but he tells us nothing of importance about human life. He tells us nothing, indeed, which any of his characters might not tell us; he writes with honesty, but as a member of the group he describes; and, accordingly, his narrative lacks proportion, which is the same thing as significance. But he is still a young writer; his gifts are original; and this first novel raises hopes of remarkable achievement. The Spanish scenes, Cohn's fight with the matador, the dance in the streets, the bull fight—these bring us in contact with a strong and original visual world.

INTRODUCTIONS AND CRITICISM

Edmund Wilson, from the introduction to *In Our Time* (New York: Scribners, 1930), pp. ix–xv.

Wilson was a well-positioned New York critic who praised Hemingway's early works, particularly the short stories. His most influential insights addressed the "Hemingway hero" and the "Hemingway code." His observation that Hemingway's characters conducted themselves according to some "principle of sportsmanship" is the germ of the concept customarily called "the Hemingway code." His reading of Jake Barnes as an older version of Nick Adams is at the base of the concept of "the composite hero"—an amalgamation of several Hemingway protagonists.

> *The Sun Also Rises* . . . has a profound unity and a disquieting reality because there is an intimate relation established between the fiesta in the little Spanish town, with its processions, its bull-fighting and its hilarity, and the atrocious behavior of the group of Americans and English who have come down from Paris to enjoy it. In the heartlessness of these people toward each other we recognize the same principle at work as in the pagan orgy of the festival. The persecution of Cohn is as much a natural casualty of a barbarous world as the unexpected fate of the man who gets accidentally gored by the bull on the way to the bull-ring. Hemingway's most remarkable effects in this book are those, as in the fishing-trip, where we are made to feel behind the gusto of the appetite for the physical world the falsity or the tragedy of a moral situation. This undruggable consciousness of something wrong seems never to arouse Hemingway to passionate violence; but it poisons him and makes him sick, and this invests with a singular sinister quality—a quality I suppose new in fiction—the sunlight and the green summer landscapes of *The Sun Also Rises*.
>
> The interest of *The Sun Also Rises* arises from the attempts of the hero and heroine to disengage themselves form such a world, or rather to find some way of living in it honorably. Life, which we devour so voraciously for the very things about it which destroy us, is always in the long run a losing game; but it is a game and at least allows of the kind of virtues proper to a game. We must stick to the code of the sportsman and lose in a sportsman-like way. And so the bull-fight itself, with which Hemingway has always been so much preoccupied, becomes a symbol of life: you stab or you get gored—and in the meantime many unoffending horses are casually

> disemboweled; the highest aim is to kill the bull, or if the time has come to die, to die game-like the old bull-fighter in "The Undefeated." This conceiving of life as a game—even though Hemingway's favorite sport is bull-fighting—is peculiarly Anglo-Saxon.

Malcolm Cowley, from the introduction to *The Viking Portable Library: Hemingway* (New York: Viking, 1944), pp. xxi–xxii.

Along with Edmund Wilson, Malcolm Cowley was among the earliest and most influential critics of Hemingway. Cowley explores the notion that *The Sun Also Rises* is Hemingway's treatise upon the wasteland theme, popularized by T. S. Eliot's poem *The Waste Land* (1922).

> Sometimes his stories come close to being adaptations of ancient myths. His first novel, for example, deals in different terms with the same legend that T. S. Eliot was not so much presenting as concealing in *The Waste Land*. When we turn to Eliot's explanatory notes, then read the book to which they refer as a principal source—*From Ritual to Romance,* by Jessie L. Weston—we learn that his poem is largely based on the legend of the Fisher King. The legend tells how the king was wounded in the loins and how he lay wasting in his bed while his whole kingdom became unfruitful; there was thunder but no rain; the rivers dried up, the flocks had no increase, and the woman bore no children. *The Sun Also Rises* presents the same situation in terms of Paris after the First World War. It is a less despairing book than critics like to think; sometimes it is gay, friendly, even exuberant; but the hero has been wounded like the Fisher King, and he lives in a world that is absolutely sterile. I don't mean to imply that Hemingway owes a debt to *The Waste Land*. He had read the poem, which he liked at first, and the notes that followed it, which he didn't like at all; I doubt very much that he bothered to look at Jessie L. Weston's book. . . . And yet when he wrote his first novel, he dealt with the same legend that Eliot had discovered by scholarship, recovering it for himself, I think, by a sort of instinct for legendary situations.
>
> And it is this instinct for legends, for sacraments, for rituals, for symbols, appealing to the buried hopes and fears, that helps to explain the power of Hemingway's work and his vast superiority over his imitators.

Robert Penn Warren, from the introduction to *A Farewell to Arms* (New York: Scribners, 1949), pp. vii–xxxvii.

The influential poet, novelist, and proponent of New Criticism, Robert Penn Warren finds in Hemingway's work defeat and death, met on their own terms by characters who have developed "an ideal of themselves" comprised of principles that allow them to endure honorably, despite their impending defeat.

> We have said that the shadow of ruin is behind the typical Hemingway situation. The typical character faces defeat or death. But out of defeat or death the character usually manages to salvage something. And here we discover Hemingway's special interest in such situations and such characters. His heroes are not defeated except upon their own terms. They are not squealers, welchers, compromisers, or cowards, and when they confront defeat they realize that the stance they take, the stoic endurance, the stiff upper lip mean a kind of victory. If they are to be defeated they are defeated upon their own terms; some of them have even courted their defeat; and certainly they have maintained, even in the practical defeat, an ideal of themselves, some definition of how a man should behave, formulated or unformulated, by which they have lived. They represent some notion of honor, that makes a man a man, and that distinguishes him from people who merely follow their random impulses and who are, by consequence, "messy."
>
> In case after case, we can illustrate this "principle of sportsmanship," as one critic has called it [Edmund Wilson, in *The Wound and the Bow*], at the center of the story. . . . It is the discipline of the code which makes man human, a sense of style or good form. This applies not only in isolated, dramatic cases . . . but in a more pervasive way which can give meaning, partially at least, to the confusions of living. . . . But to return to the subject of Hemingway's world: the code and the discipline are important because they can give meaning to life which otherwise seems to have no meaning or justification. In other words, in a world without supernatural sanctions, in the God-abandoned world of modernity, man can realize an ideal meaning only in so far as he can define and maintain the code. The effort to define and maintain the code, however limited and imperfect it may be, is the characteristically human effort and provides the tragic or pitiful human story.

Carlos Baker, from *Hemingway: The Writer as Artist* (Princeton: Princeton University Press, 1952), pp. 87–88.

While Hemingway enjoyed the attention of literary critics and reviewers during the 1920s, 1930s, and 1940s, it was not until the 1950s that the first book-length studies of his works appeared. Baker, who later wrote the first authorized Hemingway biography, *Ernest Hemingway: A Life Story* (1969), and edited *Ernest Hemingway: Selected Letters, 1917–1961* (1981), reads *The Sun Also Rises* in terms of the wasteland myth, as did Cowley; but he identifies two techniques through which Hemingway accomplished his art. The first is a "contrapuntal method" that emphasizes the "operative contrast between . . . paganism and orthodoxy, between the health and humor of Burguete and the sick neuroses of the Montparnassian ne'er-do-wells."[100] The second, the "mythical method," is described below:

> Hemingway's first novel provides an important insight into the special "mythological" methods which he was to employ with increasing assurance and success in the rest of his major writing. It is necessary to distinguish Hemingway's method from such "mythologizing" as that of Joyce in *Ulysses,* or Eliot in *The Waste Land.* For Hemingway early devised and subsequently developed a mythologizing tendency of his own which does not depend on antecedent literatures, learned footnotes, or the recognition of spot passages. *The Sun Also Rises* is the first case in point. . . .
>
> Was not Brett Ashley, on her low-lying island in the Seine, just such a fascinating peril as Circe on Aeaea? . . . When they drank her special potion of French applejack or Spanish wine, did they not become as swine, or in the modern idiom, wolves? Did not Jake Barnes, that wily Odysseus, resist the shameful doom which befell certain of his less wary comrades who became snarling beasts?
>
> There are even parallel passages. Says Jake Barnes, thinking of Brett: "I lay awake thinking and my mind jumping around. . . . Then all of a sudden I started to cry. Then after a while it was better . . . and then I went to sleep." Says Ulysses on Aeaea: "My spirit was broken within me and I wept as I sat on the bed. . . . But when I had my fill of weeping and writhing, I made answer." Or what shall be made of Robert Cohn, quietly and classically asleep on the winecasks in the back of the room of a Pamplona tavern, wreathed with twisted garlics and dead to the world

while Brett and the others carouse in the room beyond? "There was one named Elpenor," says the *Odyssey*, "the youngest of all; not very valiant in war nor sound of understanding, who had laid him down apart from his comrades in the sacred house of Circe, seeking the cool air, for he was heavy with wine. He heard the noise and bustle of his comrades as they moved about."

If he had wished to follow the mythological method of Eliot's *Waste Land* or Joyce's *Ulysses*, Hemingway could obviously have done so. But his own esthetic opinions carried him away from the literary kind of myth-adaptation and over into that deeper area of psychological symbol-building which does not require special literary equipment to be interpreted. One needs only sympathy and a few degrees of heightened emotional awareness. The special virtue of this approach to the problem of literary communication is that it can be grasped by all men and women because they are human beings. None of the best writers are without it. It might even be described as the residuum of "natural knowledge" and belief, visible in every artist after the traditional elements have been siphoned off.

Philip Young, from *Ernest Hemingway: A Reconsideration* (University Park: Pennsylvania State University Press, 1966), pp. 53–54, 87–88; a revised and expanded edition of his *Ernest Hemingway* (New York: Rinehart, 1952).

The notion of a composite "hero" is drawn from perceived similarities among the male protagonists in stories and novels; more specifically, Hemingway's adult protagonists are sometimes read as older versions of Nick Adams. As a soldier, Nick is gravely wounded, and this "wounding," sometimes physical, as with Jake Barnes, and sometimes psychological, reappears, too, in the Hemingway canon.

[Nick] is a sensitive, humorless, honest, rather passive male. He is the outdoor man, who revels in the life of the senses, loves to hunt and fish and takes pride in his knowledge of how to do such things. He is virile even as an adolescent, and very conscious of his nerve; maturity has forced a reckoning with his nerves as well. Once grown he is a man who knows his way around but he is superstitious too, and is developing a complex ritual whereby thinking can be stopped, the evil spirits placated and warded off.

This pattern, this process and this figure, with whatever distortions seen, were going to be known half the world over, for the relationship of this Nick to what is called the "Hemingway hero" is intimate, to put it mildly: Nick is the Hemingway hero, the first one. The drawing of him is very sketchy as yet, but it is true and Hemingway never takes it back to cancel half a line: the experiences of childhood, adolescence and young manhood which shape Nick Adams shaped as well Lt. Henry, Jake Barnes, Col. Cantwell, and several other heroes. They all have had Nick's childhood, Nick's adolescence, and Nick's young manhood. It is obvious that this man is not the simple primitive he was mistaken for, and it is equally clear that a good deal of what there is of the primitive in him is a defense, which trembles and cracks, against a terror which he cannot face head on. The "escapes" are escapes from horror; the Hemingway hero, the big, tough, outdoor man, is also the wounded man, and descriptions of certain scenes in the life of Nick Adams have explained how he got that way. The man will die a thousand times before his death, but from his wounds he would never recover so long as Hemingway lived and recorded his adventures. . . .

Despite quite a lot of fun *The Sun Also Rises* is still Hemingway's *Waste Land,* and Jake is Hemingway's Fisher King. This may be just coincidence, though the novelist had read the poem, but once again here is the protagonist gone impotent, and his land gone sterile. Eliot's London is Hemingway's Paris, where spiritual life in general, and Jake's sexual life in particular, are alike impoverished. Prayer breaks down and fails, a knowledge of traditional distinctions between good and evil is largely lost, copulation is morally neutral and, cut off from the past chiefly by the spiritual disaster of the war, life has become mostly meaningless. "What shall we do?" is the same constant question, to which the answer must be again, "Nothing." To hide it, instead of playing chess one drinks, mechanically and always. Love is a possibility only for the two who cannot love; once again homosexuality intensifies this atmosphere of sterility; once more the Fisher King is also a man who fishes. And again the author plays with quotations from the great of the past, as when in reply to Jake's remark that his is a taxidermist Bill objects, "That was in another country. And besides all the animals were dead."

To be sure, the liquor is good, and so are the food and the conversation. But in one way Hemingway's book is even more desperate than Eliot's. The lesson of an "asceticism" to control the aimless expression of lust would be to Jake Barnes only one more bad joke, and the fragments he has shored against his ruins are few, and quite inadequate. In the poem a message of salvation comes out of the life-giving rain which falls on western civilization. In Hemingway's waste land there is fun, but then there is no hope.

Leslie Fiedler, from *Love and Death in the American Novel* (New York: Criterion, 1960), pp. 316–320.

Fiedler, taking his cue from earlier critics and embracing the notion of a single "Hemingway hero," argues that Hemingway's men are most at home among themselves, that his American women are "unmitigated bitches," and that his British woman, Brett Ashley, is a "terrible goddess."

> Hemingway is only really comfortable dealing with "men without women." The relations of father to son, of battle-companions, friends on a fishing trip, fellow inmates in a hospital, a couple of waiters preparing to close up shop, a bullfighter and his manager, a boy and a gangster: they move him to simplicity and truth. Perhaps he is best of all with men who stand alone—in night-time scenes when the solitary individual sweats in his bed on the verge of nightmare, or arises to confront himself in the glass; though he is at home, too, with the Rip Van Winkle archetype, with men in flight from women. Certainly he returns again and again to the fishing trip and the journey to the war—those two traditional evasions of domesticity and civil life. Yet he feels an obligation to introduce women into his more ambitious fictions, though he does not know what to do with them beyond taking them to bed. All his life, he has been haunted by a sense of how simple it all was once, when he could take his Indian girl into the clean-smelling woods, stretch out beside her on the pine-needles (her brother standing guard), and rise to no obligations at all. . . .
>
> When Hemingway's bitches are Americans, they are hopeless and unmitigated bitches. . . .
>
> The British bitch is for Hemingway only a demi-bitch, however, as the English are only, as it were, demi-Americans. Catherine is delivered from her doom by death, Brett Ashley in *The Sun*

Also Rises (1926) is permitted, once at least, the gesture of herself rejecting her mythical role. But it is quite a feat at that, and Brett cannot leave off congratulating herself: "You know it makes one feel rather good deciding not to be a bitch." Yet Brett never becomes a woman really; she is mythicized rather than redeemed. And if she is the most satisfactory female character in all of Hemingway, this is because for once she is presented not as an animal or as a nightmare but quite audaciously as a goddess, the bitch-goddess with a boyish bob (Hemingway is rather fond of women who seem as much a boy as a girl), the Lilith of the '20's. No man embraces her without being in some sense castrated, except for Jake Barnes who is unmanned to begin with; no man approaches her without wanting to be castrated, except for Romero, who think naively that she is—or can easily become—a woman. Indeed, when Brett leaves that nineteen-year-old bullfighter, one suspects that, though she avows it is because she will not be "one of those bitches who ruins children," she is really running away because she thinks he might make her a woman. Certainly, Romero's insistence that she let her hair grow out has something to do with it: "He wanted me to grow my hair out. Me, with long hair. I'd look so like hell. . . . He said it would make me more womanly. I'd look a fright."

To yield up her cropped head would be to yield up her emancipation from female servitude, to become feminine rather than phallic; and this Brett cannot do. She thinks of herself as a flapper, though the word perhaps would not have occurred to her as a member of the "Lost Generation"; but the Spaniards know her immediately as a terrible goddess, the avatar of ancient archetype. She tries in vain to enter into the circle of Christian communion, but is always turned aside at the door; she changes her mind, she has forgotten her hat—the apparent reason never matters; she belongs to a world alien and prior to that of the Christian churches in which Jake finds a kind of peace. In Pamplona, Brett is surrounded by a group of riau-riau dancers, who desert a religious procession to follow her, set her up as a rival to Saint Fermín: "Some dancers formed a circle around Brett and started to dance. They were all chanting. Brett wanted to dance but they did not want her to. They wanted her as an image to dance around." Incapable of love except as a moment in bed, Brett can bestow on her worshipers nothing more than the brief joy of a drunken ecstasy—followed by suffering and deprivation and regret. In the end, not only are her physical lovers unmanned and degraded, but even Jake, who is her priest and is protected by his terrible wound, is humiliated. For her service is a betrayal not only of his Catholic faith but of his pure passion for bullfighting and trout-fishing; and the priest of the bitch-goddess is, on the purely human level, a pimp.

Mark Spilka, from "The Death of Love in *The Sun Also Rises*," in *Ernest Hemingway's The Sun Also Rises*, edited by Harold Bloom (New York: Chelsea House, 1987), pp. 25–26.

Spilka reads the novel as an allegory about the death of love.

One of the most persistent themes of the twenties was the death of love in World War I. All the major writers recorded it, often in piecemeal fashion, as part of the larger postwar scene; but only Hemingway seems to have caught it whole and delivered it in lasting fictional form. His intellectual grasp of the theme might account for this. Where D. H. Lawrence settles for the shock of war on the Phallic consciousness, or where Eliot presents assorted glimpses of sterility, Hemingway seems to design an extensive parable. Thus, in *The Sun Also Rises*, his protagonists are deliberately shaped as allegorical figures: Jake Barnes and Brett Ashley are two lovers desexed by the war; Robert Cohn is the false knight who challenges their despair; while Romero, the stalwart bullfighter, personifies the good life which will survive their failure. Of course, these characters are not abstractions in the text; they are realized through the most concrete style in American fiction, and their larger meaning is implied only by their response to immediate situations. But the implications are there, the parable is at work in every scene, and its presence lends unity and depth to the whole novel.

George Plimpton, from *Writers at Work: The Paris Review Interviews, Second Series*, edited by Plimpton (New York: Viking, 1963), pp. 235–236.

Plimpton conducted this "interview" of Hemingway by mail. In it, the aging author explained his theory of writing on "the principle of the iceberg," whereby much of the depth and power of a scene or a statement are felt by the reader but remain unseen.

The Hotel Taube in Schruns, Austria, where the Hemingways skied in the mid 1920s

INTERVIEWER: So when you're not writing, you remain constantly the observer, looking for something which can be of use.

HEMINGWAY: Surely. If a writer stops observing he is finished. But he does not have to observe consciously nor think how it will be useful. Perhaps that would be true at the beginning. But later everything he sees goes into the great reserve of things he knows or has seen. If it is any use to know it, I always try to write on the principle of the iceberg. There is seven-eighths of it under water for every part that shows. Anything you know you can eliminate and it only strengthens your iceberg. It is the part that doesn't show. If a writer omits something because he does not know it then there is a hole in the story.

The Old Man and the Sea could have been over a thousand pages long and had every character in the village in it and all the processes of how they made their living, were born, educated, bore children, etc. That is done excellently and well by other writers. In writing you are limited by what has already been done satisfactorily. So I have tried to learn to do something else. First I have tried to eliminate everything unnecessary to conveying experience to the reader so that after he or she has read something it will become a part of his or her experience and seem actually to have happened. This is very hard to do and I've worked at it very hard.

Anyway, to skip how it is done, I had unbelievable luck this time and could convey the experience completely and have it be one that no one had ever conveyed. The luck was that I had a good man and a good boy and lately writers have forgotten there still are such things. Then the ocean is worth writing about just as man is. So I was lucky there. I've seen the marlin mate and know about that. So I leave that out. I've seen a school (or pod) of more than fifty sperm whales in that same stretch of water and once harpooned one nearly sixty feet in length and lost him. So I left that out. All the stories I know from the fishing village I leave out. But the knowledge is what makes the underwater part of the iceberg.

Delbert E. Wylder, from *Hemingway's Heroes* (Albuquerque: University of New Mexico Press, 1969), pp. 64–65.

Wylder exposes the limitations of the concept of the "composite hero," the amalgamation of Nick Adams, the protagonists of the novels, and Hemingway himself. In focusing on a composite hero, critics have "frequently forced a preconceived and rigid pattern" upon the readings that denies Hemingway's "artistic versatility, his experimentation, and his increasing skill as a writer."[101]

The Sun also Rises, then, is essentially a satire on mankind, much as Ecclesiastes can be looked at as a satire on the vanity of human attempts to find the meaning of life. The novel falls into the category of those works on the "Vanity of Human Wishes" theme. Jake looks at all experience and finds it lacking. There are no simple answers for the individual—especially the wounded man—and no code is going to eliminate the problems and perplexities of human relationships . . . although it would be pretty to think so. The materialistic world of France is bereft of meaning, and the world of Spain, with its obscure value system and its rigid traditional code is too demanding for the wounded man. Jake finds some solace in nature, however, and he has learned something about integrity from the heroic Romero-Belmonte figure in the contrast to the "lost" expatriates. Jake is no hero, but he has learned something from the hero figure—a contempt for the crowd and a certain indifference to his own fate. There are to be no more illusions. And with this knowledge comes a certain compassion for Lady Brett and a recognition of the need for restraint in his association with her. Thoreau had said that he did not want to practice resignation "unless it was quite necessary." Jake Barnes the wounded man in the rapidly changing traditionless and heroless twentieth century seems to find it necessary.

Carole Gottlieb Vopat, from "The End of *The Sun Also Rises:* A New Beginning," in *Fitzgerald/Hemingway Annual 1972,* edited by Matthew J. Bruccoli and C. E. Frazer Clark Jr. (Washington, D.C: NCR Microcard Editions, 1973), pp. 245–255; reprinted in *Ernest Hemingway's The Sun Also Rises,* edited by Harold Bloom (New York: Chelsea House, 1987), pp. 91–101.

Vopat's revisionist reading of the novel challenges the prevailing view that it is essentially a study in despair that leaves the readers not better off than it found them. She argues that Jake learns from his experiences and grows to accept Brett as his friend.

While some critics, most notably Philip Young, feel that Jacob Barnes does not change at all in the course of *The Sun Also Rises,* and others, like Mark Spilka, John Rouch, and Richard Hovey, conclude that Jake changes only to realize the full extent of his inability to change, a close critical reading of the end of the novel indicates that this position needs to be reevaluated. Jake Barnes does indeed undergo profound change, and that change, which has taken place gradually and progressively throughout the novel, is summed up concisely and symbolically in the final pages of book 3.

Jake has undergone the shock of many recognitions before book 3 opens. He has been changed by the events in Pamplona: the spectacle of Romero's utter masculinity; the revelation of his own shameful role as steer and pimp; the realization that he is in his romantic dreaming little different, although quieter, than Robert Cohn. More importantly, he has recognized that what he had been calling romantic love is instead compulsion and misery, a neurotic and scarcely uncontrollable sickness to which, rather than shore up his tentative masculinity, only serves to castrate him further. Jake has changed in his estimation of himself, his wound, his crowd, and his love for Brett Ashley, who he has been discovering is not so "absolutely fine and straight."

Michael S. Reynolds, from *The Sun Also Rises: A Novel of the Twenties* (Boston: Twayne, 1988), pp.1–4.

Author of the five-volume biography of Hemingway, Reynolds has also published textual studies, edited anthologies, and catalogued Hemingway's reading from 1910–1940. He emphasizes the importance of historical context in understanding *The Sun Also Rises*.

When Hemingway arrived in Paris at Christmas, 1921, he was not prepared for the culture shock of the marginal artists, idle rich, serious painters and writers, youthful rioters, jazz musicians, black dancers, and touring Rotarians who made up a permanent but continuously shifting American/British colony in the City of Lights. This was the generation that Gertrude Stein helped label "lost," the generation of the Jazz Age. It was never really lost, nor was it at all times jazzy. It was the generation that drank more than it should have because it was illegal to drink in the United States during Prohibition; the Volstead Act (1919–33) had made half the country into criminals. In Paris, Americans were conspicuous consumers of alcohol in clubs, bars, and cafés that catered to them almost exclusively. Most Americans spoke little or no French; there was no need, for they seldom engaged natives in any real conversation. Except to provide services, few native French or Spanish appear in *The Sun Also Rises*.

This was the postwar generation, and many of Hemingway's Paris contemporaries were combat veterans. He himself bore his accidental wounding in Italy with stoic bravery, letting people think he had behaved more heroically than he had. War experience was the entry fee, the badge that got one into the select club of insiders. But the war was not over. In Germany, inflation caused by the war debt turned the country into a tourist's dream and a native's nightmare. Berlin became the most decadent town on the continent; the next war—and everyone knew there would be a next war—had to result from the Paris peace settlement that had cut the heart out of Germany's industrial economy. In the Balkans, Turks were fighting Greeks. In Italy the Fascists swept Mussolini into power, and the future was made visible. In Paris, the jazz played late in the clubs and the cheap champagne flowed on. What was the point of worrying about the next war? No one had faith any longer in the politicians who had started the last war. No one believed any longer in the values that had taken the men into the trenches of the Great War, as it was now called. Honor, glory, country no longer moved this generation of which Hemingway was a part. Politics did not interest this generation. At home the country elected Warren G. Harding, who headed the most corrupt administration since Grant's. His secretary of the interior sold the U. S. Navy's oil reserves at Tea Pot Dome to the Sinclair Oil Company. No matter. The country continued to elect conservative Republicans until the bottom fell out of the stock market and the Jazz Age went bust. The conservative politics of the twenties in America were reflected in the rise of reactionary hate groups like the Ku Klux Klan, the popularity of fundamentalist ministers, the falling numbers of union membership, the increased efforts to purify the country by censoring books and movies, and a general anti-intellectual attitude. Many of the Paris expatriates had left their native soil to avoid dealing with this conservative tide. Those were the days of the silent movies; those were the days when Chaplin was king. And they all came to Paris: the movies played along the grand boulevards and their stars played in the Paris clubs, drinking and dancing themselves silly. Or else they came to Paris for a quick divorce and a new wardrobe. Or they came to Paris like Jack Dempsey to cash in on his name and make a movie called *So This is Paris*. Dempsey, Babe Ruth, Red Grange (football), Bill Tilden (tennis), Bobby Jones (golf) and other sports figures were the other heroes of the Jazz Age. Their faces were better known than those of most political figures, and they were immortalized in newsreel footage, the first generation of highly paid superstars.

Those were also the days when women changed the rules of the mating game. From decorously trailing the floor, their skirts rose almost overnight to above their knees. Whale-bone corsets disappeared along with the pinched waist and the opulent bosom. Flat was faddish; breasts were bound and dresses were as whispy as possible. The lovely, long tresses of the previous age disappeared as hair was bobbed. The lipstick-stained cigarette was a sign of the times, and the really daring young women smoked in public. The waltz that had shocked an earlier generation was now too sedate; ministers and keepers of the public morals were enraged by the Charleston, the Black Bottom, and other jazzy dances. This was the first generation of American women to drink and smoke, the first generation to vote (1919), and the first generation for whom divorce was a reasonable solution to a bad marriage. Those who could afford a trip to Paris took advantage of easygoing divorce laws that allowed much quicker divorces than those at home. Everything was happening so quickly; speed was synonymous with the times. The automobile, no longer funereal black, increased in horsepower, beauty, and cost. Installment buying arrived just in time to allow most middle-class families to purchase the latest version of the American Dream. But the automobile was only the most obvious piece of consumer technology. Elsewhere, the airplane was speeding up mail delivery and by 1927 would fly the Atlantic with the Jazz Age's darling, Charles Lindbergh, at the controls. . . . Black jazz musicians and singers were now being heard in rooms where no Black American could enter. The Blues caught the American ear in Chicago and in Paris. Bessie Smith moaned her "Cemetery Blues" while Ruth Etting was "Shaking the Blues Away" and Ethel Waters told them 'bout "Oh Daddy." This was the generation that learned how to kiss from the movies and how to dance from records. In 1925 Black dancers and musicians took Paris by storm. Revue Negre was the rage, and its chief attraction, Josephine Baker, was the toast of the town. Hemingway's Paris was also the intellectual center of the 1920s in literature, painting, dance, and music. In Paris, Diaghilev's Ballet Russe employed modernist painters to do sets and costumes for his innovative choreography to contemporary music. In Paris, Gertrude Stein had been conducting her experiments in prose since just after the turn of the century. In her salon one could see her remarkable collection of modernist painting, perhaps even meet Picasso, Braque, Gris, or Miró. Sylvia Beach's bookstore, Shakespeare and Company, was a writer's haven and post office. Soon after Hemingway arrived, Beach published the novel that no one else dared publish—James Joyce's *Ulysses*. At the same time, Ezra Pound, mid-wife to a generation of young writers, was editing T. S. Eliot's *The Waste Land*. Eventually all the writers of the age passed through Paris, and many of the young ones became Hemingway's acquaintances: Archibald MacLeish, John Dos Passos, Sinclair Lewis, e. e. cummings, Louis Bromfield, Donald Ogden Stewart, Dorothy Parker, and F. Scott Fitzgerald, to name a few. Nowhere else could a young writer so quickly make contact with the leading edge of his times than in Paris. In less than a year Hemingway plugged into a cultural network that made him well-known before he published a single word. That was what Paris could do for a man in those days.

THE SUN ALSO RISES CRITICALLY ANALYZED

Each generation arrives at its own reading of *The Sun Also Rises:* readers in the 1920s saw it as a roman à clef, written in a splendid new style; readers in the 1930s, faced with their own crises, mustered less sympathy for the war-wearied veterans; readers in the 1940s began to focus on the work's connections to other modernist pieces, and mythological readings gained favor; in the 1950s readers became familiar with the notion of a "composite hero"—one comprised of the traits drawn from an amalgamation of Hemingway's heroes—as well as the "Hemingway Code," and the "death of love," readings that held sway for nearly two decades; critics in the 1970s generated revisionist readings—Jake was dynamic and the novel affirmative; scholars in the 1980s continued to revise received notions, explored the role of minor characters, and recast Brett Ashley; and in the 1990s, one prominent essayist asserted that "Jake narrates Brett's story."[102]

But most current readings of the story follow generally one of two veins. Some readers conclude that the story is about postwar aimlessness and malaise and, more specifically, about Jake's corruption that costs him his status as an aficionado of the bullfights and leaves him worse off at the end of the novel than he was at the beginning. Other readers embrace more affirmative readings: Jake's experience with the expatriates at Pamplona forces him to relinquish his illusion that he and Brett could "go off in the country for a while," and Brett's rejection of Romero allows her to recover the self-respect that she lost because of her affair with Robert Cohn (62). While these affirmative readings concede that Brett and Jake fail to accomplish what most readers think they most desire—a romantically and sexually fulfilling life with each other—the characters do manage to salvage their friendship as they are battered about by forces larger than themselves. Certainly this affirmative reading discovers the characters better off in Madrid than in Paris, but it scarcely attributes their growth to their own conscious actions. Jake's crucial moment of realization is typically linked to his discovery that Brett and Romero have left Pamplona together; and Brett's tearful epiphany visits her when she is, for the first time apparently, able to curb her hitherto uncontrollable passions and deny herself someone whom she really wants. Jake's knowledge results from things that seem to happen to him as if he were a passive agent; Brett's growth results from a single, conscious application of her will that finally follows a series of episodes where she has been unable to check her desires—with Jake, Robert, Mike, or Romero.

Neither of these readings is entirely satisfactory, and therein lies one of the strengths of the novel: it is specific and concrete enough to serve as a guidebook to Paris and Pamplona, but it is likewise ambiguous enough to accommodate reasonable arguments about readings that are practically diametrically opposed to one another. Certainly, the novel may be profitably read as a tragedy: Jake has been terribly wounded fighting the war to end all wars, and his wound is rendered all the more horrific in that, unlike Captain Ahab's crown-to-heel scar in *Moby-Dick*, it is invisible. Hidden too is the fact that Jake is susceptible to desire but barred from consummation. The values that he embraces are at odds with those of his contemporaries, leaving him "a most ineffectual man in a most unpromising place."[103] And Brett has lost her "true love" in the war; before the armistice, she married Lord Ashley. Her disastrous liaison with this titled dipsomaniac may well have prompted her own decline into alcoholism. While married to Ashley and serving as a nurse in the war, she met and fell in love with Jake during his convalescence that neither knew would be incomplete. Her unconsummated tryst with Jake might account for her insatiable sexual appetites. Wish as one might for a happy ending, the story remains laden with misfortune: Jake and Brett love each other—and not for a weekend or a season but for six or eight years—and, as Jake admits "there's not a damn thing we could do [about it]" (34). Even the affirmative readings allow that Brett and Jake are buffeted about by forces larger than they are and that happy coincidence as much as anything else urges them toward their discoveries at the end of the novel.

There is room, perhaps, for a still more affirmative reading, one that attributes the growth of both Brett and Jake to decisions of their own making, to acts of their own will. This reading begins by acknowledging that *The Sun Also Rises* is about a man and woman learning to live with limitations. Some of these limitations are physical: he has been emasculated, she has succumbed to the twin addictions of promiscuity and alcohol. Other limitations are metaphysical: he is uncertain about "how to live" in his radically altered condition (152); she, too, seems to be searching for a "way" to be (247). Consequently, Jake determines that his ambition is not to discover what life is all about but to learn how to live in it, and Brett, who is much more reticent about her objectives, seems to be looking not only for self-respect but also for a happy resolution to her romance with Jake.

Hemingway in 1927

In *The Scarlet Letter* Hester and Dimmesdale have consummated their affair and she has delivered her child *before* the novel opens; Captain Ahab, likewise, has lost his leg and assumed his monomaniacal preoccupation with Moby-Dick before Ishmael becomes a crew member of the *Pequod*. So, too, has Jacob Barnes met with a pair of tragic events before his narrative opens. First, he has received a war wound that has emasculated him, leaving him capable of desire but not consummation. Second, during his convalescence he and his beautiful nurse have fallen in love, presumably before realizing that his recovery will be incomplete. They have apparently tried to live together before the novel opens, but the attempt was so unsuccessful that Brett confesses "I don't want to go through that hell again" (34).

Unfortunately, the physical element of the relationship is paramount to Brett, and she simply cannot settle down with Jake, although she seems genuinely to love him. Jake's proposed solution to the problem is sensible: "We'd better keep away from each other" (34). Yet, Brett rejects this solution: "But, darling, I have to see you"—to which she quickly adds the wonderfully ambiguous line, "It isn't all that you know" (34). The referent for "it" is not immediately apparent, and the uninitiated reader may pause over the rest of the sentence as well, wondering where to place emphasis. The "it," one eventually gathers, seems a shorthand reference to "the reason why I have to see you," which would render Brett's line "The reason that I have to see you isn't all that you know."

Is she suggesting that Jake is simply unaware of one of the reasons that she needs to be with him? That he simply fails to realize something? Or is she emphasizing the word *that*—"It isn't all *that* you know"—and referring specifically to the much-discussed and sorely missed physical element of their relationship?

Jake's reply, "No, but it always gets to be," seems to support the second reading. Alone for the first time in a while, Brett and Jake slide naturally and irresistibly into each other's arms and reaffirm their love for one another, only to realize that they have played this scene out already and that the conclusion is unsatisfactory. They love each other, and Jake especially seems to enjoy this love at a distance, not unlike Gatsby's five-year vigil for Daisy in *The Great Gatsby* or Holden Caulfield's idealization of Jane Gallagher in *The Catcher in the Rye*. But because Brett cannot manage without the physical expression of that love, they have been unable to settle down permanently together. When Jake suggests that they avoid each other altogether, Brett balks and insists that she must see him for reasons that go beyond her physical attraction to him. She must see him because she loves him.

And there is half of the novel's conflict: Brett *must* see Jake. The other half of the conflict is that Jake cannot seem to see Brett without falling under her spell and being transported back to an earlier moment of their relationship, before he realized the extent of his wound, when the possibility of their spending their lives together seemed real. Brett needs Jake's physical presence, because whereas she can find sexual fulfillment elsewhere, only Jake, it seems, can be her soul mate. But Jake's strategy for dealing with his personal tragedy is entirely thwarted by Brett's presence.

How does Jake manage his life? In Chapter II, Hemingway contrasts Jake with Robert. The result is that Jake seems to be the wizened cosmopolitan man. "I like this town," he says of Paris; unlike other characters who are there vacationing, escaping creditors, or prostituting themselves, Jake has chosen to be in Paris. It is a romantic place, a city of lights where lovers stroll arm-in-arm across bridges over the Seine. He stridently encourages Cohn to "start living [his] life in Paris" because "[y]ou can't get away from yourself by moving from one place to another. There's nothing to that" (19). He speaks these words with conviction apparently born of experience: he too has been overcome by a desperate restlessness, by the gnawing question "what shall I do with myself *now*?"

His answer: distance himself from Brett Ashley; bury himself in work and play and, for an imaginative pastime, hold fast to the illusion that one day they will enjoy a life in the country together. In her absence he throws himself into work and play with the single-mindedness of a widower who is determined to postpone contemplating his loss. For work Jake has selected a field that requires him to be on the move, gathering details, sharing taxis, and writing stories against deadlines. It keeps the body busy and the mind occupied. Jake's leisure activity, going to Spain in the summertime to watch the bullfights, is much more than recreation; it is practically a calling. Year-round, he reads both of the leading bullfight magazines, knowing from long experience that whichever he reads first will ruin the pleasure of reading the other. He is not merely a casual fan, a weekend spectator, of bullfighting; he is an aficionado, so authentic that even the natives welcome this *buen hombre* into their inner circle. He has earned his *afición* by virtue of his keen observation, his steady reading, and his grasp of the historical and cultural importance of the bullfight. Just as he has chosen an occupation in which he can immerse himself, so too has he embraced an avocation that will fill his empty hours with exciting spectacle or pleasurable reading. If his interest in work or bullfighting flags, he has alternative plans cued up: "Did you ever think about going to British East Africa to shoot?" he asks the dispirited Cohn. "I'd go there with you" (18). British East Africa would be the perfect alternative to a month in Spain: the planning and execution would keep his mind occupied for months.

Judging from the way that Jake dresses down Cohn for indulging himself in his personal crisis, readers gain confidence in him, especially by virtue of his contrasts with Cohn. No self-pitying whining fool, Jake knows what he wants; he seems shaped by his own desires, not his mother's or his wife's. And while the author may have given over the first two chapters to a description of Cohn's wealth, lineage, education, and professional and athletic accomplishments, Jake seems to be shaping up as the hero of the piece. Brett, too, has been busy getting on with her life since losing her first true love and discovering the impotence of her second, Jake, before marrying one man that she did not love, Lord Ashley, and becoming engaged to repeat the error with Mike Campbell. How is Brett managing her life without Jake? There is a great deal of alcohol and a good many men. "She's slept with lots of better people than you," Mike tells Cohn (146), and to Jake he explains, "Brett's had affairs with men before. She tells me all about them" (147). There is her brassy disposition: she is a smoker, drinker, and carouser. There is her modern attire that seems to allow her to mask her femininity and flaunt it simultaneously. The cropped hair certainly departs from the nineteenth-century standards of femininity; and her man's felt hat hides those eyes that "look on and on after every one else's eyes in the world would have stopped looking" (34). But the "slipover jersey sweater and tweed skirt" cling snugly to this woman who "was built with curves like the hull of a racing yacht" (30).

Widowed by Jake's impotence, she cannot bury herself in a profession any more than the cynical Daisy Buchanan can divorce her philandering husband and join the work force to support herself and young Pammy in *The Great Gatsby.* Her instant and witty reply "We have our careers" to the Count's question "Why don't you get married, you two?" (68) belies her seldom seen capacity for introspection. Brett has no career, but she knows that she, like Jake, must keep occupied, must remain in motion. Count Mippipopolous pours her a glass of wine and says, "There, my dear. Now you enjoy that slowly, and then you can get drunk" (66). In her presence for only a matter of hours, he knows that she drinks to get drunk; that she does not savor the taste even of champagne. Nor can she abide the "quiet" of a restaurant near closing time. When the Count insists that she enjoy another brandy, "here where it is quiet," she quips, "You and your quiet. . . . What is it men feel about quiet?"(68)

For men such as Jake and the Count, who are for different reasons only able to admire Brett at a remove, a quiet and pleasant evening spent observing, drinking, and conversing with her in relative privacy during the waning hours of the evening is a valuable thing. The Count also encourages her to talk—"I should like to hear you really talk, my dear. When you talk to me you never finish your sentences at all" (65). Again the Count has tipped up the brim of that man's felt hat and taken a good look at Brett, discovering that she most often uses language to create distance from rather than intimacy with her acquaintances. Her opening conversation with Jake is elliptical, allusive, and ambiguous. Jake and Brett, longtime friends, can follow one another's meaning, but Cohn, with all his "eager, deserving expectation," probably has no idea of what has just transpired before him. Before Cohn interrupts and asks Brett to dance, she and Jake exchange a dozen lines of dialogue (Jake speaking five times, Brett seven). A full account of all of the nuance and subtlety of their exchange would cover pages, but a brief summary will suggest how the complexity of their communication keeps Cohn's understanding at arm's length.

Jake says, "It's a fine crowd you're with, Brett" (30). His comment is ironic and probably escapes Cohn, who misses the far more local irony that he, a novelist, is lulled to sleep by the sound of a typewriter. But Brett is quick to acknowledge that she has arrived in the company of several gay men. She then asks Jake "Where did you get it?" meaning that she has surmised that he is at the *bal* with Georgette. How she arrives at this inference is unknown, because as soon as the homosexuals arrive they begin dancing with Georgette and Jake spends no more of his time with her, but Brett not only knows that Georgette and Jake are there together, she knows that Georgette is a *poule,* a fact that seems to have escaped at least a few of Jake's friends. When he tells Brett that he has picked her up at the Napolitan, she asks, "And have you had a lovely evening?" (30) This question immediately highlights an irony: an impotent man has solicited a prostitute. But Jake's wit is a fine match for Brett's; his equally ironic reply—"Oh, priceless"—slices literally (there will be no charge because there will be no sex) and figuratively (the dinner was dull and the whole show at the *bal musette* makes him sick). Brett appreciates Jake's joke and laughs, then scolds him for withholding his attentions from nonworking girls such as herself, Frances, and Jo (which may be Mrs. Braddocks's first name). In turn, he appreciates Brett's humor and mocking jests, which she delivers with linguistic agility. She then remarks the irony of that sobriety: a girl might overindulge without fear of being taken advantage of when in the company of homosexuals.

All the while Cohn is standing next to Brett and Jake like a wooden Indian. He can find no crevasse in the dialogue where he might add his own witty remark, no convenient spot where he might insert himself casually. Thus, without so much as a "hello," he blurts out, "Will you dance this with me, Lady Brett?" Brett, whose title is actually "Lady Ashley," deftly parries with a lie: "I've promised to dance this with Jacob" (30). Surely Robert knows this to be false, because he has been standing with Jake and Brett since they have joined company at the *bal,* but the speed and confidence with which the line is delivered must make it seem almost believable, so Cohn, undeterred, requests the next dance. But Brett quickly pulls another arrow from her quiver of ready-made lies and, rejecting Cohn again, claims to have a date with Jake up at Montmartre. By virtue of the way that she and Jake manipulate the language, they have managed to accommodate Cohn's physical presence without having to endure his intellectual presence. Brett, especially, keeps him at a distance, just as she teases the infinitely more perceptive Count with her sentence fragments and scolds Mike for using too many words and selecting an inopportune time to ask Jake if he and Brett might join him in Burguete.

Thus, Jake and Brett have developed their own survival mechanisms. Her strategy—her attempts at marriage, her drinking and promiscuity—has served her less well than Jake's. For at odds with all of her attempts to forget him is her undeniable need to see him. He establishes routines that have become rituals. He keeps his mind busy at work and at play. As long as he is physically separated from Brett, he can carefully apportion his day so that thoughts of her do not intrude uninvited. This is not to say that he never thinks about Brett; to the contrary, he is in love with her and speaks earnestly when he tells her, "And it's a lot of fun, too, to be in love" (34). He adds, "In a way, it's an enjoyable feeling" (35). He may mean that the *idea* of being in love is appealing, provided that one controls that idea, calling it up during a serene recollection. But when thoughts of love come to call and drive out sleep and solace, then for both Brett and Jake, love becomes "hell on earth" (35). Unless this pair grows beyond the needs that they demonstrate at the beginning of the novel, their future is likely to be as tragic as their past.

Probably, reflects Jake, "I wouldn't have had any trouble if I hadn't run into Brett when they shipped me to England" (39). Early in the novel, he accuses her of only wanting what she could not have, but soon readers realize that Jake, too, desperately wants what he cannot have. Brett, Mike tells Jake, "loves looking after people. That's how we came to go off together. She was looking after me." To this, Jake can only reply, "I know" (206–207). And when Cohn massacres Romero, she looks after the matador as well. Jake may be right, for in meeting and falling in love with Brett after he was wounded, he places himself in an impossible position. Could he share a future with Brett? The answer, Jake finally admits, is no, although certainly it is "pretty to think so" (251).

For a long time, from their first falling in love in England during Jake's convalescence to the revelation of her affair with Cohn, Jake entertains the idea that he and Brett could live quietly in the country. When Bill asks Jake if he is in love with Brett, he says, "Sure. . . . Off and on for a hell of a long time" (128). Depending upon how one dates the novel, Jake's love could have spanned as many as seven years (beginning as late as 1918, the final year of the war, and continuing to 1925, the year of Bryan's passing). Presumably, his love for Brett is "off" in her absence, "on" in her presence. The novel reveals little of what Jake has been doing since the war. Mostly he seems to have established routines. Despite his relatively young age, Jake has settled into patterns that are predictable and comfortable, patterns that give him solace. He works hard, has a wide circle of friends, and likes living in Paris and vacationing in Spain (18). Having experienced one dramatic, life-altering change, Jake immerses himself in rituals of observation: he observes current events as a profession, bullfighting for pleasure. He loves to read, to watch, and to listen. Yet, he *does* very little. For example, he watches but does not engage in the running of the bulls; he fishes, but uses worms, a sedentary style of fishing contrasted with Bill's more challenging fly casting. He likes to read the papers or books and takes real pleasure in observation. Jake seems to have insulated himself since the war and the wound that it inflicted upon him. He has discovered how to keep himself busy, and as long as he stays away from Brett, he can maintain enough confidence and assurance that he is able to counsel his forlorn friend, Cohn.

But when Brett cycles back into Jake's life, as she does in the *bal musette* scene, his rituals and routines are no match for her charms and he is left acting more like Cohn's double than his foil. Her physical presence seems to hold sway over Jake's intellectual faculties; he introduces her as "damned good-looking" (30). When he is near Brett, his physical attraction to her thwarts his logic, yet, when at a remove from her, he is able to regain his composure.

He seems to have been away from her for a while before the book opens. In fact, in encouraging Robert Cohn to start living his life in Paris, Jake seems the much wiser man, although we learn shortly that, when it comes to Brett, Jake can be almost as big a boor as Cohn. But at the beginning of the novel, Jake seems to have a plan that satisfies him. He works hard during the day, keeping his mind busy. He plays tennis on the weekends and fishes for relaxation, socializes with writers and artists from the Quarter, and follows the bullfights as an aficionado, reading about them in the off season and traveling in the summers to witness the spectacle. True, he is a solitary man, but he keeps his foreground filled with work and friends, his horizon dotted with fishing trips and summers in Pamplona. Contrasted with Cohn, who at age thirty-four seems to be experiencing some kind of midlife crisis, Jake seems to have his wits about him.

But Brett's presence changes all of that. One dance with her at the *bal musette* and a taxi ride through the Parc Montsouris, bound on either end by a passionate kiss, change all of that, and he is once again bewitched by her charms and left to cry himself to sleep (39). After their initial kiss in the taxi, Brett reaffirms her passion for Jake and he wonders aloud, "Isn't there anything we can do about it?" (34). Brett responds with a silence that belies her vulnerability, and Jake is forced to answer his own question, "And there's not a damn thing we could do" (34).

There is nothing Jake can do except give up his illusion that he and Brett might live happily ever after in the country. As he is unable or unwilling to do that, he seems stuck. Brett knows this. She realizes that, given her disposition and his irreparable wound, they will *never* live quietly in the country. She has given Jake seven or eight years to come to terms with that fact, and as he has refused, so she has left with no choice but to lead him to the realization that he must make. She goes about this in a calculating and deliberate way: after telling him that she loves him, she adds, "I'm going away from you" (62). When Jake asks why she is leaving, she replies, "Better for you. Better for me" (62). She needs Jake, *must* see him, and cannot abide his indulgent illusions any longer. It would be better for Jake if he abandoned those illusions, and better for her too: then she could talk to her soul mate without his crying about his inability to be her bedmate. And she vows to bring about this "better" situation "Soon as I can" (62).

Brett's plan is relatively unsophisticated: she will sleep with one of Jake's friends. It will just be a weekend fling in San Sebastián. When she returns to Paris, Jake can choose to be angry or hurt or conciliatory, but he will not be able to wrap himself comfortably in the illusion that Brett and he might one day go off to the country together. After she announces that she is going away, Brett, Jake, and the Count spend a long evening together that ends miserably for her. The jazz drummer's refrain, "you can't two time," cuts visibly into her (70), and her happiness of a moment before dissipates. It has been a terribly trying evening for her: Jake has once again pleaded that they live together, and even the Count, sensing the chemistry between the two, inquires, "Why don't you get married, you two?" (68). Brett and Jake collaborate in deflecting the Count's question, ironically replying that they "want to lead [their] own lives" and that they "have [their] careers" to think about (68). The dramatic irony is rich here, for Jake has just finished pleading his case to Brett once again, and she, hardly trained for the professional world, has no career to consider. After she says goodnight, Brett adds, "I won't see you again" (71). Literally, she seems to be saying that she will not see Jake again before leaving for San Sebastián, a fling that, once and for all, should explode his illusion. But metaphorically, she means that after tonight, they will not see one another in the same light again.

On the day of her return from San Sebastián, Brett chances across Jake and a drunken Bill as they stroll down the boulevard (79). Jake, having no idea that Brett has been off with Cohn, is excited to see her and persuades her to have a drink with him and Bill before preparing herself for Michael's arrival. Seated at the Closerie des Lilas, she puts the seemingly innocent question to him, "How are you, Jake?" When he responds, "Great. . . . I've had a good time," she is puzzled. Did she have a good time, he asks? It was "all right. . . . Not frightfully amusing. . . . never went out. . . . Didn't do a thing" (81). This is an unsettling conversation for Brett. She apparently assumes that Jake would have learned, in her

Maxwell E. Perkins, the legendary editor at Charles Scribner's Sons

absence, of her liaison with Cohn, but his casual conversation suggests the truth—he is unaware of her fling. Their meeting later in the evening at the Select does not clarify things, but the following night at the Dingo, with Mike off getting his hair cut and Bill "out at Chantilly with some people" (88), Brett tosses down her drink, then another for good measure, and then puts her same question to Jake, this time with emphasis: "How *are* you, Jake?" Jake replies, "Fine" and then notices "Brett looked at me" as if his countenance might reveal more than his diction (89). But it does not. At last she discovers that she must be the one to tell him that she has been off with Cohn. When she does, he becomes sarcastic, which is undoubtedly a manifestation of his anger. His anger here does not flare, as it threatened to in the *bal musette,* but it is tangible, and Brett perceives it. But has it cured him? If her marrying Ashley, becoming engaged to Campbell, and sleeping with "lots of better people" than Cohn has not awakened Jake from his illusion, surely her sleeping with his tennis partner should do the trick (146).

It does. Four short sentences after she informs him of her liaison with Cohn, Jake writes, "We walked along and turned a corner" (89). Literally, their excursion has taken a new direction; figuratively Brett has shifted the course of their relationship. Has he abandoned the illusion? A week or so later Bill asks Jake if he was ever in love with Brett and he replies, "Sure. . . . Off and on for a hell of a long time." When Bill, who knows of Jake's wound, offers condolences, Jake responds, "It's all right. . . . I don't give a damn any more" (128).

In one calculated but painful act, Brett has helped Jake to arrive at a conclusion that, alone, he has been unable to reach for the better part of a decade. This is quite an accomplishment, and the story might have ended here. But just when Brett thinks that she has solved the major problem in their lives, another arises: Cohn has taken San Sebastián seriously. He believes himself to be in love with her—but of course he has confided in Jake that "I shouldn't wonder if I were in love with her"

(46)—after having only spoken to her for a moment at the *bal musette*. Having finally cured Jake of his illusions, she finds them transferred to Cohn. What was a brief dalliance to her is a budding romance to him, leaving her another conflict to resolve. But perhaps worst of all, her cure for Jake has come at the cost of her self-respect. Brett would not peddle herself to the Count for $10,000, and despite not having a sou with which to leave Romero, she refuses money from him as well, telling Jake that "He tried to give me lots of money, you know. . . . I couldn't take his money" (246). "No," Jake says, agreeing with her; of course she could not take his money, because Brett does not exchange sexual favors for cash. She has her own brand of "self-respect," and she probably could have endured compromising that self-respect for a weekend had Cohn been a good sport and left her alone afterward (187). But as he makes himself a larger and larger nuisance, the fact that she has slept with him becomes more and more of an embarrassment for Brett. A day or two into the vacation, everyone knows that she has slept with Cohn, and, unable to tell Jake why she has done so, she grows drunken, angry, and finally ashamed. Her drunkenness and Cohn's interference delay Brett's arrival at Pamplona. The anger finally bubbles forth when she scolds Cohn, "For God's sake, go off somewhere. Can't you see Jake and I want to talk? . . . If you're tight, go to bed. Go on to bed" (184–185). And the shame reveals itself when she begs Jake to introduce her to Romero: "I've got to do something. I've got to do something I really want to do. I've lost my self-respect" (187).

Sleeping with Cohn was not something that Brett really wanted to do, but she cannot very well explain that to Jake. She can, ironically enough and by virtue of having slept with Cohn, rely on Jake to help her. In a calm and reasonable tone, he repeatedly counsels her against the affair. Never once does he say, "How could you ask *me* of all people to do this for you?" There is no self-pity, no veiled illusion of a quiet life in the country. There is only one friend asking another to help her regain her self-respect. Unlike their initial dialogue in the *bal musette,* this private conversation between Jake and Brett is devoid of allusion, ambiguity, and elliptical meaning. And its irony is once again dramatic: for by now the reader knows what Jake has yet to discover—that Brett sacrificed her self-respect for him.

In capturing Romero and then releasing him, Brett concedes that she feels "set up": "I'm all right again. [Romero's] wiped out that damn Cohn" (246). Autonomy in her selection of men is paramount to Brett. She may be a "new woman," but she perceives her choices as limited: she can control with whom she sleeps and whom she allows to buy her drinks. So she puts great store in these decisions.

She is "all right again" in Book III, and so is Jake. He is finally able to be in Brett's presence, to hold her in his arms, without falling under her spell. He can be with her *and* realize that he likes to do many things—like taste food and drink wine. He has enormous appetites—for action and travel and exercise and love—but previously these passions were dwarfed by his love for Brett. Now he can manage to pursue his other passions and love Brett without being her lover. Brett has learned to live within limitations. Previously, she has engaged in excessive drinking and promiscuity. Now, having regained her self-respect through her affair with Romero, she stops—or at least she reins in—her excessive drinking. And she claims that she will return to Mike, who is just her "sort of thing" (247). Just as Jake has postponed dealing with his tragedy by burying himself in work and play and clinging to impossible illusions, Brett's drinking and promiscuity have only helped her to pass the time before she is able to be around Jake without making his life miserable.

In the taxi in Madrid, Brett can finally "rest comfortably" against Jake and say "we could have had such a damned good time together." The dull ache that accompanies their knowledge that they can be friends but not lovers leaves them somber but no longer paralyzed. Brett is now ready to settle—to settle for Michael, who is "so damned nice and . . . so awful" (247)—and to settle for friendship with Jake, whom she has helped to discard his own illusions and admit that the pretty fantasy of their living together in the country is impossible. And Jake is ready to invent a new ritual, perhaps shooting in British East Africa, that will supply his evening reading as he prepares for the trip, as well as his summer vacation. And where does this leave Brett and Jake? They are friends, at last, who have helped each other through their most difficult moments and learned not only what life is all about but also how to live in it.

NOTES

1. Audre Hanneman, *Ernest Hemingway: A Comprehensive Bibliography* (Princeton: Princeton University Press, 1967; corrected, 1969), pp. 5–11.
2. Jeffrey Meyers, ed., *Hemingway: The Critical Heritage* (London & Boston: Routledge & Kegan Paul, 1982), p. 12.
3. Ibid., pp. 92, 95, 96.
4. Ibid., p. 94.
5. Ibid., p. 104.

6. Hugh Walpole, "Contemporary American Letters," *Nation & Athenaeum,* 41 (4 June 1927): 302–303; reprinted in James Nagel, ed., *Critical Essays on Ernest Hemingway's The Sun Also Rises* (New York: G. K. Hall, 1995), p. 4.

7. Carlos Baker, *Hemingway: The Writer as Artist,* fourth edition (Princeton: Princeton University Press, 1972), p. 78.

8. Bertram D. Sarason, *Hemingway and The Sun Set* (Washington D.C.: NCR/Microcard Editions, 1972), pp. 209–210.

9. Ibid., p. 223.

10. Michael Reynolds, *Hemingway: The Paris Years* (Oxford: Basil Blackwell, 1989), pp. 306–355.

11. James T. Farrell, "The Sun Also Rises," in John K. M. McCaffery, ed., *Ernest Hemingway: The Man and his Work* (Cleveland: World, 1950), p. 221.

12. *Hemingway: The Critical Heritage,* p. 93.

13. Farrell, "The Sun Also Rises," p. 222.

14. Ibid., p. 224.

15. Malcolm Cowley, *Exile's Return: A Literary Odyssey of the 1920s* (New York: Viking, 1951), pp. 225–226.

16. Joseph Warren Beach, "Ernest Hemingway: The Esthetics of Simplicity," in his *American Fiction: 1920–1940* (New York: Macmillan, 1941), pp. 101–102.

17. Robert Penn Warren, "Hemingway," *Kenyon Review,* 19, no. 1 (1947): 18.

18. Harry Levin, "Observations on the Style of Ernest Hemingway," *Kenyon Review,* 13, no. 4 (1951): 597.

19. Ibid., p. 599.

20. Ibid., p. 600.

21. Richard Bridgman, *The Colloquial Style in America* (New York: Oxford University Press, 1966), pp. 219–220.

22. Ibid., pp. 228–229.

23. T. S. Eliot, *Selected Prose of T. S. Eliot,* edited by Frank Kermode (New York: Harcourt Brace Jovanivich, 1975), pp. 177–178.

24. Cowley, introduction, *The Viking Portable Library: Hemingway,* edited by Cowley (New York: Viking, 1944), p. xxii.

25. Richard P. Adams, "Sunrise Out of The Waste Land," *TSE: Tulane Studies in English,* 9 (1959): 119–131; reprinted in James Nagel, ed., *Critical Essays on Ernest Hemingway's The Sun Also Rises* (New York: G. K. Hall, 1995), pp. 58–59.

26. Ibid., p. 58.

27. Philip Young, *Ernest Hemingway: A Reconsideration* (University Park: Pennsylvania State University Press 1966), p. 86.

28. *Hemingway: The Writer as Artist,* p. 88.

29. Young, *Ernest Hemingway* (New York: Rinehart, 1952), pp. 28–50; revised as *Ernest Hemingway: A Reconsideration.*

30. Ernest Hemingway, *In Our Time* (New York: Scribners, 1988), n. pag.

31. *Ernest Hemingway: A Reconsideration,* p. 40.

32. Ibid., pp. 55, 63.

33. Earl Rovit, *Ernest Hemingway* (New York: Twayne, 1963), p. 55.

34. Dewey Ganzel, "*Cabestro* and *Vaquilla:* The Symbolic Structure of *The Sun Also Rises,*" *Sewanee Review,* 76 (Winter 1968): 26–48; Donald T. Torchiana, "*The Sun Also Rises:* A Reconsideration," in *Fitzgerald/Hemingway Annual 1969* (Washington, D.C.: NCR Microcard Editions, 1969), pp. 77–103.

35. "*The Sun Also Rises:* A Reconsideration," p. 81.

36. *The Viking Portable Library: Hemingway,* p. xxi.

37. "*The Sun Also Rises:* A Reconsideration," p. 99.

38. Carole Gottlieb Vopat, "The End of *The Sun Also Rises:* A New Beginning," in *Fitzgerald/Hemingway Annual 1972* (Washington, D.C.: NCR Microcard Editions, 1973), pp. 245–255; reprinted in *Ernest Hemingway's The Sun Also Rises,* edited by Harold Bloom (New York: Chelsea House, 1987), pp. 91–101.

39. Arthur Waldhorn, *A Reader's Guide to Ernest Hemingway* (New York: Farrar, Straus & Giroux, 1972), p. 112.

40. Mark Spilka, "The Death of Love in *The Sun Also Rises,*" in *Twelve Essays on Great American Novels,* edited by Charles Shapiro (Detroit: Wayne State University Press, 1958), pp. 238–256; reprinted in *Ernest Hemingway's The Sun Also Rises,* pp. 25–37.

41. Sibbie O'Sullivan, "Love and Friendship/Man and Woman in *The Sun Also Rises,*" *Arizona Quarterly,* 44, no. 2 (1988): 76–97.

42. Ibid., 96.

43. See Kelli A. Larson, *Ernest Hemingway: A Reference Guide 1974–1989* (Boston: G. K. Hall, 1991).

44. Matthew J. Bruccoli, ed., *Ernest Hemingway: The Sun Also Rises. A Facsimile Edition,* 2 volumes (Detroit: Omnigraphics, 1990).

45. For explication of "Zizi," see Robert E. Fleming, "The Fun Also Rises: A Tribute to Jim Hinkle," *Hemingway Review,* 13, no. 1 (1993): 90–91; see also James Hinkle, "What's Funny in *The Sun Also Rises,*" *Hemingway Review,* 4, no. 2 (1985): 31–41; and Scott Donaldson, "Humor in *The Sun Also Rises,*" in *New Essays on The Sun Also Rises,* edited by Linda Wagner-Martin (New York: Cambridge University Press, 1987), pp. 19–41.

46. Michael Reynolds, *The Young Hemingway* (Oxford: Basil Blackwell, 1986); *Hemingway: The Paris Years* (Cambridge, Mass: Blackwell, 1989); *Hemingway: The American Homecoming* (Cambridge, Mass: Blackwell, 1992); *Hemingway: The 1930s* (New York: Norton, 1997); and *Hemingway: The Final Years* (New York: Norton, 1999).

47. Reynolds, "The *Sun* in Its Time: Recovering the Historical Context," in *New Essays on The Sun Also Rises,* p. 44.

48. See Harold Bloom, ed., *Brett Ashley* (New York: Chelsea House, 1991); Wendy Martin, "Brett Ashley as New Woman in *The Sun Also Rises,*" in *New Essays on The Sun Also Rises,* pp. 65–82; Linda Patterson Miller, "Brett Ashley: The Beauty of It All," in *Critical Essays on Ernest Hemingway's The Sun Also Rises,* pp. 170–184; and James Nagel, "Brett and the Other Woman in *The Sun Also Rises,*" in *The Cambridge Companion to Hemingway,* edited by Scott Donaldson (New York: Cambridge University Press, 1996), pp. 87–108.

49. *Hemingway: The Critical Heritage,* p. 58.

50. See Kenneth S. Lynn, *Hemingway* (New York: Simon & Schuster, 1987); and Mark Spilka, *Hemingway's Quarrel with Androgyny* (Lincoln: University of Nebraska Press, 1989).

51. *Hemingway's Quarrel with Androgyny,* p. 2.

52. See Nancy R. Comley and Robert Scholes, *Hemingway's Genders: Rereading the Hemingway Text* (New Haven: Yale University Press, 1994); and Carl P. Eby, *Hemingway's Fetishism: Psychoanalysis and the Mirror of Manhood* (Albany: State University of New York Press, 1999).

53. Review of *The Sun Also Rises, Chicago Daily Tribune,* 27 November 1926, p. 13; review of *The Sun Also Rises, Dial,* 82 (January 1927): 73; review of *Fiesta, Observer,* 12 June 1927, p. 8; review of *Fiesta, Times Literary Supplement,* 30 June 1927, p. 454; Edwin Muir, review of *Fiesta, Nation & Anthenaeum,* 151 (2 July 1927): 450, 452; all reviews quoted in Audre Hanneman, *Ernest Hemingway: A Comprehensive Bibliography* (Princeton: Princeton University Press, 1967; corrected, 1969), pp. 352–355.

54. Conrad Aiken, review of *The Sun Also Rises, New York Herald Tribune Books,* 31 October 1926, p. 4; reprinted in *Hemingway: The Critical Heritage,* edited by Jeffrey Meyers (London & New York: Routledge & Kegan Paul, 1982), p. 90.

55. Edwin Muir, review of *Fiesta,* pp. 450, 452; reprinted in *Hemingway: The Critical Heritage,* p. 96.

56. Andre Maurois, review of *The Sun Also Rises, This Quarter,* 2 (October 1929): 212–215; reprinted in *Hemingway: The Critical Heritage,* p. 97.

57. Herbert Gorman, review of *The Sun Also Rises, New York World,* 14 November 1926, p. 10M; reprinted in *Hemingway: The Critical Heritage,* p. 92.

58. Burton Rascoe, review of *The Sun Also Rises, New York Sun,* 6 November 1926, p. 10; quoted in *Ernest Hemingway: A Comprehensive Bibliography,* p. 351.

59. *Hemingway: The Critical Heritage,* p. 90.

60. Ibid., p. 93.

61. Ibid., p. 91.

62. Edmund Wilson, introduction to *In Our Time* (New York: Scribners, 1930), p. xiii.

63. Edmund Wilson, "Hemingway: Gauge of Morale," *Atlantic,* 164 (July 1939): 36–46; reprinted in *Modern Critical Views: Ernest Hemingway,* edited by Harold Bloom (New York: Chelsea House, 1985), pp. 17–33.

64. Alfred Kazin, *On Native Grounds: An Interpretation of Modern American Prose Literature* (New York: Harcourt, Brace, 1942), p. 262.

65. *Modern Critical Views: Ernest Hemingway,* pp. 19, 20; John Peale Bishop discusses the lost generation's failed spirituality in "The Missing All," *Virginia Quarterly Review,* 13, no. 1 (1937): 106–121; reprinted in *Ernest Hemingway: The Man and his Work,* edited by John K. M. McCaffery (New York: World, 1950), pp. 292–307.

66. Robert Penn Warren, introduction to *A Farewell to Arms* (New York: Scribners, 1949), pp. vii–xxxvii; quoted in *Modern Critical Views: Hemingway,* p. 40.

67. Wilson, review of *Men without Women, New Republic,* 53 (14 December 1927): 102–103; reprinted in *Hemingway: The Critical Heritage,* p. 113.

68. *Modern Critical Views: Ernest Hemingway,* pp. 24, 26.

69. Lionel Trilling, review of *The Fifth Column and the First Forty-Nine Stories, Partisan Review,* 6 (1939): 52–60; reprinted in *Hemingway: The Critical Heritage,* p. 280.

70. *Hemingway: The Critical Heritage,* p. 31.

71. Cowley, "Hemingway at Midnight," *New Republic,* 111 (14 August 1944): 190, 192, 194–195; expanded as introduction to *The Viking Portable Library: Hemingway,* edited by Cowley (New York: Viking, 1944), p. vii.

72. Ibid., pp. xxi–xxii.

73. *Hemingway: The Writer as Artist*, pp. 92–93.

74. Ibid., p. 88.

75. Philip Young, *Ernest Hemingway: A Reconsideration* (University Park: Pennsylvania State University Press 1966), pp. 40, 54–55.

76. Ibid., p. 63.

77. Ibid., p. 86.

78. Mark Spilka, "The Death of Love in *The Sun Also Rises*," in *Twelve Essays on Great American Novels*, edited by Charles Shapiro (Detroit: Wayne State University Press, 1958), pp. 238–256; reprinted in *Ernest Hemingway's The Sun Also Rises,* pp. 25–37.

79. Ibid., pp. 36–37.

80. Earl Rovit, *Ernest Hemingway* (Boston: Twayne, 1963), pp. 148–149.

81. Ibid., pp. 149, 151.

82. Ibid., p. 161.

83. Torchiana, "*The Sun Also Rises*: A Reconsideration," in *Fitzgerald/Hemingway Annual 1969* (NCR Microcard Editions, 1969), p. 77.

84. Ibid., pp. 98–100.

85. Scott Donaldson, "Hemingway's Morality of Compensation," *American Literature,* 43, no. 3 (1971); reprinted in *Ernest Hemingway's The Sun Also Rises,* pp. 74, 77.

86. *Ernest Hemingway's The Sun Also Rises,* pp. 91, 100.

87. Donald A. Daiker, "The Affirmative Conclusion of *The Sun Also Rises,*" *McNeese Review,* 21 (1975): 3–19.

88. Arthur Waldhorn, *A Reader's Guide to Ernest Hemingway* (New York: Farrar, Straus & Giroux, 1972), pp. 96, 100.

89. Ibid., p. 112.

90. "The Unpublished Opening of *The Sun Also Rises,*" *Antaeus,* 33 (Spring 1979): 7.

91. For an annotated listing of articles, see Linda Welshimer Wagner, *Ernest Hemingway: A Reference Guide* (Boston: G. K. Hall, 1997); and Kelli A. Larson, *Ernest Hemingway: A Reference Guide, 1974–1989* (Boston: G. K. Hall, 1990); see also James Nagel's thorough bibliographic review essay of criticism on *The Sun Also Rises* in his *Critical Essays on Ernest Hemingway's The Sun Also Rises* (New York: G. K. Hall, 1995), pp. 1–31.

92. Linda Wagner-Martin, introduction to *New Essays on The Sun Also Rises* (Cambridge & New York: Cambridge University Press, 1987), p. 15.

93. Delbert E. Wylder, "The Two Faces of Brett: The Role of the New Woman in *The Sun Also Rises,*" *Kentucky Philological Association Bulletin* (1980): 27–33.

94. Gene D. Phillips, *Hemingway and Film* (New York: Ungar, 1980); Frank M. Laurence, *Hemingway and the Movies* (New York: Da Capo Press, 1981); *A Moving Picture Feast:*

The Filmgoer's Hemingway, ed. Charles M. Oliver (New York: Praeger, 1989). John Raeburn, *Fame Became of Him: Hemingway as Public Writer* (Bloomington: Indiana University Press, 1984); Leonard J. Leff, *Hemingway and His Conspirators: Hollywood, Scribners, and the Making of American Celebrity Culture* (Lanham, Md.: Rowman & Littlefield, 1997).

95. Jim Steinke, "Brett and Jake in Spain: Hemingway's Ending for *The Sun Also Rises*," *Spectrum*, 27 (1985): 131–141.

96. Sibbie O'Sullivan, "Love Friendship/Man and Woman in *The Sun Also Rises*," *Arizona Quarterly*, 44 (Summer 1988): 81, 98.

97. Roger Whitlow, *Cassandra's Daughters: The Women in Hemingway's Fiction* (Westport, Conn.: Greenwood Press, 1984).

98. Charles M. Oliver, ed., *Hemingway Review*, 6, no. 1 (1986).

99. James Nagel, *Critical Essays on Ernest Hemingway's The Sun Also Rises* (New York: G. K. Hall, 1995); Robert E. Fleming, *The Face in the Mirror: Hemingway's Writers* (Tuscaloosa: University of Alabama Press, 1994); Scott Donaldson, *The Cambridge Companion to Hemingway* (Cambridge: Cambridge University Press, 1996).

100. Harold Bloom, ed., *Major Literary Characters: Brett Ashley* (New York : Chelsea House, 1991); J. Gerald Kennedy and Jackson R. Bryer, eds., *French Connections: Hemingway and Fitzgerald Abroad* (New York: St. Martin's Press, 1998); Kennedy, *Imagining Paris: Exile, Writing, and American Identity* (New Haven: Yale University Press, 1993); Peter Hays, *Ernest Hemingway* (New York: Continuum, 1990); Peter Messent, *Ernest Hemingway* (New York: St. Martin's Press, 1992); Marc D. Baldwin, *Reading The Sun Also Rises: Hemingway's Political Unconscious* (New York: Peter Lang, 1997).

101. *Hemingway: The Writer as Artist*, p.93.

102. Delbert E. Wylder, *Hemingway's Heroes* (Albuquerque: University of New Mexico Press, 1969), pp. 4–5.

103. Linda Patterson Miller, "Brett Ashley: The Beauty of it All," in *Critical Essays on Ernest Hemingway's The Sun Also Rises*, edited by James Nagel (Boston: G. K. Hall, 1995), p. 171.

104. Michael Reynolds, "The Sun in Its Time: Recovering the Historical Context," in *New Essays on The Sun Also Rises*, edited by Linda Wagner-Martin (New York: Cambridge University Press, 1987) p. 64.

THE SUN ALSO RISES IN HISTORY

The *man* and the *work* in Hemingway studies are sometimes indistinguishable. Hemingway seems scarcely to exist separately either as a writer or as an adventurer; therefore, both the man and the work account for retrospective assessments of his influence. Busts in Cojimar Bay, Cuba, in Ketchum, Idaho, and in Pamplona, Spain, commemorate both the artist and his art. His birthplace in Oak Park, Illinois, and his beloved Finca Vigía in Cuba (now museums), join two other preserved homes in Key West and Ketchum. The Hemingway Bar at the Hotel Ritz in Paris, the avenues in Spain and France named for him, and the annual writing awards and even imitation contests—all of these honors betoken a life lived "all the way up," as Jake says in *The Sun Also Rises* (18), and art that has begun to enjoy immortality. His face on a postage stamp and his papers housed at the John F. Kennedy Library are signs that his cultural and literary reputations are secure.

The Sun Also Rises is not exclusively responsible for all of this recognition, but certainly the novel contributed to the public's first view of Hemingway, which was as a serious artist and as a character in a roman à clef. The initial sensation was literary, biographical, and cultural, and in each of these categories the changes wrought were profound and lasting. Literary critics, while divided about the appropriateness of Hemingway's subject matter, were nearly unanimous in acknowledging the effective new style of his novel. Unlike his predecessors, Hemingway revealed character mainly through dialogue and action, limiting his interior monologue and reserving his exposition for the landscape. The reticence of his characters and their "hard-boiled" attitudes have been imitated by generations of writers. Thematically, his novel confronts the controversial issues of its day—including prohibition, World War I and its aftermath, sexual mores, and the religious debate that pitted fundamental beliefs against their more modern counterparts. His protagonist, Jake Barnes, was hardly a hero in the traditional sense: he loses the girl, the fight, and his status among the aficionados. Hemingway's successful battles over the

Sketch of Hemingway by John Blomshield, which appeared on the dust jacket of the first edition of *The Sun Also Rises*

use of particular words also made using all of the words available to them easier for artists who followed.

When the models for the characters of *The Sun Also Rises* faded from view in the 1930s, the novel was read as a "period piece" depicting the "lost generation" that was cut loose from its moral and spiritual moorings by World War I. At the same time, readers began to pursue its relation to the myth of the Fisher King and its "code" hero. By the 1950s *The Sun Also Rises* was widely seen as a study of the exhaustion of the postwar generation that left the characters—as the epigraph had left the wind, rain, and sun—just as it found them. Not until the 1970s did revisionist readings inject a note of optimism, suggesting that the events of the novel have taught Jake and Brett that, although they have no future as lovers, they do have a genuine friendship that they might continue to cultivate. Brett, who for half a century was regarded as an alcoholic nymphomaniac and a bitch, rose in stature among readers to the point that one commentator cogently argues that the novel rightfully belongs to her and not to Jake.[1]

"Good writing is true writing. If a man is making a story up it will be true in proportion to the amount of knowledge of life that he has and how conscientious he is; so that when he makes something up it is as it would truly be. If he doesn't know how many people work in their minds and actions his luck may save him for a while, or he may write fantasy. But if he continues to write about what he does not know about he will find himself faking. After he fakes a few times he cannot write honestly any more."

Ernest Hemingway

From "Monologue to the Maestro: A High Seas Letter," *Esquire* (October 1935): 21.

The Sun Also Rises changed Hemingway's life, as well. Before the novel, he was well known among the expatriates, who were significant but relatively few in number. After 22 October 1926 his novel and his name were forever a part of the public domain. A sketch of the author, which appeared on the dust jacket of the first edition (others appeared thereafter on even more widely circulated paperbacks), assured that his countenance would become as universally recognized as his name and his works. Hemingway, of course, welcomed and encouraged such recognition. A man who intends to earn his living by writing books must necessarily court his audience. Yet, he must also produce his art in relative solitude. To achieve this solitude, Hemingway took up residence at the margin of America—Key West, Florida—then on an island still further removed from the mainstream in Cuba, and finally in sparsely populated Ketchum, Idaho. After *The Sun Also Rises,* Hemingway was no longer just a journalist turned fiction writer from the Midwest; he was the spokesman for the Lost Generation, and his style became one of the distinctive elements of American literature.

American culture, too, was changed by Hemingway's first novel. Malcolm Cowley remembers college girls in the 1920s "modeling themselves after Lady Brett" and young men from the Midwest "trying to be Hemingway heroes, talking in tough understatements from the sides of their mouths."[2] According to Richmond Barrett, the novel became a guide for living. Students "learned it by heart and, deserting their families and running away from college, immediately took ship to Paris to be the disciples of the new faith under the awnings of the Dôme and the Rotonde and the other sidewalk cafes."[3] Of course, he influenced more than the manners of college students, as Alfred Kazin explains: he supplied themes, an attitude toward life, and a standard of craftsmanship:

"If a writer of prose knows enough about what he is writing about he may omit things that he knows and the reader, if the writer is writing truly enough, will have a feeling of those things as strongly as though the writer had stated them. The dignity of movement of an iceberg is due to only one-eighth of it being above water."

Ernest Hemingway

From *Death in the Afternoon* (New York: Scribners, 1932), p. 192.

> Technically and morally Hemingway was to have a profound influence on the writing of the thirties. As a stylist and craftsman his example was magnetic on younger men who came after him; as the progenitor of the new and distinctively American cult of violence, he stands out as the greatest single influence on the hard-boiled novel of the thirties, and certainly affected the social and the left-wing fiction of the period more than some of its writers could easily admit. No one save Dreiser in an earlier period had anything like Hemingway's dominance over American fiction, yet even Dreiser meant largely an example of courage and frankness during the struggle for realism, not a standard of craftsmanship and a persuasive conception of life, like Hemingway's.[4]

John W. Aldridge captures the sense of Hemingway's literary and personal presence for his peers:

> For members of my generation, the young men born between 1918, roughly, and 1924, there was a special charm about Hemingway. By the time most of us were old enough to read him he had become a legendary figure, a kind of twentieth-century Lord Byron; and like Byron, he had learned to play himself, his own best hero, with superb conviction. . . . But even without the legend he created around himself . . . his impact upon us was tremendous. The feeling he gave us was one of immense expansiveness and freedom and, at the same time, of absolute stability and control. We could put our whole faith in him and he would not fail us. We could follow him, ape his manner, his cold detachment, through all the doubts and fears of adolescence and come out pure and untouched.[5]

The "Hemingway time," for Aldridge, was not the 1920s but the 1930s, and it "was a good time to be young."[6] Subsequent generations, as well, have found their "Hemingway time," a moment when his works or example influenced their attitudes toward art or love or life.

American humorist David Ogden Stewart, one of the originals for Bill Gorton in *The Sun Also Rises*

Not only did the novel offer a model for speech and behavior; it also introduced readers to Spain and its bullfight, to Paris and its Left Bank. Visitors may retrace Hemingway's footsteps using John Leland's *A Guide to Hemingway's Paris* and Noel Riley Fitch's *Walks in Hemingway's Paris;* Hemingway figures prominently in Fitch's *Literary Cafés of Paris.* Parisians continue to commemorate Hemingway by naming streets and bars in his honor, and a plaque outside of Hemingway's apartment at 74, rue du Cardinal-Lemoine commemorates the time and words he invested in Paris.

However, *The Sun Also Rises* changed Spain more than it did France. The running of the bulls in Pamplona was, when Hemingway first witnessed it in 1923, a rural festival attended by so few foreigners that the visitors were singled out for thanks—"Hurray for the Foreigners!" (158)—in the novel. The bullfight, too, was hardly known and less understood by Westerners when Hemingway introduced it to the reading public in 1926. All of that changed. When Hemingway returned to Pamplona while writing what was to become *The Dangerous Summer* (1985), he observed:

> Pamplona was rough as always, overcrowded with tourists and characters, but with a hard core of all that is fine in Navarre. For a week we averaged something over three hours sleep a night to the pounding of the war drums of Navarre, the piping of old tunes and the dancers swirling and leaping. I've written about Pamplona once and for keeps. It is all there as it always was except forty thousand tourists have been added. There were not twenty tourists when I first went there nearly four decades ago. Now on some days they say there are close to a hundred thousand in the town.[7]

Some growth in the provincial fiesta was inevitable, but that American college students flock yearly to Pamplona to run with the bulls is attributable to Hemingway and *The Sun Also Rises*. Unlike such summer visitors, Hemingway was, in the words of the Spanish writer Salvador de Madariage "no longer the gaping tourist, the go-getter businessman, the Protestant ever ready to frown at Catholic superstition, the progressive commiserating on backward Spain."[8] In fact, Madariage adds, he "may well have been the non-Spaniard who of all time has come closest to the core of this strange form of Spanish life."[9] Edward F. Stanton asserts that "it would be almost impossible to conceive of Hemingway without Spain"; however, for many American readers, the inverse is also true: Spain has come alive for them through Hemingway's *The Sun Also Rises, Death in the Afternoon, For Whom the Bell Tolls,* several short stories, and his coverage of the Spanish Civil War.[10]

Hemingway is, for biographer Michael Reynolds, "an authentic artifact, a piece of the continent, an American author whose career changed the face of fiction."[11] Hemingway's career and his novel that launched it have become part of the international landscape and remain linked, in bronze and stone, to the places that his words brought to life.

NOTES

1. Linda Patterson Miller, "Brett Ashley: The Beauty of It All," in *Critical Essays on Ernest Hemingway's The Sun Also Rises,* edited by James Nagel (New York: G. K. Hall, 1995), pp. 170–184.

2. Malcolm Cowley, *Exile's Return: A Literary Odyssey of the 1920s* (Harmondsworth, U.K.: Penguin, 1976), pp. 225–226.

3. Richmond Barrett, "Babes in the Bois," *Harper's*, 66 (May 1928): 724, quoted in John Raeburn, *Fame Became of Him: Hemingway as Public Writer* (Bloomington: Indiana University Press, 1984), p. 22.

4. Alfred Kazin, *On Native Grounds: An Interpretation of Modern Prose Literature* (Garden City, N.Y.: Doubleday, 1956), p. 265.

5 John W. Aldridge, *After the Lost Generation: A Critical Study of the Writers of Two Wars* (New York: McGraw-Hill, 1951), pp. 23–25.

6. Ibid., p. 25.

7. Ernest Hemingway, *The Dangerous Summer* (New York: Scribners, 1985), p. 136.

8. Salvador de Madariage, "The World Weighs a Writer's Influence," *Saturday Review*, 44 (29 July 1961): 18, quoted in Allen Josephs, "Hemingway's Spanish Sensibility," in *The Cambridge Companion to Hemingway*, edited by Scott Donaldson (Cambridge: Cambridge University Press, 1996), p. 234.

9. Ibid.

10. Edward F. Stanton, *Hemingway and Spain: A Pursuit* (Seattle: University of Washington Press, 1989), p. xii.

11. Michael Reynolds, "Hemingway as American Icon," *Picturing Hemingway: A Writer in His Time*, edited by Frederick Voss (New Haven: Yale University Press, 1999), p. 9.

ADAPTATIONS OF *THE SUN ALSO RISES*

MOVIE AND TELEVISION ADAPTATIONS

More than fifty movie, stage, television, and radio adaptations of Hemingway's works have appeared, including a movie (1957) and a television version (1984) of *The Sun Also Rises*.[1] Neither production was particularly satisfying from a literary scholar's perspective, but the earlier production, though it "fails to catch the excitement and haunted gaiety of the book," manages to "stick admirably close to the novel."[2]

The movie version of *The Sun Also Rises*, by 20th-Century Fox, was produced by Darryl F. Zanuck and directed by Henry King. Peter Viertel wrote the screenplay. The movie stars Tyrone Power as Jake Barnes, Ava Gardner as Brett Ashley, Mel Ferrer as Robert Cohn, Eddie Albert as Bill Gorton, Errol Flynn as Mike Campbell, Gregory Ratoff as Count Mippipopolous, Juliette Greco as Georgette, Marcel Dalio as Zizi, Henry Daniell as the "doctor," Bob Cunningham as Wilson-Harris, Danik Patisson as "the girl," Robert Evans as Romero, Eduardo Noriega as Mr. Braddocks, Jacqueline Evans as Mrs. Braddocks, Carlos Muzquiz as Juanito Montoya, Rebecca Iturbi as Frances Clyne, and Carlos David Ortigos as "Romero's manager."

Peter Viertel's script manages to include most of the important scenes from the book and some of the dialogue.[3] Jake's impotence and Romero's heroism are depicted well; yet, much of the nuance, such as the contrast between the complications of Paris and the simplicity of Burguete, is absent. Brett's "predatory aspects" are captured by Ava Gardner, but Gardner "simply doesn't, or can't, convey the lady's innate, poignant air of breeding."[4] Zanuck's production focuses on the major characters, and critic Hugh Ford explains what is lost by omitting the minor characters.[5] Without Harvey Stone, viewers miss the opportunity to see the latent antagonism between Jake and Robert. By eliminating the homosexuals from the scene at *bal musette*, the movie prevents a glimpse of the sexual incomplete-

Le Rotonde, a Paris café popular with expatriates

ness of Brett and Jake. Without the scene involving Woolsey and Krum, viewers fail to observe Jake in his professional environment. Likewise, the movie omits Frances's annihilation of Cohn at the Café Select. The depiction of Paris is wanting as well, for director Henry King "decided to present a tinsel touristy Paris, garnished with spicy romantic nonsense that would satisfy a gullible public. King's Paris is an embarrassment of poverty, a colossal Busch Gardens."[6] The movie also fails "to convey the characters' mental and moral fatigue, their feelings of futility, ennui, that spiritual bankruptcy that haunts Mike."[7]

Q: "What is your own attitude toward writing for Hollywood?"

A: "Never done it."

Ernest Hemingway

From "Hemingway in the Afternoon," *Time,* 50 (4 August 1947): 80.

The two-part television play of *The Sun Also Rises* by NBC 20th-Century Fox was produced by John Furia and directed by James Goldstone. Credit for writing went to Hemingway and Robert L. Joseph. Hart Bochner stars as Jake Barnes, Jane Seymour as Brett Ashley, Robert Carradine as Robert Cohn, Zeljko Ivanek as Bill Gorton, Ian Charleson as Mike Campbell, and Leonard Nimoy as Count Mippipopolous.

Frank M. Laurence's scene-by-scene breakdown of the television version reveals that forty-two of eighty-three scenes from the NBC version are not related to the novel.[8] Instead of being a wounded aviator, Jake is depicted as an infantryman who suffers a grenade wound. Hemingway's gregarious Bill Gorton is cast as a sullen and moody aviator who continues thrill seeking after the war. He dies in Jake's arms, if not by suicide then by taking suicidal risks in pushing his plane past its limits. NBC's Romero saves Brett from having her throat cut by Count Mippipopolous (a Russian court-assassin for Czar Nicholas) by stabbing him with a killing sword. NBC's plot is only tangentially related to Hemingway's novel; moreover, instead of the dialogue that Hemingway made famous, NBC supplies exclamations such as "Applesauce!" suitable for prime-time audiences. Discussing the poor reviews that greeted the miniseries, a representative of the network asserted that "*The Sun Also Rises* could not find an audience because 'it is a classic, it has an episodic nature, it is more a portrait of an era than a story with a beginning, a middle, and an end.'"[9] The screenwriter, Robert L. Joseph, defended his divergence from the text by saying "Hemingway's novel is a great set, but nothing happens."[10]

NOTES

1. For a comprehensive list of adaptations see *Ernest Hemingway A to Z: The Essential Reference of His Life and Work*, by Charles M. Oliver (New York: Facts on File, 1999), pp. 398–399.
2. Review of the movie *The Sun Also Rises*, "Hemingway's Lost Souls," *Life* (16 September 1957): 61–66.
3. See Gene D. Phillips, *Hemingway and Film* (New York: Ungar, 1980), p. 125 ff.
4. Review of the movie *The Sun Also Rises*, "Hemingway Classic," *New York Times* (24 August 1957): 12.
5. Hugh Ford, "Hemingway's Hollywood Paris," in *A Moving Picture Feast: The Filmgoer's Hemingway*, edited by Charles M. Oliver (New York: Praeger, 1989), pp. 114–121.
6. Ibid., p. 118.
7. Ibid., p. 119.
8. Frank M. Laurence, "*The Sun Also Rises:* The NBC Version," in *A Moving Picture Feast: The Filmgoer's Hemingway*, edited by Charles M. Oliver (New York: Praeger, 1989), pp. 91–113.
9. Anne Tremblay, "Taking Some Liberties with *The Sun Also Rises*," *New York Times* (26 August 1984): sec. 2, p. 23.
10. Ibid.

RESOURCES FOR STUDY OF *THE SUN ALSO RISES*

STUDY QUESTIONS

BOOK I, CHAPTERS I–II

1. Identify the point of view of the novel. What are the advantages and disadvantages of this point of view? What specific details from the narrative generate trust or suspicion about the narrator? How might this story be different if it were written from another point of view?

2. Identify the narrator's tone (his attitude toward subject or character). Does he admire Robert Cohn? Identify details that reveal the author's feeling toward Robert. Why does Jake devote the first two chapters of the novel to a description of Robert?

3. Describe the narrator's personality. Does he seem content? Cynical? Honest? What details lead you to your conclusion?

4. Consider the setting (place and time in the story). What details reveal the setting and how are they important?

5. Judging from the conversation at the Café de Versailles (end of chapter I), explain what causes tension in the relationship between Cohn and Frances Clyne.

6. In chapter II Robert and Jake begin a discussion in Jake's office that continues in a café. What do readers learn about the different ambitions and values of each man through their conversation?

CHAPTER III

1. Georgette tells Jake "Everybody's sick. I'm sick, too" (23). Describe her personality and explain what she means by "sick." Why does she believe that everyone is sick?

2. The scene at the *bal musette* involves several ironies surrounding Jake, Georgette, Brett, and the group of men with whom Brett arrives. Identify these ironies and explain their significance.

3. Describe Brett's physical appearance and her manner of speaking. In her brief conversation with Jake, what do we learn about their relationship?

4. What effect does the sight of Brett Ashley have upon Robert?

CHAPTER IV

1. What do we learn about Brett and Jake as they ride in the taxi together? What causes conflict in their relationship?

2. After Jake leaves Brett at the Café Select with Count Mippipopolous, he returns to his room and reads his mail, including a bank statement and a wedding invitation. Explain the significance of the two themes, money and love, to this point in the novel.

3. During the ensuing interior monologue, Jake reveals some of his passions as well as his "old grievance" (38). Explain the sources of Jake's joys and sorrow.

4. When Brett visits Jake at half-past four in the morning, she tells him that Count Mippipopolous is "one of us" (40). What does she mean by this statement?

CHAPTER V

1. This chapter opens with a description of Jake's observations. What does he see en route to his office? How does he differ from the tourists he sees on the street?

2. Contrast Jake with Woolsey and Krum, fellow journalists who share a cab with Jake as they return from a press conference.

3. During lunch at Wetzel's, Robert and Jake have another conversation that further differentiates them from one another. How does Jake characterize Brett? Does Robert accept Jake's assessment of her? Explain why or why not.

CHAPTER VI

1. When Brett fails to appear for her date at the Crillon with Jake, we are reminded of their earlier exchange: "Try and be there," says Jake. "Don't worry," Brett replies, "I've never let you down, have I?" To this, Jake replies "Heard from Mike?" (37). How do Brett's actions later in this chapter help us to interpret this earlier conversation with Jake?

2. Drunken and unshaven, Harvey Stone is friendly to Jake but nasty to Robert. What does Stone represent and why does he dislike Robert?

3. When Frances Clyne takes Jake aside to explain that her relationship with Robert is ending, what does she identify as the cause of their break-up? What do we learn about her feelings for Robert and her personal ambitions?

4. As Frances berates Robert, he remains silent. What does this behavior suggest about him? What is Jake's response to this bitter scene?

CHAPTER VII

1. After Brett sends the count for champagne, Jake and Brett engage in a conversation that reveals much about their affection for each other. Explain their feelings.

2. The count and Brett do most of the talking during the evening. The count insists that one must "get to know the values" (67); what "values" are suggested in his dialogue?

3. The last stop is Zelli's, where Brett and Jake dance. What accounts for Brett's feeling "miserable" (70) and pushing Jake away as he kisses her goodnight?

BOOK II, CHAPTERS VIII–IX

1. Characterize Jake's friend Bill Gorton. What does his explanation of the Vienna prizefight reveal about him? Describe his humor; does it seem to be aimed at people, institutions, or ideas?

2. Identify Mike Campbell's chief attributes. What do we learn about Mike from his own speech and actions? What do we learn about him through others?

3. What is Jake's response when he learns that Brett has been to San Sebastián with Robert?

4. Sharing a compartment on the train with Bill and Jake are a couple from Montana and their son, Hubert. What values do these Americans represent?

CHAPTER X

1. As Jake, Bill, and Robert ride in their rented car from Burguete to Pamplona, Jake carefully records his observations. What does he see? How do Bill and Robert respond to the scenery?

2. What does Robert say to irritate Bill and Jake during lunch at the Montoya?

3. What specific reasons does Jake offer to explain his hatred for Robert?

CHAPTERS XI–XII

1. Describe the atmosphere on the bus as Bill and Jake leave Pamplona for Burguete. How does this journey differ from the train ride from Paris to Bayonne?
2. During breakfast at the inn in Burguete, Bill teases Jake about being "an expatriate" (120). Does Jake actually fit Bill's description of expatriates?
3. When Jake stops fishing, he reads an A. E. W. Mason story. In what ways is the complication of that story similar to the conflict in Hemingway's novel?
4. Explain Bill's humorous discussion of the chicken and the egg. Why does he "reverse the order" (126) for William Jennings Bryan's sake? (See Glossary)
5. Jake and Bill joke about many things during lunch. Using the Glossary to identify the people and universities, identify the objects of their humor.
6. This portion of the novel seems calm and uncomplicated. What makes it so?

CHAPTER XIII

1. Characterize Wilson-Harris. Why do he, Bill, and Jake develop a friendship so quickly? How does their camaraderie reveal itself?
2. The friendship between Jake and Montoya is based on Jake's status as an aficionado. Define this term and explain the importance of aficionados to Montoya.
3. Jake explains that the steers play an important role in the unloading of the bulls. Explain the relationship between the bulls and the steers. In what ways is this relationship analogous to the interactions among the expatriates?
4. In response to Robert's question "Were you in the war, Mike?" (139) Brett's fiancé relates a humorous anecdote about giving away another man's war medals. What does Mike's story reveal about him and his attitude toward his military service?
5. Explain Brett's reaction to the first unloadings. What impresses her? How does Jake help her to appreciate what she sees?
6. Not long after Mike berates Robert for following Brett around like a steer, the expatriates reconvene for dinner, which Jake describes as "a

very pleasant meal" with "such nice people" (150). Is Jake's tone here serious or ironic? Explain.

CHAPTERS XIV–XV

1. Hearing Brett and Mike laughing in the hotel room next door, Jake has difficulty falling asleep and begins reflecting on his personal philosophy. Describe Jake's "fine philosophy" (152). Does it seem realistic or idealistic? Jake reveals much about himself through interior monologues; are these details consistent with his external actions?
2. How does each of the expatriates spend his or her days in Pamplona prior to the beginning of the fiesta? What do their activities suggest about them?
3. Describe the opening of the fiesta and contrast it to the preceding day.
4. A group of *riau-riau* dancers attach themselves to the expatriates and lead them to a wineshop. How does this quasi-religious festival contrast with the pilgrimage to Lourdes made by the Americans from Ohio in chapter IX?
5. How is Robert's status as an outsider reinforced in the scene in the wineshop?
6. Why does Montoya invite Jake to meet Pedro Romero? What are Jake's impressions of the young matador?
7. Explain why Jake admires Romero's performance on the second day.

CHAPTER XVI

1. Having received a request to invite Pedro Romero and Marcial Lalanda to the Grand Hotel to have coffee with the American ambassador and his entourage, Montoya solicits Jake's opinion. What is Jake's advice and how does Montoya respond to it? What do their actions and reactions suggest about them?
2. In the dining room, Jake again encounters Romero; their discussion of bulls is interrupted first by Brett and then by Mike. What conflict is developing and who is aware of it?
3. After Romero leaves, Mike again tells Robert that he is not wanted. Why does Mike select this moment for his outburst?
4. Explain the role of Edna, Bill's friend from Biarritz.
5. When Brett discovers that she is in love with Romero, she asks Jake for help. Why does she seek Jake's assistance and what is his response?

CHAPTER XVII

1. Bill, Mike, and Edna are removed from the Bar Milano by the police in an episode that Edna finds hilarious. What serious feelings lie beneath the surface of this episode?
2. Minutes later, at the Café Suizo, Robert accosts Jake and calls him a "damned pimp" (194). To what extent is his accusation true?
3. After knocking Jake out, Robert begs for forgiveness. Does Jake finally forgive him? Why or why not?
4. After knocking out Jake, Robert intrudes on Romero and Brett. What transpires in this encounter and how does it shape our perception of Brett, Romero, and Cohn?
5. The following morning Vincente Girones is fatally gored while running with the bulls. Jake mentions this fact to a waiter and to Bill. Contrast their responses.
6. Mike reveals some background information about Brett's husband, Lord Ashley. How does this new information affect readers' attitudes toward Brett?

CHAPTER XVIII

1. After rejoining the expatriates for lunch the following day, Brett leaves with Jake. Where does she propose that they go and why? What accounts for her sudden concern for the wind?
2. Back at the hotel, Montoya passes Jake and Brett on the stairs and says nothing. Why is he silent?
3. Jake describes Belmonte's performance in the bullring as "very good" (217) but ultimately less satisfying than Romero's. Why is the older fighter insulted by the crowd?
4. Describe Romero's style of fighting and killing bulls that so impresses the crowd.

BOOK III, CHAPTER XIX

1. After the fiesta concludes, Mike, Bill, and Jake prepare to go in separate directions and roll poker dice to determine who pays for the drinks. What does Bill finally learn about Mike in this scene?
2. Alone in Bayonne, Jake spends a quiet evening considering his upcoming time in San Sebastián. Examine the paragraph that begins "At a newspaper kiosque . . ." (236) and list the qualities of San Sebastián that seem attractive to Jake.
3. What does Jake enjoy most about his time in San Sebastián?

4. Jake and the manager of a French team share a long conversation about cycling, but Jake ultimately decides not to rise early the next morning to see the riders depart. Compare and contrast French cycling and Spanish bullfighting. Is Jake likely to come to view cycling as "the greatest sporting event in the world"? Why or why not?
5. Jake observes a young couple floating upon a raft in San Sebastián just as in chapter VIII he has noticed a man and a girl "walking with their arms around each other." How does the vision of the two couples affect Jake?
6. Do readers expect Jake to answer his summons to retrieve Brett from Madrid? Why or why not?
7. Why has Brett decided to send Romero away? Does this action suggest that Brett's character has developed? Why or why not?
8. In what ways did Romero propose to change Brett and why?
9. Dining at Botín's, Jake consumes a great deal of alcohol whereas Brett scarcely drinks. Is this merely a coincidence or does it suggest a change in their characters?
10. In response to Brett's observation "You like to eat, don't you?" Jake replies, "I like to do a lot of things" (250–251). What does Jake mean by this remark?
11. Explicate Jake's closing line, "Isn't it pretty to think so?" (251).

GLOSSARY OF LITERARY TERMS

Allusion: a figure of speech making casual reference to a famous historical or literary figure or event that readers are expected to relate to the current context.

Archetype: an image, detail, pattern, or character type that recurs in literature, myth, religion, or folklore and is therefore believed to evoke profound emotions in the reader.

Double entendre: (double meaning) intentional ambiguity, often sexual in nature and intended to be humorous.

Existentialism: a philosophy centered upon the analysis of existence and stressing the individual's responsibility for his or her own choices.

Hedonism: a philosophical doctrine stating that pleasure is the chief good of man; generally associated with sensual gratification.

Iceberg theory: Hemingway explains in an interview with George Plimpton (see Critical Excerpts): "If it is any use to know it, I always try to write on the principle of the iceberg. There is seven eighths of it under water for every part that shows. Anything you know you can eliminate and it only strengthens your iceberg. It is the part that doesn't show. If a writer omits something because he does not know it, then there is a hole in the story."

Image: a single mental creation that amalgamates several of the impressions of one or more senses.

In medias res: opening a narrative in the middle of the action and then supplying background information.

Irony: a broad term referring to the recognition of a reality different from the masking appearance.

Metaphor: an implied analogy that imaginatively identifies one object with another and ascribes to the first one or more of the qualities of the second, or invests the first with emotional or imaginative qualities associated with the second.

Modernism: a conscious break with traditional themes and techniques characterizing the years 1910–1930. Responding in part to changing technology, modern psychology, and the perceived increase in the complexity of life, modernists sought to "make it new," a phrase that meant experimentation, stream of consciousness and objective narration, and emphasis on showing rather than telling.

Motif: recurrent images, words, objects, phrases, or actions that tend to unify a literary work.

Nihilism: an attitude or doctrine that regards traditional values and beliefs as unfounded and existence as senseless and useless.

Objective correlative: a pattern of objects, actions, or events; or a situation that can serve effectively to awaken in the reader the emotional response that the author desires without being a direct statement of that emotion. Poet T. S. Eliot popularized this expression in his essay "Hamlet and His Problems" (1919).

Roman à clef: a novel in which actual persons and events are presented under the guise of fiction.

Tone: the attitude that the writer takes toward his subject, characters, or audience.

GLOSSARY OF UNFAMILIAR WORDS OR TERMS IN *THE SUN ALSO RISES*

Absinthe: a green aromatic liquor made with anise and wormwood that is 68% alcohol and has a bitter, licorice flavor; harmful to the central nervous system, it is now banned in most Western countries.

Afición: passion, fondness, or liking for; especially, passion for bullfighting.

Aguardiente: (unmatured) brandy distilled on the Isla de Margarita in the Caribbean Sea, a part of Venezuela.

Arrobas: a weight of about 25 pounds or 11.5 kilograms.

Ayuntamiento: a corporation or body of magistrates, a town council.

Bal Musette: a dancing club.

Barreras: ringside seats in a bullring.

Bois: the Bois de Boulogne, a park on the west side of Paris by the Seine, famous for its restaurants and cafés.

Carabineers: soldiers armed with carbines, which are short-barreled, lightweight rifles.

Centime: the hundredth part of a franc.

Cogida: gore, goring.

Col: French term for a mountain pass; separates the French from the Spanish landscape in Chapter 10.

Comment: how, in what manner, why, wherefore.

Consigne: cloakroom.

Cornada: thrust with a bull's horn, gore.

Darb: a slang term for a person or thing that is remarkable or superior.

Desencajondada: context (136 of *The Sun Also Rises*) suggests that this term refers to the unloading of bulls.

Encierro: Hemingway says in *Death in the Afternoon* (1932): "In Pamplona the running of the bulls through the streets with the crowd running ahead of them from the corral and the edge of the town into and through the bullring into the corral of the ring. The bulls to be fought in the afternoon are run through the streets at seven o'clock in the morning of the day they are fought."

Fiacre: a hackney coach; a horse-drawn cab.

Flamenco: Flemish; an Andalusian gypsy; a flashy, ostentatious, cocky individual.

Flapper: an unconventional woman of the 1920s who often worked outside of the home, drank and smoked in public, kept her own hours, and flouted the prevailing sexual mores.

Flemish: the Germanic language of the Flemings, who are members of a Germanic people inhabiting chiefly northern Belgium.

Fonda: an inn or eating house.

Kepi: a military hat, peak cap.

Liège: a province in East Belgium.

Lost Generation: after World War I, the many writers and artists who, unhappy in America, became expatriates, residing in Europe and especially Paris, where living was cheaper. The phrase is attributed to Gertrude

Stein in the first epigraph of *The Sun Also Rises;* soon came to describe this disillusioned group of expatriated artists who had participated in World War I.

Paseo: a social stroll whereby young people meet in Spain.

Pelouse: the grass within the racetrack.

Pernod: a green aromatic anise- and licorice-flavored liqueur first produced by Henri-Louis Pernod in 1797.

Pesage: weighing-in room; paddock at a racetrack.

Peseta: bronze coin equal to 100 centimos.

Posada: an inn.

Snappers: shortened from "mackerel-snapper"; a derogatory term for Roman Catholics.

Sol, sol y sombra, sombra: sol: sun, sunlight, day; sombra: shade.

Tromper: to deceive, to be unfaithful to.

Zizi: slang term for penis, according to Robert E. Fleming in "The Fun Also Rises: A Tribute to Jim Hinkle," *Hemingway Review* (1993).

GLOSSARY OF HISTORICAL EVENTS, PEOPLE, AND PLACES*

Alexander Hamilton Institute: founded in 1914 and lasting for over seventy years, it published books on management, investments, and business; named for the first secretary of the Treasury, who was a supporter of a strong central government.

Alger, Horatio, Jr.: American novelist who wrote about 125 popular books for children, all based on the premise that if a boy works hard and eschews temptation, he will rise to power. Ragged Dick and Tattered Tom were two of his protagonists.

Bonaparte: patent-leather hat.

Bryan, William Jennings: American orator and politician who favored the silver standard, was a pacifist who opposed American participation in World War I, supported Prohibition, and argued for a fundamentalist reading of the Bible. He ran for U.S. President on the Democratic ticket in 1896, 1900, and 1908 and was defeated three times.

Burguete: a town in the Pyrenees Mountains of northern Spain that is about twenty-four miles north of Pamplona.

* The sources of many details in this glossary are Miriam Mandel's *Reading Hemingway: The Facts in the Fictions* (Metuchen, N.J.: Scarecrow Press, 1995) and Charles M. Oliver's *Ernest Hemingway A to Z: The Essential Reference of his Life and Work* (New York: Facts on File, 1999).

Circe: in Greek legend, a dangerous enchantress who turned men into swine.

"The Colonel's Lady and Judy O'Grady": in Rudyard Kipling's poem "The Ladies," the speaker entreats the reader to "learn about women from me" and concludes, "For the Colonel's Lady an' Judy O'Grady / Are sisters under their skins!" a phrase that Bill Gorton jokingly modifies.

Crillon: luxury hotel located on the Place de la Concorde.

Davis, Jefferson: president of the Confederacy from 1862 to 1865, the duration of the Civil War.

Dempsey, William Harrison "Jack": American world heavyweight champion from 1919 through 1926; toured Europe in 1926; lost the title to Gene Tunney in 1926 in a match in Philadelphia and lost in a rematch against Tunney in 1927 in Chicago. He was the first boxer to draw a million-dollar gate.

Dingo: bar on the rue Delambre, behind the boulevard Montparnasse; a favorite Hemingway rendezvous.

Dôme: popular café in Paris on the boulevard Montparnasse near its intersection with the boulevard Raspail; favorite of the expatriates.

Dun reports, R. G.: reports supplying information about the strength of American businesses for creditors and investors.

Flowers, Tiger ("The Georgia Deacon"): African American boxer and world middleweight champion in 1926.

Foyots: rated the best restaurant in the Latin Quarter by Baedeker.

Franc: Prades rate of exchange.

France, Anatole: French novelist, literary critic, and influential man of letters; won the Nobel Prize in 1921.

Kid Francis (Francisco Buonaugrio): French bantamweight boxer born in 1907 who fought Charles Ledoux on 9 June 1924.

Fratellinis: Italian family of clowns and horseback performers who were popular between the world wars.

Fritsch (Frisch), Frankie: American baseball player and manager who played for Fordham University and the New York Giants; was elected to baseball's Hall of Fame in 1947.

Hardy, Thomas: English novelist and poet, known for novels set in rural England.

Hoffenheimer: a fictionalized version of a friend of H. L. Mencken, American novelist Joseph Hergesheimer, whose name was used in the manuscript.

Hudson, W. H.: English naturalist and writer whose novel *The Purple Land that England Lost* (1885) features romantic but improbable adventures.

Jacob (of Genesis): son of Isaac, he is a wanderer who goes to great lengths to secure his love, Rachel, with whom he has thirteen children. He wrestles all night with the Lord, who strikes Jacob's thigh, causing the sinew to shrink.

James, Henry: an American short-story writer, novelist, and essayist about whom Jake and Bill joke; possibly rendered impotent as the result of an accident.

K.K.K.: the Ku Klux Klan; founded in Tennessee after the Civil War to advocate white supremacy; active in the 1920s, when Klansmen lynched blacks and terrorized Catholics and Jews.

Ledoux, Charles ("Kid Ledoux"): French boxer who was European featherweight champion from 1920 to 1924 and on 9 June 1924 lost to Kid Francis, fifteen years his junior.

Left Bank: Bohemian section of Paris on the Seine where many artists and writers lived.

Lenglen, Suzanne: a highly competitive French lawn-tennis player who won many championships, including Wimbledon.

Lourdes: the town in the Pyrenees Mountains where, in 1858, Bernadette Soubirious saw a vision of the Virgin Mary several times. Bernadette had recently been canonized at the time Hemingway wrote *The Sun Also Rises.*

Manning, Bishop: conservative and controversial Episcopal bishop of New York in 1921; opposed the marriage of divorced persons and had strong views against divorce. Jake and Bill joke that they have studied with Manning, an impossibility since Manning was a generation older and would have had no contact with the Catholic institution Loyola.

Marlowe, Christopher: a dramatist and poet of the English Renaissance who was admired by William Shakespeare. When joking about the taxidermist, Gorton makes an allusion to Marlowe's *The Jew of Malta* (first performed 1592, published 1633).

Mason, A. E. W.: Jake reads this Englishman's story "The Crystal Trench" from *The Four Corners of the World* (1917), in which a young husband is killed in a climbing accident and his bride vows to wait twenty-four years for the crevasse to give up the body—waiting, too, is a young man who has fallen in love with her. When the body reappears, it bears a locket with another woman's picture in it.

McGinty flies: a lure used by Bill for trout fishing.

Mencken, H. L.: American writer, journalist, editor, and critic whose views of American democracy and culture were controversial and usually in opposition to prevailing notions.

Miura (bulls): a breed of bulls famous for their bravery.

Mumms [Mumm], Baron: nobleman whose family, German Protestants who never became French citizens, began producing champagne in 1827 but saw their firm confiscated by the French government during World War I.

Ney, Marshal: French military hero who fought Napoleon's rear-guard action in Russia, was known for his bravery, and was one of the original sixteen marshals of France.

Primo de Rivera: Spanish lawyer, soldier, and politician who in 1923 took over the Spanish government as dictator until he was exiled in 1930.

Riff: the disputed territory along the coast of Morocco colonized by Spain and France; the Riff War (1919–1926) was fought between the Spanish and the Moroccan Riff and Jibala tribes. France joined the war in 1925 on the side of Spain; the Arab leader, Abd el-Krim, surrendered to Spain in 1926.

Right Bank: section of Paris on the Seine where the luxury hotels are located.

Roncesvalles (Roncevaux in France): monastery in the Pyrenees Mountains, thirty miles northeast of Pamplona, where Roland, fighting rear guard for Charlemagne, died in 778.

Rotonde: popular café in Paris on the boulevard Montparnasse near its intersection with the boulevard Raspail; favorite of the expatriates.

San Fermín: second-century Spanish prelate who, with Francisco Javier, has been patron saint of the province of Navarre. The first bishop of Pamplona, he was martyred by being beheaded, an action symbolically represented by the red neckerchiefs worn by participants in the fiesta.

Scott, Dred: an African American slave, Scott lived with his owner in free territory but, at the time of his owner's death, they were living in slave territory. Because Scott had lived so long in free territory, he sued for his freedom; however, in 1856–1857, the U.S. Supreme Court denied that Scott had any civil rights.

Select: popular café in Paris on the boulevard Montparnasse near its intersection with the boulevard Raspail; favorite of the expatriates.

Stein, Gertrude: an important experimental writer and art collector. Her remark about the "lost generation," which was included as an epigraph of the novel, was later attributed to the owner of the garage that serviced her car.

Turgenieff, Ivan: Russian novelist and short-story writer whose collection *A Sportsman's Sketches* (1852) realistically and sympathetically describes the conditions of Russian peasant life.

Wheeler, Wayne B.: an American lawyer and prohibitionist, he defended the constitutionality of Prohibition laws before state and federal courts as well as the U.S. Supreme Court. A graduate of Oberlin College and thirty years older than Jake and Bill, he could not have been their classmate.

Wilson, Sir Henry Hughes: British politician and distinguished military man, he was murdered by the Irish Republican Army on 22 June 1922.

BIBLIOGRAPHY

Adams, Richard P. "Sunrise Out of *The Waste Land*," *TSE: Tulane Studies in English*, 9 (1959): 119–131; republished in *Critical Essays on Ernest Hemingway's The Sun Also Rises*, edited by James Nagel. New York: G. K. Hall, 1995, pp. 52–62. Links Brett to fertility myths and Cohn to the Grail knight.

Aiken, Conrad. Review of *The Sun Also Rises*. *New York Herald Tribune Books* (31 October 1926): 4; republished in *The Critical Heritage*, edited by Jeffrey Meyers. London & New York: Routledge, 1982; republished, 1997, pp. 89–91.

Alderman, Taylor, and Kenneth Rosen, eds. *Hemingway Notes*. Carlisle, Pa.: Dickinson College, 1971–1974.

Aldridge, John W. *After the Lost Generation: A Critical Study of the Writers of Two Wars*. New York: McGraw-Hill, 1951.

Baker, Carlos. *Hemingway: A Life Story*. New York: Scribners, 1969. The standard single-volume biography.

Baker. *Hemingway: The Writer as Artist*. Princeton: Princeton University Press, 1952; revised and enlarged, 1972. Emphasizes counterpoint and mythological rather than roman à clef elements of narrative.

Balassi, William. "The Trail to *The Sun Also Rises*: The First Week of Writing," in *Hemingway: Essays of Reassessment*, edited by Frank Scafella. New York: Oxford University Press, 1991, pp. 33–51.

Balassi. "The Writing of the Manuscript of *The Sun Also Rises*, with a Chart of Its Session-by-Session Development," *Hemingway Review*, 6, no. 1 (1986): 65–78.

Baldwin, Marc D. *Reading The Sun Also Rises: Hemingway's Political Unconscious*. New York: Peter Lang, 1997.

Barrett, Richmond. "Babes in the Bois," *Harper's*, 66 (May 1928): 724; quoted in John Raeburn, *Fame Became of Him: Hemingway as Public Writer*. Bloomington: Indiana University Press, 1984, p. 22.

Baskett, Sam S. "An Image to Dance Around: Brett and her Lovers in *The Sun Also Rises*," *Centennial Review*, 22 (Winter 1978): 45–69. Examines what Jake learns from Brett's admirers.

Beach, Joseph Warren. "Ernest Hemingway: The Esthetics of Simplicity," in his *American Fiction: 1920–1940*. New York: Macmillan, 1941, pp. 97–119.

Bishop, John Peale. "The Missing All," *Virginia Quarterly Review*, 13, no. 1 (1937): 106–121; republished in *Ernest Hemingway: The Man and his Work*, edited by John K. M. McCaffery. Cleveland & New York: World, 1950, pp. 292–307.

Bloom, Harold, ed. *Ernest Hemingway's Modern Critical Interpretations: The Sun Also Rises*. New York: Chelsea House, 1987.

Bloom, ed. *Major Literary Characters: Brett Ashley*. New York: Chelsea House, 1991.

Bloom, ed. *Modern Critical Views: Ernest Hemingway.* New York: Chelsea House, 1985.

Bridgman, Richard. "Ernest Hemingway," in his *The Colloquial Style in America.* New York: Oxford University Press, 1966, pp. 195–230.

Bruccoli, Matthew J. *Scott and Ernest: The Authority of Failure and the Authority of Success.* New York: Random House, 1978; revised as *Fitzgerald and Hemingway: A Dangerous Friendship.* New York: Carroll & Graf, 1994. Describes Hemingway's and Fitzgerald's relationship and includes much primary material.

Bruccoli, ed. *Conversations with Ernest Hemingway.* Jackson & London: University of Mississippi Press, 1986. Collection of interviews.

Bruccoli, ed. *Ernest Hemingway: The Sun Also Rises. A Facsimile Edition,* 2 volumes. Detroit: Omnigraphics, 1990. Includes the manuscript and related materials.

Bruccoli, C. E. Frazer Clark, and others, eds. *Fitzgerald/Hemingway Annual.* Washington, D.C.: NCR Microcard Editions, 1969–1974; republished, Englewood, Colo.: Information Handling Services, 1975–1976; republished, Detroit: Gale, 1977–1980.

Bruccoli, ed., with Judith S. Baughman. *A Life in Letters: F. Scott Fitzgerald.* New York: Simon & Schuster, 1994.

Bruccoli, ed., with Robert W. Trogdon. *The Only Thing that Counts: The Ernest Hemingway/Maxwell Perkins Correspondence, 1925–1947.* New York: Scribners, 1996.

Bruccoli and Trogdon, eds. *Dictionary of Literary Biography, Documentary Series,* volume 15: *American Expatriate Writers: Paris in the Twenties.* Detroit: Bruccoli Clark Layman/Gale, 1997, pp. 168–202. Primary material, including photographs.

Catalog of the Ernest Hemingway Collection of the John F. Kennedy Library, 2 volumes. Boston: G. K. Hall, 1982.

Colvert, James B. "Ernest Hemingway's Morality of Action," *American Literature,* 27 (1955): 372–385. Emphasizes the pursuit of values.

Comley, Nancy R. and Robert Scholes. *Hemingway's Genders: Rereading the Hemingway Text.* New Haven: Yale University Press, 1994.

Cowley, Malcolm. *Exile's Return: A Narrative of Ideas.* New York: Norton, 1934; revised as *Exile's Return: A Literary Odyssey of the 1920s.* New York: Penguin, 1951; republished, Harmondsworth, U.K.: Penguin, 1976.

Cowley. "Hemingway at Midnight," *New Republic,* 111 (14 August 1944): 190, 192, 194–195; expanded as the introduction to *The Viking Portable Library: Hemingway,* edited by Cowley. New York: Viking Press, 1944, pp. vii–xxiv. Links Hemingway to Eliot and pursues allusions to mythology.

Daiker, Donald A. "The Affirmative Conclusion of *The Sun Also Rises,*" *McNeese Review,* 21 (1975): 3–19. Argues that the novel is affirmative and teaches Jake how to live.

Donaldson, Scott. "Hemingway's Morality of Compensation," *American Literature,* 43, no. 3 (1971): 399–420; republished in *Ernest Hemingway's The Sun Also Rises,* edited by Bloom. New York: Chelsea House, 1987, pp. 71–90. Contrasts French materialism with Spanish disregard for material wealth.

Donaldson. "Humor in *The Sun Also Rises,*" in *New Essays on The Sun Also Rises,* edited by Linda Wagner-Martin. New York: Cambridge University Press, 1987, pp.19–41.

Donaldson, ed. *The Cambridge Companion to Hemingway.* Cambridge: Cambridge University Press, 1996. Excellent anthology including thirteen articles on the phases and themes of Hemingway's works.

Eby, Carl P. *Hemingway's Fetishism: Psychoanalysis and the Mirror of Manhood.*

Albany: State University of New York Press, 1999.

Eliot, T. S. "Tradition and the Individual Talent," in *Critical Theory Since Plato,* edited by Hazard Adams. New York: Harcourt Brace Jovanovich, 1971, pp. 784–787.

Farrell, James T. "The Sun Also Rises," in his *The League of the Frightened Philistines and Other Papers.* New York: Vanguard, 1945, pp. 20–24; republished in *Ernest Hemingway: The Man and His Work,* edited by John K. M. McCaffery. Cleveland & New York: World, 1950, pp. 221–225.

Fleming, Robert E. *The Face in the Mirror: Hemingway's Writers.* Tuscaloosa: University of Alabama Press, 1994.

Fleming. "The Fun Also Rises: A Tribute to Jim Hinkle," *Hemingway Review,* 13, no. 1 (1993): 90–91.

Ford, Hugh. "Hemingway's Hollywood Paris," in *A Moving Picture Feast: The Filmgoer's Hemingway,* edited by Charles M. Oliver. New York: Praeger, 1989, pp. 114–121.

Frohock, W. M. "Violence and Discipline 1947," *Southwest Review,* 32 (Winter 1947): 89–97, Part I; (Spring 1947): 184–193, Part II; republished in *Ernest Hemingway: The Man and His Work,* edited by McCaffery. Cleveland & New York: World, 1950, pp. 262–291.

Ganzel, Dewey. "*Cabestro and Vaquilla:* The Symbolic Structure of *The Sun Also Rises,*" *Sewanee Review,* 76 (Winter 1968): 26–48.

Gorman, Herbert. Review of *The Sun Also Rises. New York World* (14 November 1926): 10 M; republished in *The Critical Heritage,* edited by Jeffrey Meyers. London & New York: Routledge, 1982; republished, 1997, p. 92.

Hanneman, Audre, *Ernest Hemingway: A Comprehensive Bibliography.* Princeton: Princeton University Press, 1967; corrected, 1969. Primary and secondary bibliography.

Hanneman, *Supplement to Ernest Hemingway: A Comprehensive Bibliography.* Princeton: Princeton University Press, 1975. Primary and secondary bibliography.

Hays, Peter. *Ernest Hemingway.* New York: Continuum, 1990.

Hemingway, Ernest. *The Complete Short Stories of Ernest Hemingway,* Finca Vigía Edition. New York: Scribners, 1987; republished, New York: Collier's, 1991.

Hemingway. *The Dangerous Summer.* New York: Scribners, 1985.

Hemingway. *Death in the Afternoon.* New York: Scribners, 1932.

Hemingway, "The Unpublished Opening of *The Sun Also Rises,*" *Antaeus,* 33 (Spring 1979): 7–14. Publishes the excised opening of the typescript.

Hinkle, James. "What's Funny in *The Sun Also Rises,*" *Hemingway Review,* 4, no. 2 (1985): 31–41.

Hinkle, James. "'Dear Mr. Scribner'—About the Published Text of *The Sun Also Rises,*" *Hemingway Review,* 6, no. 1 (1986): 43–64. Addresses errors in the typescript.

Josephs, Allen. "*Toreo:* The Moral Axis in *The Sun Also Rises,*" *Hemingway Review,* 6, no. 1 (1986): 88–99. Places *toreo* at the center of the novel and author's artistic vision.

Kazin, Alfred. *On Native Grounds: An Interpretation of Modern American Prose Literature.* New York: Harcourt, Brace, 1942.

Kennedy, J. Gerald. *Imagining Paris: Exile, Writing, and American Identity.* New Haven: Yale University Press, 1993.

Kennedy and Jackson R. Bryer, eds. *French Connections: Hemingway and Fitzgerald Abroad.* New York: St. Martin's Press, 1998.

Kobler, J. F. "Confused Chronology in *The Sun Also Rises,*" *Modern Fiction Studies,* 12 (Winter 1967–1968): 517–

520. Shows that neither the historical nor fictive chronology is correct.

Lajoie, Ronald and Sally Lentz. "Is Jake Barnes Waiting?" *Fitzgerald/Hemingway Annual* (1975): 229–233. Explicates allusion to A. E. W. Mason's "The Crystal Trench," the story that Jake reads while fishing in Burguete.

Larson, Kelli A. *Ernest Hemingway: A Reference Guide 1974–1989*. Boston: G. K. Hall, 1991. Secondary bibliography, well annotated and indexed.

Laurence, Frank M. "*The Sun Also Rises*: The NBC Version," in *A Moving Picture Feast: The Filmgoer's Hemingway*, edited by Oliver. New York: Praeger, 1989, pp. 91–113.

Lauter, Paul. "Plato's Stepchildren, Gatsby and Cohn," *Modern Fiction Studies*, 9 (1963–1964): 338–346.

Leff, Leonard J. *Hemingway and His Conspirators: Hollywood, Scribners, and the Making of American Celebrity Culture*. Lanham, Md.: Rowman & Littlefield, 1997.

Leland, John. *A Guide to Hemingway's Paris*. Chapel Hill, N.C.: Algonquin, 1989.

Levin, Harry. "Observations on the Style of Ernest Hemingway," *Kenyon Review*, 13, no. 4 (1951): 97.

Lewis, Robert W. *Hemingway on Love*. Austin: University of Texas Press, 1965, pp. 19–35. Argues that romantic love is examined and rejected.

Lowenkron, David Henry. "Jake Barnes—A Student of William James in *The Sun Also Rises*," *Texas Quarterly*, 19, no. 1 (1976): 147–156. Posits a pragmatic rather than stoic code.

Lynn, Kenneth S. *Hemingway*. New York: Simon & Schuster, 1987.

Madariage, Salvador de. "The World Weighs a Writer's Influence." *Saturday Review*, 44 (29 July 1961): 18; quoted in Allen Josephs, "Hemingway's Spanish Sensibility," in *The Cambridge Companion to Hemingway*, edited by Donaldson. Cambridge: Cambridge University Press, 1996, p. 234.

Mandel, Miriam B. *Reading Hemingway: The Facts in the Fictions*. Metuchen, N.J.: Scarecrow Press, 1995. Identifies all of the people, animals, and cultural constructs in the novel.

Martin, Wendy. "Brett Ashley as New Woman in *The Sun Also Rises*," in *New Essays on The Sun Also Rises*, edited by Wagner-Martin. New York: Cambridge University Press, 1987, pp. 65–82.

McCaffery, John K. M., ed. *Ernest Hemingway: The Man and His Work*. Cleveland & New York: World, 1950.

McIlvaine, Robert. "Robert Cohn and *The Purple Land*," *Notes on Modern American Literature*, 5, no. 2 (1981): item 8.

Mellow, James R. *Hemingway: A Life without Consequences*. Boston: Houghton Mifflin, 1992.

Messent, Peter. *Ernest Hemingway*. New York: St. Martin's Press, 1992.

Meyers, Jeffrey. *Hemingway: A Biography*. New York: Harper & Row, 1985.

Meyers, ed. *Ernest Hemingway: The Critical Heritage*. London & New York: Routledge, 1982; republished 1997. Reprints contemporary reviews.

Miller, Linda Patterson. "Brett Ashley: The Beauty of It All," in *Critical Essays on Ernest Hemingway's The Sun Also Rises*, edited by James Nagel. New York: G. K. Hall, 1995, pp. 170–184. Places Brett rather than Jake at the center of the novel.

Muir, Edwin. Review of *The Sun Also Rises*. *Nation and Athenaeum*, 41 (2 July 1927): 450, 452; quoted in *The Critical Heritage*, edited by Meyers. London & New York: Routledge, 1982; republished, 1997, p. 96.

Nagel, James. "Brett and the Other Women in *The Sun Also Rises*," in *The Cambridge Companion to Hemingway*, edited by Donaldson. Cambridge: Cambridge University Press, 1996, pp. 87–108. Considers Brett's role as "New Woman" and contrasts her to the other female characters.

Nagel, James, ed. *Critical Essays on Ernest Hemingway's The Sun Also Rises*. New York: G. K. Hall, 1995. Nagel's introduction provides the best survey of criticism of the novel.

Newman, Paul B. "Hemingway's Grail Quest," *University of Kansas City Review*, 28 (1962): 295–303. Links the novel to Jesse Weston's discussion of Fisher King.

Oliver, Charles M. *Ernest Hemingway A to Z: The Essential Reference of His Life and Work*. New York: Facts on File, 1999.

Oliver, ed. *Hemingway Review*, 6, no. 1 (1986). Special issue on *The Sun Also Rises*.

Oliver, ed. *A Moving Picture Feast: The Filmgoer's Hemingway*. New York: Praeger, 1989.

O'Sullivan, Sibbie. "Love and Friendship/Man and Woman in *The Sun Also Rises*," *Arizona Quarterly*, 44, no. 2 (1988): 76–97; republished in *Hemingway: Seven Decades of Criticism*, edited by Linda Wagner-Martin. East Lansing: Michigan State University Press, 1998, pp. 61–79.

Parker, Hershel. "Textual Criticism and Hemingway," in *Hemingway: Essays of Reassessment*, edited by Frank Scafella. New York: Oxford University Press, 1991, pp. 17–31.

Phillips, Gene D. *Hemingway and Film*. New York: Ungar, 1980.

Plath, James L. "*The Sun Also Rises* as 'A Greater Gatsby': 'Isn't it pretty to think so,'" in *French Connections: Hemingway and Fitzgerald Abroad*, edited by Kennedy and Bryer. New York: St. Martin's Press, 1998, pp. 257–275.

Plimpton, George, "An Interview with Ernest Hemingway," *Paris Review*, 18 (Spring 1958): 60–69; republished in *Ernest Hemingway: Five Decades of Criticism*, edited by Linda Welshimer Wagner (East Lansing: Michigan State University Press, 1974), pp. 21–38. Here Hemingway discusses his "iceberg principle" and denies that Jake has been castrated.

Raeburn, John. *Fame Became of Him: Hemingway as Public Writer*. Bloomington: University of Indiana Press, 1984. Explains how the novel transformed its author into the spokesman for his generation.

Review of the movie *The Sun Also Rises*. "Hemingway Classic," *New York Times*, 24 August 1957, p. 12.

Review of the movie *The Sun Also Rises*. "Hemingway's Lost Souls," *Life* (16 September 1957): 61–66.

Reynolds, Michael. "False Dawn: *The Sun Also Rises* Manuscript," in *A Fair Day in the Affections: Essays in Honor of Robert B. White Jr.*, edited by Jack D. Durant and M. Thomas Hester. Raleigh, N.C.: Winston Press, 1980, pp. 171–186.

Reynolds. *Hemingway: The American Homecoming*. Oxford: Blackwell, 1992.

Reynolds. *Hemingway: The Final Years*. New York: Norton, 1999.

Reynolds. *Hemingway: The 1930s*. New York: Norton, 1997.

Reynolds. *Hemingway: The Paris Years*. Oxford: Blackwell, 1989.

Reynolds. *Hemingway's First War: The Making of A Farewell to Arms*. Princeton: Princeton University Press, 1976.

Reynolds. "Putting on the Riff," *Hemingway Review*, 5, no. 1 (1985): 30–31. Explicates allusion to General Miguel Prima Rivera and the war on the Riff in 1925.

Reynolds. "The *Sun* in Its Time: Recovering the Historical Context," in *New Essays on The Sun Also Rises*, edited by Linda Wagner-Martin. New York: Cambridge University Press, 1987, pp. 43–64.

Reynolds. "Words Killed, Wounded, Missing in Action," *Hemingway Review,* 6, no. 2 (1981): 5.

Reynolds. *The Young Hemingway.* Oxford: Blackwell, 1986.

Rood, Karen, ed. *Dictionary of Literary Biography 4: American Writers in Paris, 1920–1939.* Detroit: Bruccoli Clark/Gale, 1980.

Rovit, Earl, and Gerry Brenner. "*The Sun Also Rises:* An Essay in Applied Principles," in their *Ernest Hemingway.* Boston: Twayne, 1963; revised edition, 1986. Succinct overview of major themes, characters, and techniques; especially good on Jake as narrator.

Sarason, Bertram D. *Hemingway and the Sun Set.* Washington, D.C.: NCR Microcard, 1972. Excellent source for interviews and testimony from the models for the roman à clef.

Schonhorn, Manuel. "*The Sun Also Rises:* I: The Jacob Allusion; II: Parody as Meaning," *Ball State University Forum,* 16 (Spring 1975): 49–55. Reads allusion to biblical patriarch as affirmative.

Skipp, Frances E. "What was the Matter with Jacob Barnes?" *Carrell,* 6 (December 1965): 17–22. Suggests that Jake learns to live within the limitations imposed by his world.

Spilka, Mark. "The Death of Love in *The Sun Also Rises,*" in *Twelve Essays on Great American Novels,* edited by Charles Shapiro. Detroit: Wayne State University Press, 1958, pp. 238–256; quoted in *Ernest Hemingway's The Sun Also Rises,* edited by Bloom. New York: Chelsea House, 1987, pp. 25–37. Influential allegorical reading that posits Cohn as false knight, Brett and Jake as desexed by war, and Romero as hero.

Spilka. *Hemingway's Quarrel with Androgyny.* Lincoln: University of Nebraska Press, 1989.

Sprague, Claire. "*The Sun Also Rises:* Its 'Clear Financial Basis,'" *American Quarterly,* 21 (Summer 1969): 259–266. Explains the metaphoric exchange of values in the novel.

Stanton, Edward F. *Hemingway and Spain: A Pursuit.* Seattle: University of Washington Press, 1989.

Steinke, Jim. "Brett and Jake in Spain: Hemingway's Ending for *The Sun Also Rises,*" *Spectrum,* 27 (1985): 131–141. Argues that Jake and Brett learn to become friends.

Stephens, Robert O., ed. *Ernest Hemingway: The Critical Reception.* New York: Burt Franklin, 1977. Republishes initial reviews and discusses the critical reception.

Stoneback, H. R. "'For Bryan's Sake': The Tribute to the Great Commoner in Hemingway's *The Sun Also Rises,*" *Christianity and Literature,* 32 (Winter 1982): 29–36. Allies Jake with William Jennings Bryan.

Stoneback. "From the Rue Saint-Jaques to the Pass of Roland to the 'Unfinished Church on the Edge of the Cliff,'" *Hemingway Review,* 6, no. 1 (1986): 2–29. Explores Jake's Catholic sensibility.

Stoneback. "Hemingway and Faulkner on the Road to Roncevaux," in *Hemingway: A Revaluation,* edited by Donald R. Noble. Troy, N.Y.: Whitston, 1983, pp. 135–163. Considers Jake's search for spiritual values.

Svoboda, Frederic Joseph. *Hemingway & The Sun Also Rises: The Crafting of a Style.* Lawrence: University Press of Kansas, 1983. Excellent study of the writing of the novel.

Tamke, Alexander. "Jacob Barnes' 'Biblical Name': Central Irony in *The Sun Also Rises,*" *English Record,* 18 (December 1967): 2–7. Posits Jake as ironic contrast to the biblical Jacob, who was very prolific.

Torchiana, Donald T. "*The Sun Also Rises*: A Reconsideration," *Fitzgerald-Hemingway Annual 1969.* Dayton, Ohio: NCR Microcard Editions, 1970, pp. 77–103.

Tremblay, Anne. "Taking Some Liberties with *The Sun Also Rises,*" *New York Times,* 26 August 1984, sec, p. 2: 23.

Trilling, Lionel. Review of *The Fifth Column and the First Forty-nine, Partisan Review,* 6 (1939): 52–60; quoted in *Ernest Hemingway: The Critical Heritage,* edited by Meyers. London & New York: Routledge, 1982; republished, 1997, p. 280.

Vance, William L. "Implications of Form in *The Sun Also Rises,*" in *Ernest Hemingway's The Sun Also Rises,* edited by Harold Bloom. New York: Chelsea House, 1987, pp. 39–49.

Vanderbilt, Kermit. "*The Sun Also Rises:* Time Uncertain," *Twentieth Century Literature,* 15 (October 1969): 153–154. On the inconsistencies of real and fictional time in the novel.

Vopat, Carole Gottlieb. "The End of *The Sun Also Rises:* A New Beginning," *Fitzgerald/Hemingway Annual, 1972,* edited by Matthew J. Bruccoli & C. E. Frazer Clark Jr. Washington D.C.: NCR Microcard Editions, 1973; quoted in *Ernest Hemingway's The Sun Also Rises,* edited by Bloom. New York: Chelsea House, 1987, pp. 91–101.

Voss, Frederick. "Hemingway as American Icon," in *Picturing Hemingway: A Writer in His Time,* edited by Michael Reynolds. New Haven: Yale University Press, 1999, pp. 1–9.

Wagner, Linda Welshimer. *Ernest Hemingway: A Reference Guide.* Boston: G. K. Hall, 1997. Secondary bibliography, well annotated and indexed.

Wagner-Martin, Linda. "Hemingway's Search for Heroes, Once Again," *Arizona Quarterly,* 44 (Summer 1988): 58–68. Explicates allusion with emphasis on endurance of the biblical Jacob in his loyalty to Rachel.

Wagner-Martin. "*The Sun Also Rises*: One Debt to Imagism," *Journal of Narrative Technique,* 2, no. 2 (1972): 88–98. Traces the influence of Ezra Pound and the Imagist movement, focusingon methods, suggestion, and speed of presentation.

Wagner-Martin, ed. *New Essays on The Sun Also Rises.* New York: Cambridge, 1987.

Waldhorn, Arthur. "The World, The Hero, and the Code," and "*The Sun Also Rises,*" in his *A Reader's Guide to Ernest Hemingway.* New York: Farrar, Straus & Giroux, 1972, pp. 21–29, 93–112. Succinct overview of compositional history, roman à clef elements, structure, theme, and character; argues that Jake recovers self-respect and rejects "false hope and empty illusion."

Warren, Robert Penn. "Hemingway," *Kenyon Review,* 19, no. 1 (1947): 18.

Warren. Introduction to *A Farewell to Arms.* New York: Scribners, 1949, pp. vii–xxxvii; quoted in *Modern Critical Views: Ernest Hemingway,* edited by Bloom. New York: Chelsea House, 1985, pp. 35–62.

Watts, Emily Stipes. *Ernest Hemingway and the Arts.* Urbana: University of Illinois, 1971. Explores Hemingway's indebtedness to Cézanne.

White, William, ed. *The Merrill Studies in The Sun Also Rises.* Columbus, Ohio: Merrill, 1969.

Whitlow, Roger. *Cassandra's Daughters: The Women in Hemingway's Fiction.* Westport, Conn.: Greenwood Press, 1984.

Wilson, Edmund. "Ernest Hemingway: Burbon Guage of Morale," *Atlantic,* 164 (July 1939): 36–46; collected in his *The Wound and the Bow: Seven Studies in Literature.* Boston: Houghton Mifflin, 1941.

Wilson. Introduction to *In Our Time.* New York: Scribners, 1930.

Wilson. Review of *Men without Women. New Republic,* 53 (14 December 1927): 102–103; republished in *Ernest Hemingway: The Critical Heritage,* edited by Jeffrey Meyers. London & New York: Routledge, 1982; republished, 1997, p. 113.

Wylder, Delbert E. "The Two Faces of Brett: The Role of the New Woman in *The Sun Also Rises*," *Kentucky Philological Association Bulletin* (1980): 27–33. Considers Brett as a "New Woman," free of Victorian restraints.

Wylder. "*The Sun Also Rises:* The Wounded Anti-Hero," in his *Hemingway's Heroes*. Albuquerque: University of New Mexico Press, 1969, pp. 31–65. Distinguishes Jake from the expatriates and focuses on his search for a meaningful existence.

Young, Philip. *Ernest Hemingway.* New York: Rinehart, 1952; revised as *Ernest Hemingway: A Reconsideration*. University Park: Pennsylvania State University Press, 1966. Young's influential theory allies Hemingway and his protagonists, positing the importance of a traumatic wound and a code in their lives.

Young and Charles Mann. "Fitzgerald's Sun Also Rises: Notes and Comment." *Fitzgerald/Hemingway Annual 1970*. Washington, D.C.: NCR Microcard Editions, 1970.

MASTER INDEX

A

B

C

D

E

F

G

H

I

J

K

L

M

N

O

P

Q

R

S

T

U

V

W

Y

Z